THE
FRONTII
PART 3: FRINGE WORLDS
EPISODE 6

EVOLUTION
RYK BROWN

CHAPTER ONE

"What have you got?" Nathan asked as he and Jessica walked onto the Aurora's bridge.

"A mayday relay, sir," Sima reported. "A cargo ship in the Tunc system is under attack."

"Pirates?" Nathan inquired as he came to stand by his command chair.

"Unknown," Sima admitted. "The communications tech on Tunc picked up the distress call. All he could make out was that they were under attack by several small ships and one larger one."

"*Tunc is on the edge of Brodek space,*" Aurora stated. "*Only four light years from the border with Morden territory.*"

"That's the third time this week," Jessica commented. "I'd say the Morden clan has figured out the Brodek aren't around any longer."

"They're testing us," Nathan said. "Recon drone?" he asked Laza.

"Link coming online now," Laza replied.

"We can just send Dragons," Jessica reminded him.

Nathan paid her recommendation no attention, instead waiting for Laza.

"Link active," Laza reported. "Three raiders and an assault ship. The cargo ship is powered down. It looks like they've surrendered, sir. The assault ship is moving in to board her."

"How many souls aboard?" Nathan asked.

"The cargo ship, fifty-four," Laza replied. "Fifty of them are grouped together in the same compartment, so they're probably passengers."

"How many on the assault ship?"

"Twenty-three."

"Dragons in the tubes?" Nathan inquired, taking his seat.

"Stacked and racked," Jessica replied.

"Sound general quarters," Nathan ordered. "Aurora, set course for the Tunc system and prepare to jump us in close," Nathan added as the bridge trim lighting changed from blue to red, and the alert klaxon echoed in the ship's corridors beyond the bridge.

"*Changing course for Tunc,*" Aurora acknowledged. "*Spinning up all weapons and shields.*"

"Launch the Alert Dragons," Nathan added. "Keep the rest in the tubes for now."

"*Alert One, cleared for launch.*" Sima announced over comms.

"Light 'er up, sweetie," Josh instructed.

His AI immediately complied, and Josh's Dragon quickly accelerated forward into the launch tube, shooting out of the forward end into space alongside the Aurora's bow.

"Alert One, away," Josh announced as he took the controls but waited for his wings to unfold before maneuvering.

"*Alert Two, away,*" Nikolas announced over comms as his fighter was spit out of the starboard tube.

"*Alert Three, away,*" Allet announced next.

"*Alert Four, away,*" Tika followed.

Josh glanced at his tactical display, which was linked to the recon drone the Aurora had sent to the Tunc system. "Looks like three raiders and a big boy."

"*Alert One, Aurora Actual*," Nathan called over comms. "*Engage the raiders. Standard ROE. We'll take care of the assault ship.*"

"You got it, boss," Josh replied. "You heard the man. Let's go de-claw some raiders." With his wings now fully deployed, Josh rolled his fighter onto the intercept course. "One's got jump lead," he announced, glancing at his display to ensure that the other three Dragons in his flight were linked up.

A second later, he pressed the jump button.

"Dragons are away," Sima reported.

"*On course for the Tunc system*," Aurora announced. "*How close to the assault ship would you like to arrive?*"

"Close enough to scare the piss out of them," Nathan replied.

"*Will five hundred meters be close enough to cause them to void their bladders, or should I jump us in closer?*"

Nathan recognized sarcasm in her tone, even if it wasn't really there. "Five hundred meters will be fine."

"*Jump plotted and ready.*"

"Drone link shows that Dragons have engaged the raiders and are leading them away from the cargo ship," Laza reported.

"The moment we jump in, target their weapons and fire to disable," Nathan instructed.

"I know the drill," Jessica assured him.

"Aurora, jump us in."

Ryk Brown

"Jumping in three......two......one......"

The jump flash washed over the bridge, and the Morden assault ship, along with the cargo ship they were docked with, suddenly filled their forward window screens.

"Jump complete," Aurora reported. *"Holding relative position."*

"Locked onto their guns," Jessica announced. "Firing to disable."

———

The Aurora's two forward ventral fixed gun emplacements opened fire, sending both plasma bolts and rail gun slugs into the assault ship's main gun turrets, ripping them apart. Having been caught by surprise, they were unable to adjust their shields and bring them online to protect themselves in time.

The array of smaller guns, rolling down the tracks along the Aurora's grav-lift wing on her ventral side, moved into position and opened fire as well, picking off smaller point-defense turrets, comm-arrays, and other items that would help disable, but not destroy, the enemy ship.

A single missile launched from the Aurora's port tube. It pitched up over the Morden assault ship, passing overhead before coming about and detonating near her single main engine thrust port at her stern.

———

"Assault ship's weapons are neutralized," Laza reported. "Their main propulsion is offline, and they are running on backup power."

"Can they jump?" Nathan asked.

"I do not believe so," Laza replied.

"Sima, open a channel."

"Channel open."

"Attention, unidentified vessel. This is Captain Scott of the Free Ship Aurora. You are committing an act of piracy in free space. Power down all systems and prepare to be boarded, or we will destroy you."

"Go to hell! We were here first!"

"Wrong answer," Nathan said, closing the channel. "Jess?"

"Locking main guns on the target, increasing strike power to maximum," Jessica replied.

"Assault ship is undocking from the cargo ship," Laza warned. "They're firing maneuvering thrusters. I believe they're making a run for it, sir."

"Which means they can still jump," Nathan surmised. "Jess, take them out."

"With pleasure," Jessica replied.

The Morden assault ship thrust away from the cargo ship and then pitched up, firing her aft forward translation thrusters to give herself enough of a course change to clear the Aurora and get a safe jump line.

The Aurora's main guns opened fire again, this time at full power. The rail gun slugs tore through the assault ship's hull, and the plasma bolts plowed deep inside her, setting off secondary explosions that tore the ship apart.

"Target is breaking up," Jessica announced.

"Captain, I'm now detecting *sixty* life signs aboard

the cargo ship...make that fifty-nine. Six of them are armed," Laza reported.

"They've been boarded," Jessica realized.

Nathan tapped his comm-set. "Kit, six boarders on the cargo ship. Can you take them?"

"*Just hold position*," Kit replied. "*We'll take care of them.*"

————————

Kit and the other Ghatazhak gathered in the starboard boarding foyer, dressed in their pressurized combat armor. "Ready to fly," Kit announced over his helmet comms.

"*Activating inner and outer pressure shields,*" Jessica reported over comms.

The opening from the boarding foyer to the corridor filled with a pale blue haze as the pressure shield activated.

"*Opening inner and outer doors,*" Jessica announced.

The inner door to the boarding airlock opened first, followed by the outer door, each of them sliding into the bulkheads.

"*Alpha, in three...*" Jessica began.

Kit turned and nodded to the other three men in his team. All of them nodded back, ready to go.

"*Two...*"

"Alpha Team, stand ready," Kit instructed.

"*One...*"

Kit crouched slightly, ready to spring forth.

"*Alpha, deploy.*"

Kit ran across the foyer, through the airlock, and leapt out into space, firing his suit's maneuvering thrusters as soon as he cleared the hatch. Three more Ghatazhak followed, all of them maneuvering in the same way.

Kit checked the tactical display in his visor, noting that he was on course for the forward breach point. "Touchdown in thirty seconds."

"*Bravo, in three...*"

Kit fired his thrusters again, rotating just enough to land feet first.

"*Two...*"

"*Two more passengers have died,*" Laza reported over comms.

"*One...*"

Kit didn't care. His job was the same: save as many as possible. There was nothing he could do about those who were killed before his team was in play.

"*Bravo, deploy,*" Jessica instructed.

Kit glanced at his tactical display as four more friendly icons appeared on his display behind him, headed toward the aft end of the target vessel. "Fifteen seconds to touchdown."

His thrusters fired again, this time to slow him down, to avoid slamming into the cargo ship and breaking his legs. Instead he landed hard, but not so hard that his combat suit couldn't absorb the excess energy. He immediately pulled the bag he had slung from his hip up and removed eight small emitters, sticking them to the hull in a three-meter-diameter circle.

Mori was the next one down. He pulled out a wiring harness and began plugging it into each of the emitters, securing the wires outside of the imaginary circle the emitters formed.

Jokay landed immediately after Mori, squatting down and connecting a small, self-powered pressure shield generator to the wiring harness. As soon as he was down, he flipped the switch, and a pressure shield formed along the hull in between the eight emitters.

Abdur was the last down, immediately deploying a breach ring. *"Fire in the hole,"* he announced over comms. All four stepped back, their mag-boots holding their feet to the ship's hull. There was a small flash of light, and a meter-wide section of hull drifted away, leaving an opening to the interior of the ship, the pressure shield preventing decompression.

Wordlessly, Kit turned around and stepped through, dropping inside, pulled by the ship's artificial gravity. As expected, he was greeted with low-yield blaster fire which simply bounced off his combat armor. He calmly walked toward the aggressors, clearing the drop zone so that Mori could follow.

The two pirates who had fired at him holstered their weapons, realizing they were useless, instead pulling sabers and grinning.

"You've got to be kidding me," Kit chuckled as he continued toward them. He reached down and pulled out two combat knives nearly as long as his forearm. One in each hand, holding them with the tips down, bending his wrists so that the blades were nearly parallel to his forearms.

The two men charged, their sabers up over the heads, ready to slash Kit when they reached him. Both men did exactly that, and Kit deflected them both with his blades. He spun around as he passed between the two men, flipping the horizontal blades in opposite directions as he rotated, so that the knife in his right hand pierced the left chest of the attacker on his right, and the knife in his left hand entered the right flank of the man to his left. He withdrew both knives as he continued his rotation, continuing down the corridor and leaving the two wounded men for Mori to finish off.

Weapons fire sounded in the next compartment, red-orange blasts lighting up the corridor as Kit approached the entrance. The compartment was full of passengers, all of whom were now climbing out of their seats in panic as two more pirates began firing on them. Kit launched the knife in his right hand, sending it across the room between two fleeing passengers and into the face of one of the attackers.

His action drew fire from the other pirate, who immediately grabbed a female passenger, holding her in front of him as a shield as she screamed in terror.

"Back off or I'll fry the bitch!" the pirate threatened.

Kit just kept walking toward the man as passengers scattered left and right, inadvertently clearing a path for him.

At that moment, two more pirates came rushing in from behind the one holding the hostage as a shield. Kit quickly drew his side arm, bringing it to bear on the man and firing a single shot that whizzed so close to the hostage's head that her hair was singed by the tiny plasma bolt. The shot landed exactly where Kit had intended, entering the man's left eye and burning through his skull, brains, and out the back of his head. The man dropped, and the woman fell to her knees.

Kit swung his weapon to take out the two pirates who had just entered from behind, but both men succumbed to weapons fire coming from behind them before he could get another shot off. A moment later, Chief Anson stepped into the compartment, followed by Uray Teece.

"*Bravo, clear,*" the chief announced calmly.

"Alpha, clear," Kit reported. "Bravo, sweep aft. Alpha, sweep forward." Kit stepped up to the female passenger, opening his visor so that he could speak to her. He knelt down, putting his hand on her shoulder. "Are you injured, ma'am?"

The woman, still severely shaken, checked herself over briefly. "No, I don't think so."

"Think you can help check for wounded passengers?"

"Yes, I think..." The woman looked at him. "Who are you people?"

Kit smiled. "We're the Free Fleet, ma'am. We're the good guys."

"The ship is secure," Jessica reported. "Eight dead, sixteen wounded, including two pirates."

"What about the crew?" Nathan asked.

"Two survivors," Jessica replied. "The captain and the chief engineer."

"What about the raiders?" Nathan asked Sima.

"Alert flight reports all three raiders bugged out."

"Tell them to fly cover while we rescue the passengers," Nathan instructed. "And get both shuttles over there to evac."

"Yes, sir."

Nathan tapped his comm-set. "Medical, Captain."

"*Medical,*" Doctor Chen answered.

"You're going to have sixteen wounded coming in about fifteen minutes," Nathan warned.

"*We're ready,*" Melei assured him.

"Launch Beta flight, and put them on extended BARCAP," Nathan told Jessica. "I don't want any surprises."

"You got it," Jessica assured him.

"I'm going down to the flight deck," Nathan said as he headed for the exit. "I want to talk to the captain of that ship. You have the conn, Jess."

"I've got the conn."

* * *

Robert studied the shuttle's sensor screen as Cameron piloted the ship over the surface of Libertara. "Let's look at grid one five seven next."

"What was wrong with this one?" Cameron wondered as she entered the course change.

"Not enough open grassland and not enough water flowing through it," Robert explained.

"It was pretty though."

"Yes it was. I'm looking for something a little less hilly and without forests bordering the open range."

"What's wrong with forests?"

"That's where the predators live."

"Aren't you going to use shields?"

"In the beginning, yes, but eventually it will become too large to fully shield. Besides, I'd prefer to keep it as 'low tech' as possible."

Cameron looked at him as if he was crazy. "Why?"

"Fewer problems, less dependency."

"And more work," Cameron pointed out.

"Hard work is good for you," Robert argued. "Besides, a reliable supply of meat will be essential for a new settlement, especially this far away from the rest of civilization."

Cameron seemed to accept his reply, which surprised Robert.

"Why did you volunteer to come along?" Robert wondered. "I mean, you of all people."

"Because I've always been opposed to eating animals?"

"I believe the correct phrase would be *radically opposed*."

"Yeah, well radical changes require radical adaptations," Cameron explained. She looked at him. "Don't tell anyone, but I really *like* the taste of dollag, especially when it's barely seared and still raw inside."

Robert was shocked. "Just when I thought there was nothing left that could surprise me."

"I'm still opposed to eating animals," Cameron insisted. "And maybe someday I'll be able to go back to an animal-free diet, but for now—well a girl's gotta eat, you know?"

"A very practical attitude."

"That's me. Practical to the end."

"I do appreciate the company," Robert assured her.

"I was bored anyway. Not much to do now that the fleet is parked. And it will be a few more days before Dominic can give us a full report on what needs to be overhauled and how the process should be prioritized."

"Coming up on one five seven," Robert commented, studying his sensor display again. "Plenty of flat land. A nice big river running right through the middle of it, and it eventually joins the main branch that skirts the settlement site, so we could use the river to ship fresh meat to you."

"It's nice," Cameron agreed. "And there's a mountain range to the northeast that will shield it from weather."

"Good thinking," Robert agreed as he peered out of the windows at the range below. "We could build the main complex right at the edge of the range, tucked in against the foothills."

"You don't want to put it in the middle of the range?" Cameron wondered.

"Oh hell no," Robert insisted. "I want to be able to sleep with the windows open and not smell dollag dung."

Cameron laughed. "Good point. I'd like a little place for myself right over there, next to the river."

"Really? I figured you for a lifer."

"I am," Cameron admitted. "But that doesn't mean I can't have a place to get away now and then. And I'll have to retire someday. It may as well be here."

"Then I guess we'll be neighbors," Robert said.

"Maybe."

"Just promise me one thing. That you're not going to come over and try to tell me how to run my ranch."

"You know I will," Cameron admitted.

* * *

Nathan entered the Aurora's medical treatment ward, which was packed with wounded from the cargo ship they had just rescued. Although a few of them were in bad shape, most had been lucky, coming in with only minor sprains, bruises, lacerations, and a few broken bones. Considering the number of patients, his medical staff seemed to be handling the situation quite well.

"I'm looking for the captain of that ship," Nathan told one of the med-techs.

"Sitting next to bed one," the med-tech replied, pointing.

Nathan went over, finding a woman in her late forties sitting next to a younger man who was unconscious and appeared to have multiple injuries. "Ma'am?" Nathan asked. "Are you the captain of that cargo ship?"

"I am," the woman replied, eying Nathan suspiciously.

"Nathan Scott, captain of this ship."

"Tapani Helder," the woman replied. "But people just call me Tap."

"A pleasure to meet you." Nathan looked at the man in the bed. "Is this man someone close to you?"

"Remi. My chief engineer. Kind of like a son I guess."

"Is he going to be alright?"

"Doc says he should recover. Probably take a few weeks though. Don't know how I'm gonna get the ship running again without him."

"I'm sure we can help you with that," Nathan told her.

She didn't acknowledge his words. "I need to find a way to get him home so he can rest."

"He is welcome to stay here as long as necessary. You both are."

"That's generous of you, Captain. But we wouldn't want to put you out. You've done enough already. Those bastards would've executed every last one of us and left the Traverna adrift, just to send a message."

"To whom?" Nathan wondered.

"To anyone thinking about trying to navigate this region of space."

"Well they may be thinking twice about pulling something like that again, at least around here," Nathan insisted.

"Don't bet on it," Tap replied. "There's no shortage

of people who are willing to die rather than work for a living."

"Hopefully we'll be able to change that."

Tap looked up at him. "What ship did you say this was?"

"I didn't. It's the Aurora."

"Bad enough that your parents saddled you with a notorious name, but then you go and name your ship *Aurora*?" Tap laughed. "You've got balls, kid. I'll give you that. Wait till I tell the other captains back on Peredine that I was rescued by Captain Scott and the Aurora."

"Maybe it would be better if you didn't," Nathan suggested. "You might chase business away."

"You're probably right."

"How many did you lose?" Nathan asked.

"Two crew but no civilians."

"Well you should be proud of that," Nathan insisted.

"Nothing to be proud of. We just got lucky." She cast a suspicious gaze Nathan's way. "How did you know we were in trouble?"

"You put out a mayday."

"My pilot, Torga, must've done so. Still, it's lucky you were in the system."

"We weren't," Nathan told her. "In fact, we were about eight hundred light years away when the communications officer on Tunc alerted us to your mayday."

"Then how the hell did you get here so fast?"

"Eight hundred light years is well within our single-jump range," Nathan explained.

"Then I guess you don't care about damaging the interdimensional barrier?"

"Why would I care about a lie?"

Captain Helder shot Nathan an odd look.

"We'll talk later," Nathan told her. "If you don't mind, I'm sending an engineering team to check out your ship and see what needs to be done to get her safely down on Tunc."

"Thank you...I think."

Nathan smiled, then turned to depart, nodding to Doctor Barra as she passed, headed for the Traverna's wounded engineer.

"Your friend was very lucky," Doctor Barra said as she studied the bio-monitor screen on the wall at the head of the bed.

"God takes care of drunks and fools," Tap said. "So he got help on two counts."

"I see."

"What was that man's name?" Tap asked, nodding in the direction Nathan had departed.

"Captain Scott?"

"So that's *really* his name? That's a cruel thing to do to a kid."

"I'm pretty sure his parents didn't know his name would become infamous when they gave it to him," Doctor Barra insisted.

"Huh?" Now Tap was staring at Doctor Barra, confused.

"He really *is* Nathan Scott and not just in name. He's *the* Nathan Scott."

"As in the one who *died* five hundred years ago," Tap confirmed, extremely skeptical.

"That's the one."

"So you're in on it too then," Tap surmised.

"Yeah, I didn't believe it at first either," the doctor admitted. "Don't worry, you'll come around," she added as she left.

Tap looked around, a different look on her face.

Finally, she turned to her unconscious engineer. "These people are daft."

* * *

"She's out of Easton," Jessica said as she and Nathan walked down the corridor. "A mid-sized colony in the fringe, about three hundred and eighty-seven light years from Tunc."

"That's kind of a long haul, isn't it?"

"Well that may be where she's based, but that's not where she's been spending most of her time lately," Jessica continued. "Seems our good Captain Helder is a bit behind on her mortgage payments. I have a feeling she's staying as far away from Easton as she can."

"So she's skipped out on her ship loan then," Nathan surmised as they entered the elevator.

"That's how it looks."

"How are you getting all this?"

"I cracked her logs, both ship and personal," Jessica bragged.

"Not very nice of you," Nathan commented as the elevator doors opened.

"Fuck nice. I'm protecting this ship," Jessica insisted.

"Any idea why she was headed for Tunc?"

"All I know is that she picked up the run on Pykamay a few days ago. And someone paid her double the going rate."

"For what I wonder?" Nathan said as they entered the bridge.

"I don't know yet. We scanned all her cargo and didn't find anything suspicious. There are a few sections of the ship that are shielded though, so those may be smuggler's bays. I didn't want to tear them open until I spoke with you."

"That's uncharacteristic of you."

"I'm feeling lazy today."

"I'll speak with Captain Helder again later today and see if I can squeeze more details from her."

"We need to know if this was a random attack, which would indicate that the Morden are testing to see if the Brodek are still around or not, or was a targeted attack, and they were looking for something specific."

"I'll do what I can," Nathan promised. "What about the passengers?"

"I'll be interviewing most of them later today, once Doc Chen clears them."

"Very well," Nathan agreed, heading into his ready room without her. He went to his desk, calling up the data they had collected on the Traverna, looking it over in the hopes that something would stand out to him. But nothing did. As best he could tell, it was just a standard cargo ship, old, like every other ship operating outside Alliance space. Like most ships in this century, it was slow, barely able to accelerate much past orbital velocity without burns lasting weeks. And their jump logs showed at least an hour between each ten-light-year jump, indicating that they needed to recharge between each max-jump event.

"*Nathan?*" Vladimir called over Nathan's comm-set.

"What's up?" Nathan replied.

"*You and Jessica need to come to the Traverna. There's something you need to see.*"

"What is it?"

"*Just come.*"

* * *

Nathan and Jessica stood in the Traverna's

compact engineering compartment, looking down at the small window on the large container that Vladimir had pulled out of the cargo ship's reactor compartment.

"And this container was in the reactor compartment?" Nathan asked.

"Directly under the reactor," Vladimir confirmed.

"Why?"

"Probably because it would just look like part of the reactor to anyone scanning the compartment from outside," Vladimir theorized. "The only reason I even opened the compartment was because I was curious. I've never seen this reactor design."

"How is she still alive?" Jessica wondered, pointing to the radiologic warning placard on the door to the compartment.

Vladimir looked at the sign, waving it off dismissively. "There's no radiation in there," he insisted. "Not unless the reactor fails, in which case this whole section would be in trouble. Besides, the container is shielded."

"So it's just an SA pod then?" Nathan said.

"Pretty much," Vladimir agreed. "A nice one but nothing unusual about it."

"Any idea who she is?" Nathan asked.

"*Nyet*," Vladimir replied. "No markings of any kind."

Nathan sighed. "Well I guess I'd better speak to Captain Helder again."

"If that's her *real* name," Jessica commented.

* * *

Cameron stepped out from the Celestia's forward cargo ramp toward the newly arrived shuttle from the Anastianus just as a middle-aged woman stepped down from its boarding hatch. The woman was dressed in a uniform similar to those worn on the other ships owned by Jakome Ta'Akar, and she wore it well.

"Captain Taylor?" the woman asked Cameron as they approached one another.

"Captain Klim, I assume," Cameron replied, offering her hand. "I was surprised when I got your hail. I thought you had only just arrived at the gate."

"That is true," she replied, looking around. "Beautiful spot Doctor Goff chose."

"It is," Cameron agreed.

"The positioning of your ships changes our deployment plans," Captain Klim stated.

"We positioned them to better support one another during the refit process," Cameron explained. "We *can* move them if you need us to."

"I don't think that will be necessary," the captain insisted. "I'm sure we can make it work."

"I understand your *entire ship* is to be broken down and used to create the settlement. I'd love to see the specs on how that's done."

"It's not all that impressive. At its heart, the Anastianus is really just a barge pusher, built with a post-mission utility career in mind. It's the design of the cargo modules that's key."

"How long will it take you to get broken down and through the gate?"

"A few days I expect."

"Is this your first colonization mission?" Cameron asked.

"Fifteenth actually," Detta replied. "First one I'm not going home from though."

"You're staying on Libertara permanently?"

"I've been flying colonization missions for thirty plus years," Detta explained. "This is by far the furthest out I've ever hauled, and even if I continued hauling for another thirty years, I doubt I'd surpass it by much. So I figure this rock has my retirement written all over it."

"I was thinking the same thing," Cameron agreed, "but not for another decade or two."

"Do you have any decent food on your ship?"

"Surprisingly good actually."

"Then I'll make you a deal. Feed me, and I'll explain to you just how the Anastianus will be turned into a colony."

"You've got a deal," Cameron replied, smiling.

* * *

"In the *reactor* compartment?" Captain Helder questioned. "That can't be."

"It is," Nathan replied. "Where is your engineer?"

"In the medical scanner."

"So you're saying you know *nothing* about this stowaway on your *own* ship?"

"The Traverna is hardly *my* ship," Captain Helder insisted.

"We know about your mortgage problems," Nathan told her.

Captain Helder looked at him, squinting. "Someone's been going through my personal records."

"I apologize, but there is too much at stake."

"I wasn't referring to the mortgage."

"What then?"

"The Traverna was my husband's dream," Tap explained.

"Where is your husband now?"

"Gone."

"I'm sorry. I didn't realize."

"Don't be. The asshole ran off with some slut and stuck me with *his* failing business and a fucking mortgage that's been sucking the life out of me for five years now."

"Good reason to take up smuggling," Nathan pointed out.

"I wouldn't even know how to begin," she admitted. "Hell, I don't even know how to fly that damned thing. And the only thing I know about the reactor compartment is that there's a big red warning sign on the hatch telling me to keep out."

Nathan wasn't sure how much of what Tap was telling him was true, but at this point it didn't matter. His main goal was to learn the identity of the stowaway, not Captain Helder's life history. "What about your engineer?" Nathan asked. "Could he have arranged to take on this stowaway?"

"I suppose," Tap admitted. "But why not just bring the stowaway on with the rest of the passengers? And why in SA?"

"People in suspended animation don't return life signs on most sensors, and by putting the SA pod so close to the reactor, the device would appear to be part of the reactor itself," Nathan explained. "So you can see why we might assume that your engineer had a hand in this."

Captain Helder had no response.

"How well do you know your engineer?"

"Pretty well I suppose. When my husband split, his engineer quit. Remi was just a loader, but he was pretty handy with systems, so he just sort of took over the engineer's position. He's become like a son to me."

"Do you think he's done this before?"

"You're assuming that he *did*. There were two more people on my crew."

"You mentioned your pilot last time we talked. How long was he with you?"

"A little over a year I'd say."

"What about the other crewman?" Nathan asked.

"Iros Bandura. This was his first trip."

"What was his job?"

"Loader, basically a grunt. It's an entry-level position, and we seem to have a pretty high turnover. I guess no one likes being the low man on the totem pole."

"How much did you know about him?" Nathan wondered.

"I didn't," Tap admitted. "My last loader got arrested in port, and we needed someone quick. This guy just happened to be in the right place at the right time."

Nathan thought for a moment. He was starting to believe the Traverna's captain. Her answers felt quick and real, so if she wasn't telling the truth, then she was very well rehearsed. "I understand your engineer is awake?"

"Yes."

"See if he knows anything about this woman in SA and then let me know."

"The stowaway was a *woman*?" Tap asked, seeming surprised.

"Late twenties, early thirties. Had to have some resources to arrange an SA pod like that. So it makes me wonder who she's sneaking away from."

* * *

"You weren't kidding," Captain Klim said after her first bite. "You eat like this every day?"

"We didn't at first," Cameron replied. "Luckily, the Navarro had staff on board and a fully stocked pantry when she was taken."

"I can't believe you guys *stole* three ancient warships. Seriously, who does that?"

"I thought you said you read up on our histories?"

"I did, but to be honest, I assumed most of it was exaggerated. History usually is."

"You sound like Nathan."

"How much of *his* history was exaggerated?" Captain Klim wondered.

"I'm not sure," Cameron admitted. "I haven't had the time to read what it says about him. But from what others have told me, there are more than a few things in there that aren't true."

"Such as?"

"Well we didn't *start* the war with the Ilyan Gamaze, and we certainly didn't go into their space against orders."

"History says you were ordered to remain *outside* the Ilyan," Captain Klim stated.

"Our orders were *quite* specific," Cameron insisted. "We were to determine if the crew of the Lawrence, which was attacked *outside* of Ilyan space, had survived, and if so, to effect rescue."

"But you went all the way to the Gamazan home system and attacked them."

"That's also a lie," Cameron defended. "Our orders also dictated that we were to assume the Lawrence's existing mission, which was to establish contact with one of our covert operatives on Gamaze and extract her if necessary. Those orders clearly gave us the discretion to enter the Gamazan home system. In fact, Captain Scott received his orders directly from the president at the time."

"His sister."

"That is correct."

"You can see how some people might twist that around."

"Of course," Cameron admitted. "But the truth is we were following our orders to the letter. And while our actions may have precipitated a war, they were not in violation of our orders. In fact, we strongly suspect that the Alliance orchestrated the entire thing in order to *start* the war."

"Yeah, I've heard that conspiracy theory before," Captain Klim admitted.

"And what do you think?"

"I think it's hard to imagine anyone *wanting* to see millions of people die needlessly just for the sake of power and profit."

"Nathan will be the first to tell you that history is full of just such examples."

"I know, but that doesn't make it any easier to believe."

"That's why they get away with it," Cameron said.

"I never thought about it that way," Captain Klim admitted.

"How long have you worked for Jakome Ta'Akar?" Cameron asked, hoping to change the topic.

"This is actually my first flight for him."

"Really. I assumed you knew him."

"I do," Captain Klim corrected. "He approached me more than a decade ago, just after I returned from my mission in the Onerason system. He had this crazy idea to start a new, utopian empire, far enough away from the Alliance to remain free of their influence. To be honest, I thought he was nuts. But he was so passionate about the idea and so open-minded about *how* to go about the task. Most people with such high-minded plans think they have everything figured out, and they won't listen to the advice of others. But Jakome was different. He *sought* the advice of others. He *craved* it. And not just from specialists or people like myself who had been there and done that. From *anyone.* I watched him listen to the ideas of a park maintenance tech on the proper landscaping of a city. He was enthralled by the man's ideas, and he had never *met* the guy before. He believes that *anyone* can be a source of inspiration. That's why I decided to take the mission. He not only wanted me to command the flight, but he also wanted my input on designing the ship and the load-out. And he wasn't just looking for confirmation of his *own* ideas. He wanted to learn from others."

"I didn't realize," Cameron admitted.

"At times he scares me. He's so driven and so single-minded. Yet with all his time and wealth being poured into his dream, he still manages to run his house and lands better than any of the other nobles."

"Sounds a lot like someone I once knew," Cameron said.

"Casimir?"

"Exactly," Cameron confirmed.

"Imagine what Casimir might have accomplished had he not had the leadership of Takara on his shoulders."

"I understand that Jakome spent hours listening to Deliza's stories about her father."

"Imagine that," Captain Klim said. "Visiting with an old woman who is like a grandparent to you but is actually the *daughter* of the man whose DNA you were cloned from."

"I think I know the feeling in a way," Cameron told

the captain. "When I first met the *clone* of Nathan Scott, he was, well...*different*. He *looked* the same, and for the most part, he acted the same, but there were differences about him. He didn't remember some things at first, and it kind of worried me. But eventually, he became more like himself but better."

"How so?"

"He always had really good instincts. I'm talking *unbelievably* good. It irritated me. Especially since he was so hesitant to embrace his role and utilize the talents he had been blessed with. But his clone seemed far less so. He embraced his role and excelled at it. His instincts were better, his coordination, his physical abilities, even his mind. Everything about him had improved as a result of the cloning process. I don't know how, but it did. *Plus* he had the added experiences of having lived for five years as someone else *without* knowing his true identity."

"History never said anything about *that*."

"I'm not surprised."

"What was he doing all those years?"

"He was a privateer with his own cargo shuttle, jumping all around the Pentaurus sector, barely scrapping out enough credits to keep the ship flying and feed his crew. Those experiences gave him an entirely new perspective on things, one that he never would have developed had he been *aware* of his true identity while living as Connor Tuplo."

"Connor Tuplo?"

"His alter ego," Cameron explained. "Don't bother searching for it. You won't find anything other than a fake background they created for him."

Captain Klim finished her last bite, leaning back

in her chair as she set her utensils down. "The man has led a storied life. There's no doubt about that."

"That's the thing about Nathan Scott," Cameron said. "He has two settings. Absolutely boring and full-speed out of control about to die."

"Where are we now?" Captain Klim wondered.

"Closer to the latter as usual," Cameron replied.

CHAPTER TWO

Nathan and Jessica stood just inside the hatch of the Traverna's reactor compartment, watching as Vladimir and Doctor Barra examined the suspended animation pod.

"It appears to be a fairly standard SA pod," Kayci stated as she cycled through the pod's various technical displays on the small control screen built into its side. "But there are no medical records for its occupant."

"What are you talking about?" Nathan asked.

"No one goes into SA these days unless they're in an escape pod or they've got some disease that medical science doesn't yet have a cure for."

"What about the Anastianus?" Jessica asked. "All of their passengers are in SA."

"The Anastianus?" Kayci asked, not familiar with the name.

"It's the colonization ship due to arrive at Libertara in a few days," Nathan explained. "The ship was originally designed for a months-long journey carrying a thousand colonists. All of them in suspended animation."

"Well *this* is a medical SA pod, which means it should have medical records in its data unit."

"Is that a problem?" Vladimir wondered.

"Maybe yes, maybe no," Kayci replied. "Why put her in a medical SA pod if there's nothing wrong with her? And if there *is* something wrong with her, why no medical records? And where's the accompanying physician? At the very least, there should be a pod-tech traveling with this unit."

"So you're saying she might be carrying some terrible disease?" Jessica asked.

"I'm saying that without medical records or someone who *knows* why she's traveling in a medical SA pod, we have no way of knowing. Not without reviving her."

"Can you scan her?" Nathan asked.

"I could, but that wouldn't tell me what's wrong with her."

"Why not?"

"Because suspended animation is just that. 'Suspended.' All metabolic processes are virtually halted. So the most I'd get is a snapshot of her current condition. While that might tell me a little, it won't give me anything close to an accurate diagnosis. For that, she must be taken completely out of SA."

"But if she is carrying a disease, we'd be risking the entire ship," Nathan surmised.

"Maybe one of the passengers was traveling with her?" Vladimir said.

"We interrogated all of them," Jessica replied.

"So. Maybe they lied?" Vladimir stated.

Jessica just sneered at him. "Trust me, I'd know."

"So we're back to the crew," Nathan decided. "If it was the engineer, then we might still get some useful information from him. But if it was one of the others..."

"We're shit outta luck," Jessica finished for him.

"Then we'd better bring her out of SA," Kayci opined.

"I'm not risking the entire ship over the mystery of one woman in SA," Nathan insisted. "I'd just as soon fix this ship and let Captain Helder complete the delivery."

"Assuming she wants to," Jessica pointed out.

Kayci stared at Nathan and Jessica, then at Vladimir. "For command-level officers, you people don't know much about your own ship's medical department."

Nathan looked at her, curious.

"We have medical isolation fields you know," Kayci explained. "There won't be any risk to the ship."

"We also cannot afford to put *you* at risk, Doctor," Nathan replied.

"Trust me, Captain. I don't wish to be put at risk either," Kayci assured him. "Fortunately the fields will protect me as well."

"Then I guess we'd better get this pod to medical," Nathan decided.

"That's going to be a little tricky," Vladimir admitted.

"Why?" Nathan asked, his tone implying that he was not happy about the surprise.

"The battery on this thing is nearly depleted," Vladimir explained. "The only reason it's still operating is because I connected it to the Traverna's power grid, which is currently being fed by the Aurora's power grid."

"Can't you rig a battery pack for it?" Nathan asked.

"Or recharge its existing battery?" Jessica suggested.

"It wasn't *originally* connected to this ship's power grid," Vladimir admitted. "I did that when I noticed its battery was low. But the power frequencies of this ship are very different than the Aurora's. The only reason we're able to provide power to keep basic systems running on this thing is because of its frequency converter. But I'm afraid to feed it too much power."

"You do realize this is all going over our heads, right?" Jessica complained.

"The *reactor* wasn't on your initial damage report for this ship," Nathan stated.

"Correct. I took it offline when I discovered this pod."

"Then just fire it back up and recharge the pod," Jessica insisted.

"There had to be a *reason* the pod wasn't connected to the ship's power grid," Vladimir reminded her. "For all we know, they aren't compatible. Plugging it in might destroy it."

"Which means the occupant dies, right?" Nathan asked, looking to Doctor Barra for the answer.

"She could still be successfully revived, but the odds would *not* be in her favor."

"Well we certainly don't have the right to put the *occupant* at risk just to satisfy our own curiosity," Nathan decided. Nathan looked at the doctor, noticing her sigh of relief. "You were expecting me to say otherwise?"

"Actually..."

Nathan turned back to Vladimir. "How long will it take you to get this thing rigged to move?"

"Then we *are* taking it back to the Aurora?" Jessica surmised.

"I'm just asking."

"A couple of hours if I stop fixing *this* ship," Vladimir estimated.

"How much more is there to do?" Nathan asked.

"We've got basic maneuvering barely working, as well as limited main propulsion. But all the grav-lift emitters on her starboard side are shot."

"How long to repair them?"

"Days," Vladimir warned. "Not only do we have to

fabricate new ones, but installing them is an *exterior* task, which means either EVAs or crawler work."

"Could one of our tugs get her down?" Jessica suggested.

"They're only designed to move a ship through space, not bring them down to the surface," Nathan told her.

Jessica looked at Nathan. "It's your call."

Nathan sighed. "As much as I'd like to know who she is and why she's in a medical SA pod, I don't think we have the right to make that decision."

"Who does?" Jessica wondered.

"Captain Helder I'm afraid. After all, she's a stowaway on *her* ship, not ours. But let's find a way to recharge her battery pack just in case."

"I'll take care of it," Vladimir promised.

"I need to get back to medical," Doctor Barra stated. "We still have several patients who require close attention, and Doctor Chen probably needs my help."

"Of course," Nathan agreed. "We'll escort you back."

* * *

"It's gotta be boring as hell," Josh insisted as he checked his jump nav display.

"*I don't know,*" Nikolas replied over comms. "*It might be kind of interesting. Every mission is slightly different.*"

"But you don't get to shoot anything."

"*But no one is shooting at you either.*"

"Exactly!" Josh exclaimed as he initiated their next patrol jump. "Where's the fun in that?"

"*You'd think differently if you had a wife and family to worry about,*" Nikolas replied as both

Dragons jumped in unison to the next waypoint on their patrol.

"Which is *exactly* why I make damn sure *that* never happens."

"*What, you don't like women?*" Nikolas teased.

"I love 'em," Josh insisted. "I just don't want to marry them. Takes all the fun out of 'em."

"*Spoken like a true, die-hard bachelor.*"

"I'll take that as a compliment." Suddenly, an alarm sounded in his cockpit, and the warning light along the top edge of his threat display began flashing red. "Uh-oh."

"*I see it,*" Nikolas confirmed. "*I'm not getting an ID though.*"

"Whoever the fuck he is, he's... Oh shit! Aurora! Dragon One! Four jump missiles inbound! Two five seven by one four!"

* * *

Erica's first shift on the Aurora's bridge had been uneventful. In fact, with the Aurora's AI monitoring everything, she had virtually nothing to do. The only reason she was there was to provide any immediate authorization needed by their AI in case of an emergency. But since Aurora had authorizations to take any action necessary to protect the ship and her crew, Erica couldn't imagine what authorization she might need to give.

Most of her time was spent answering comms from various sources, most of which were from the four Dragons currently patrolling the one-light-year perimeter around the Aurora and the Traverna docked to her port side. For some odd reason, Josh especially enjoyed constantly reporting 'no contacts' as he jumped from sector to sector, despite the fact that his sensors were directly linked to the Aurora's.

Should there be a contact, the Aurora's AI would be aware of it before Josh even keyed his mic.

In between comms calls, Erica spent her time studying the Aurora's operations manuals. She had just reached the point where she felt she knew everything about flying the Mirai when she had suddenly been thrown into her new role as a pilot for the Aurora herself. Although all spacecraft flew in relatively the same manner, being a large, complex warship, the Aurora had far more procedures and protocols than her shuttles. And she hadn't even looked at the section on weapons and combat yet.

"How's it going?" Aiden asked as he entered from behind.

Erica spun around, startled by his arrival. "You scared me."

"You're on the bridge. How's that even possible?"

"I wasn't expecting you back so soon."

"I *said* I'd be right back."

"But you went to get dinner. That usually takes more than ten minutes."

"Have you tasted Neli's goramon enchiladas?"

"What's a goramon?"

"I'm still trying to figure that one out," Aiden admitted, holding his belly as if he had indigestion.

"I guess I'm fasting tonight," Erica decided.

"Good choice. Anything to report?"

"Everything is quiet."

The bridge trim lighting suddenly turned red, and a single alert klaxon sounded on the bridge, immediately followed by the repeating alert echoing from the corridors outside the bridge.

"All hands, general quarters," Aurora announced over the loudspeakers. Meanwhile, the ship began to roll to starboard, initiating a turn and accelerating.

"What the..." Aiden began.

"*Incoming ordnance,*" Aurora continued. "*Brace, brace, brace.*"

The boarding tunnel connecting the Aurora to the Traverna shook suddenly, and the lights at the Aurora's end turned red. At the same time, the outer hatch to the Aurora rapidly slid shut.

"The ship is under attack, Captain," Aurora warned over Nathan's comm-set. "Recommend immediate return to the Traverna and quite possibly, her escape pods."

The gravity suddenly vanished, and the three of them found themselves floating in the tunnel that had previously connected the two ships.

"What's happening?" Kayci asked as she found herself weightless for the first time in her life.

"Get back to the Traverna!" Nathan barked. "Use the handrails!" he added, pushing Kayci toward the nearest handhold.

"Are we under attack?"

Nathan and Jessica ignored her. Nathan positioned himself to help Kayci by shoving her back toward the cargo ship to get her moving, then began pulling himself along the rails behind her, with Jessica doing the same to his right.

"They came back, didn't they?" Jessica assumed as she pulled herself along.

The tunnel shook violently. Nathan felt himself being sucked backward and flipping over due to the uneven forces suddenly being applied to him. As he tumbled, he saw the open end of the boarding tunnel, which had been ripped open by something.

The end of the tunnel lit up, covered by a pale blue pressure shield, and the sucking stopped. Nathan scrambled to get hold of the rail and avoid continuing through the pressure shield, which wasn't designed to stop solid matter from passing through it. After a second or two of fumbling, he finally caught hold of the rail, just in time to reach out and grab Kayci as she passed by him, also headed toward the pressure shield protecting them from the vacuum of space.

Jessica, who had also managed to get a firm grasp of the railing, also reached out to grab Kayci. "We gotta move!" she barked, pushing them both toward the Traverna again. "Haul ass!" she added as a flash of light from outside translated through the pressure shield, filling the tunnel.

All three of them pulled hard, building up speed toward the cargo ship they had just left. The moment they passed through the outer hatch, the Traverna's gravity took over and pulled them crashing downward onto the airlock deck.

Jessica rolled over, looking back toward the tunnel as it began to come apart. She jumped to her feet, slapping the hatch's close button hard. "Grab onto something!" she warned, bracing herself.

Again, sudden decompression threatened to pull them out into space, despite their efforts to hang on. Luckily, just as Doctor Barra was losing her grip on the interior hatch frame, the Traverna's outer hatch slid closed and sealed, halting the decompression process.

"Inside! Inside!" Jessica barked, pushing them out of the airlock into the cargo ship and closing the inner hatch as soon as they were inside.

"*What the hell's going on?*" Vladimir asked over

comm-sets as the cargo ship rocked violently, nearly knocking them off their feet.

"We're under attack!" Nathan replied. "Get that reactor to full power fast!" he added as he headed out.

"Where are you going?" Jessica asked.

"The flight deck."

"Will this thing even fly?" Jessica asked, following him out.

"It won't if we don't start pushing buttons!"

"What about me?" Doctor Barra wondered.

"Go back to engineering and help Vlad!" Nathan barked.

"But I'm a doctor, not an engineer!"

———————

"We're maneuvering!" Erica exclaimed as she jumped into the helmsman's seat.

"Aurora! Report!" Aiden barked as the ship rocked from detonations.

"*Four jump missiles were just intercepted and destroyed at close range,*" Aurora reported in her usual, calm, matter-of-fact manner. "*Shields are up, and I'm taking evasive action in case of a second wave.*"

"What about the Traverna?"

"I was forced to seal the docking tunnel and disconnect."

Aiden tapped his comm-set. "Captain Scott! How do you copy?"

"I've got contacts!" Erica warned. "Three two five by two one five, twenty kilometers out!"

"Multiple contacts," Aurora reported. "Fighters

and assault shuttles. Several of them are closing on the Traverna."

"*We're here!*" Jessica exclaimed. "*We're headed for the flight deck! We're gonna try to get this bucket under way!*"

"Six missile launches," Aurora reported. "Point-defenses activated."

"*Aiden!*" Nathan yelled over comm-sets. "*Take command!*"

"Aurora!" Aiden called. "All weapons hot. Maximum force is authorized!"

"*All weapons hot, going offensive,*" Aurora confirmed.

"Captain, you've got assault ships closing on you! They may be looking to try and board you again!"

"Two more contacts!" Erica declared. She glanced back up at the forward window screens as two Dragons streaked across their bow, close enough that Erica could swear she saw Josh smiling as he passed. "They're Dragons!"

––––––––––

"Those are *not* pirate ships," Josh stated as they passed over the Aurora's bow. He pushed his stick down, diving toward the assault shuttles closing on the Traverna.

"*Josh, we've got people on that cargo ship,*" Aiden warned over comms.

"We're on it," Josh assured him as he opened fire on the first shuttle. "Have you launched the Dragons?"

"*They're scrambling now,*" Aiden assured him. "*You guys protect that cargo ship. We'll deal with the heavies.*"

Josh passed over the assault shuttles, then flipped his ship over so that his nose was pointing aft. He fired his plasma cannons again, decimating one of the shuttles as Nikolas destroyed the other. He then thrusted downward, putting his fighter into a backwards descent on the port side of the cargo ship, pushing his main engine throttles to full power to arrest his motion and reverse direction. A few seconds later, he was headed nose first under the Traverna, at which point he pulled back his throttles and pitched up, blasting the last shuttle as it was about to attach to the cargo ship's starboard side.

"*Four more inbound,*" Nikolas warned as his fighter streaked past Josh, having followed him through the entire maneuver.

"Traverna! You're clear for now! Suggest you haul ass!"

"*Dragons Seven and Eight, engaging!*" Allet announced over comms.

"Kusya! Pound those shuttles before they get here," Josh instructed. "Remo and I will ride escort on the Traverna!"

Nathan entered the Traverna's flight deck, pausing momentarily to get his bearings. It was larger than the cockpit of the Seiiki, but much smaller than the bridge of the Aurora, with a total of six stations. Deciding that the helm was at one of the two forward stations, he went for the left station, spotting manual flight controls to the left of the seat and a throttle quadrant in the center.

"Where's that power, Vlad?" Nathan demanded

over comm-sets as he plopped down into the pilot's seat.

"*This is a cargo ship, Nathan, not a warship,*" Vladimir protested. "*You can't just flip a switch and expect her to come alive!*"

"Well if it doesn't, we won't be," Nathan said as he began turning on systems. "We've at least got some battery power," he informed Jessica as she took the seat next to him.

Jessica peered out the starboard windows, spotting four small flashes of light revealing tiny forms that she couldn't quite make out. "This can't be good."

———

"Four more contacts," Laza reported as she took her station. "Three assault shuttles and what looks like a jump tug."

"Comms, warn Josh about that tug. Don't let it get near the Traverna.

"Aye, sir."

"Have our Dragons launched?"

"*Affirmative,*" Aurora replied.

"More incoming missiles," Laza reported.

"*Taking evasive action,*" Aurora followed. "Jumping."

"Jesus," Aiden exclaimed as the jump flash washed over them for the third time in less than a minute. He glanced up at the tactical display on the center overhead view screen, trying to keep track of where they were in relation to the fight, but the Aurora was already coming about hard and jumping again.

"*Locking four missiles, two on each of the larger*

vessels," the ship's AI reported. "*I assume I still have authorization to fire?*"

"Please," Aiden insisted.

"*Missiles away.*"

"I can barely keep track of where we are," Erica admitted with frustration.

"Don't feel bad," Aiden told her. "Neither can I."

"New contacts," Laza warned. "Dozens of them, coming from the warships."

"Dozens?" Aiden asked. "What are they?"

"I'm not sure," Laza admitted. "But they're small."

"*They are drones,*" Aurora reported, "*and they are armed.*"

Nikolas's eyes widened as he watched the dozens of icons moving toward them on his tactical display. "Those are swarm drones."

"*What the fuck are swarm drones?*" Josh asked.

"Dozens of small drones acting in unison," Nikolas explained. "By themselves not much of a threat, but in groups of ten or twenty?"

"*Well they're not vectoring on us,*" Josh said.

"They're headed for the Traverna," Nikolas realized. "They'll make sure she can't get away."

"*How do we kill 'em?*"

"Like everything else I'm guessing."

"*That's all I needed to hear,*" Josh exclaimed.

"What are you doing here?" Vladimir asked as he worked.

"The captain told me to come and help you," Doctor Barra explained.

"You're a doctor, not an engineer."

"That's what I told him!"

There was a sudden bang that rocked the ship, eliciting a tiny yelp from the startled doctor.

"*Vlad!*" Jessica called over comm-sets. "*Boarders aft! Don't let them take engineering, or we're screwed.*"

"*Gospadee*," Vladimir exclaimed. "No gun and a doctor," he added as he scrambled to find something to defend himself.

"What are you doing?" Kayci asked.

"Looking for a weapon. They've boarded us."

"What?" A noise from the corridor caught Kayci's attention. She leaned out, withdrawing with widened eyes when she heard both voices and footfalls. "Someone's coming!" she exclaimed as she ran toward Vladimir.

With nothing else in sight, Vladimir picked up the nearest object, a metal toolbox. Kayci screamed, and Vlad spun around as two men entered, weapons drawn. Vlad raised the toolbox as the first man fired, but the blast of energy ricocheted off the toolbox, bouncing off the overhead, the deck, one bulkhead and then another before it finally passed only millimeters behind the man who had fired it. It slammed into the neck of the second man, toppling him over. The first man turned to look at his fallen comrade, surprised that his personal shield had not protected him. That was Vladimir's opportunity, and he took it, charging forward, swinging the toolbox around and slamming it into the side of the first man's head. The man tried to duck back to avoid the object, but the corner of the metal box caught him in the cheek, ripping it open and slinging blood, and a few teeth, across the compartment.

Vladimir's decades-old training came back to him

in that instant, and he continued around, letting the momentum of the toolbox carry it in a full circle, landing in his opponent's side next, and sending him to the deck. Vlad then raised the toolbox up and dropped to his knees, straddling the man as he drove the toolbox into his face, smashing his nose and driving it into the intruder's brain.

Kayci stood in horror, stunned by what she had just witnessed. Until this moment, she had seen Vladimir as a big teddy bear with a data pad and wrench. Now he seemed more like a grizzly.

Vladimir paused for a moment, dropping the toolbox to the side. Then he heard more voices and footfalls, and scrambled for the dead man's gun two meters away.

Two more men entered just as Vladimir reached the weapon. He rolled over, firing repeatedly without really aiming. Again, tiny bolts of energy, strong enough to inflict deadly wounds but not powerful enough to penetrate the alloy bulkheads of the ship, ricocheted off the walls, ceiling, deck, and various pieces of machinery. Miraculously, none of them found a human target.

The two men fired back, rounds bouncing off the deck on either side of Vlad, but the burly engineer continued firing as he brought his weapon to bear on the first man and then the second. To his surprise, his assumption had been correct. Something about the systems in this compartment interfered with the intruders' protective shields.

Without pause, Vladimir scrambled to his feet, quickly grabbing the weapons dropped by the second pair of men, tossing one of them to Doctor Barra, who nearly dropped it.

"I'm a *doctor!*" she reminded him.

"Not today," Vladimir said as he stepped into the hatch, checking down the corridor for boarders. "Get to the flight deck! You'll be safer there with Nathan and Jessica!"

"What if there are more of them out there?"

"That's what the gun is for," Vladimir insisted, pushing her out the door. "I'll get you halfway there!" he added, following her out and sweeping his weapon down the corridor behind them.

"You're not going there?"

"My place is back here," Vladimir insisted.

The drone swarms split up, half of them heading for the Traverna and the other half toward the Aurora. Every gun emplacement along the Aurora's three gun tracks opened fire, targeting the rapidly approaching drones.

"*The drones are moving too fast for our guns to accurately track,*" Aurora warned. "*Less than one percent of our shots are hitting them.*"

"What are they doing?" Aiden asked, unable to discern their tactics.

"*I believe they are searching for openings,*" their AI stated. "*I have sealed up all openings in the exterior hull, including the Dragon recovery deck and the hangar bay. But I will be unable to relocate our weapons turrets as long as the swarm is active.*"

"Well just jump us!" Aiden exclaimed.

"*The drones are very close,*" Aurora warned. "*Most of them will be jumped with us.*"

"Well if we can't do anything about the swarm, how about the ships they came from?" Aiden suggested.

"*We are limited to guns,*" Aurora replied. "*Launching missiles requires opening exterior doors, which is not recommended.*"

"Son of a bitch," Aiden exclaimed. "For little drones that aren't even shooting at us, these things are a hell of a nuisance."

"*Agreed.*"

"Maneuver in close to the nearest warship and hit them with every gun we've got," Aiden instructed. "But jump clear if we start losing shields."

———————

"Reactor is at five percent and rising," Jessica reported. She peered out of the window again, spotting the swarm of drones and the four ships coming toward them, one of which was much larger than the others. "I think that's a tug!"

"What?" Nathan strained to see for himself but was unable to spot anything.

"They're deploying something," Jessica said as the drones swarmed around them. "Fuck. Those are jump rescue nets!"

Nathan jammed his flight control stick forward. Although the response was more than sluggish, his nose did begin to pitch down a bit. Then he moved his stick all the way to the right, starting an agonizingly slow roll maneuver at the same time.

"What the hell are you doing?"

"Whatever I can to make it more difficult for them," Nathan replied, frustrated. "Come on, Vlad! Where's that power?"

"*We're a little busy back here!*" Vladimir replied,

the sound of energy weapons fire nearly drowning out his voice.

"I'm on it," Jessica said, jumping from her seat.

"Christ! What the hell kinda shields has that thing got?" Josh exclaimed as his barrage of fire seemed to bounce off the tug's flashing shields.

"*You've got eight drones on your ass!*" Nikolas warned.

"*Josh! Another one of those shuttles just attached itself to the Traverna's hull!*" Allet announced over comms.

"Well shoot the fucker!" Josh told him. "They're probably trying to put boarders on."

Josh felt a thud, followed by several flashing warning lights. "Fuck! I lost my starboard drive! I've gotta jump clear and shake these buggers!"

"*Do it, Josh!*" Nikolas replied. "*I'll follow you and try to force them off you!*"

"Just don't shoot *me* in the process!"

"*No promises,*" Nikolas replied.

Josh sighed as he moved his thumb to the jump button on his flight control stick. "I fucking hate drones."

"The drones are targeting our shields and jump emitters," Abby warned, having just arrived and taken her station.

"How the hell are they getting *inside* our shields?" Aiden demanded.

"They may appear to be fast-moving, but they are

well below our shields' effective defense threshold," Laza explained.

"In English?"

"They're too small and too slow for our shields to stop them," Abby translated.

"You couldn't just say *that*?" Aiden asked Laza.

"If we don't jump in the next minute, we may not be able to jump at all," Abby warned.

"Shit!" Nikolas exclaimed as he jinked back and forth, trying to stay on Josh's tail as his leader attempted to shake the drones that were attempting to latch onto him.

"*What the hell are they doing?*" Josh barked.

"They're trying to latch onto you!"

"*Fucking why?*"

"That's probably how they inflict damage. Maybe drill into you or something!"

"*Or something?*"

"Well how the hell do I know?"

"*You're the drone geek!*"

"Would you hold still a moment?" Nikolas complained. "I'm trying to shoot these things and you're making it harder!"

"*Oh yeah? Well watch this!*"

Josh's Dragon suddenly entered a very fast roll, pitching over at the same time, finally adding in a rapid starboard yaw just to make it even more ridiculous.

"Holy crap, Josh! What the hell are you doing?"

"*Let's see them try to latch onto me now!*"

Nikolas got a surprised look on his face, noticing that the drones were actually spreading out, probably to avoid colliding with the wildly spinning fighter. "Gina, lock onto those drones and fire, but *don't* hit Dragon One!"

"*Understood,*" his AI confirmed.

One by one, pinpoint bolts of plasma fired by Dragon Two's gun turrets began picking off the drones as they maneuvered to avoid colliding with the wildly spinning fighter.

Josh concentrated on his three-way spin maneuver, trying to keep track of his fighter's orientation in relation to his path of flight. At some point, he would have to recover from this absurd maneuver, which, even with his AI's help, was not going to be easy. "Talk to me, Remo!"

"It's working!" Nikolas replied over comms. "Thirty seconds! Just give me thirty seconds!"

"*In thirty-two seconds, this maneuver will become unrecoverable,*" his AI warned.

"Nothing's unrecoverable!" Josh insisted.

"Dragon Three, away," Talisha reported as her fighter left the port launch tube. "Kusya, Slider! Help is on the way!" she added as she turned toward the Traverna to join Allet and Tika in defending the besieged cargo ship.

"*Dragon Three, Aurora,*" Sima called over comms. "*Unable to launch remaining Dragons.*"

"What? Why not?"

"*Ship is on external lockdown to prevent the drones from getting inside,*" Sima explained.

"Well isn't that lovely," Talisha commented. She glanced at her tactical display, hoping to see her wingman's icon, but he wasn't there.

"*Sorry, boss,*" Evan said over comms.

"Launch when you can," she replied.

"*We can't force that tug off the Traverna,*" Allet said. "*They're too well shielded.*"

"Have you tried A-Sams?" Talisha asked.

"*Too risky. The blast would rip the Traverna apart. All we can do is keep those assault shuttles off them.*"

Talisha glanced up, looking out her forward windows for the first time since she launched. The Traverna and the jump tug attached to her were directly ahead, broadening as she closed in on them. She could see Allet's and Tika's Dragons as they fired on the assault ships, one of which had managed to attach itself to the Traverna's hull. Allet's fighter opened fire, tearing apart the assault shuttle that was still maneuvering. "Don't shoot the shuttle attached to the Traverna!" Talisha insisted. "If they've already breached the hull and you destroy them, the entire ship might decompress!"

"*Fuck!*" Allet exclaimed in frustration as his fighter peeled off.

"Captain Scott! This is Talisha! You've got boarders entering midship. Do you copy?"

The Traverna suddenly became engulfed in blue-white light that quickly brightened and then flashed, fading a second later.

The Traverna and the jump-tug were gone.

"Leta! Can you calculate their jump range and heading?" Talisha asked.

"*Affirmative.*"

"Send the trail to the Aurora and jump when ready." Talisha instructed her AI.

"Ten seconds," Josh's AI warned.

"*Two more to go!*" Nikolas reported.

Josh grabbed his flight control stick and began his attempt to stop the wild spin he had started, firing tiny bursts to measure the effect and get a feel for how much thrust it would take and from which thrusters, in order to regain control over his fighter.

"*You are doing it incorrectly,*" his AI cautioned.

"Oh please," Josh replied as he continued his efforts to regain control.

"*Five seconds,*" his AI cautioned. "*Would you like me to take over?*"

"I've got this," Josh insisted. He suddenly felt his flight controls lock up. "Hey!"

"*I was being polite,*" his AI clarified as the ship's wild roll began to slow. A few seconds later, the roll was completely gone, and the fighter was flying nose-first.

"I told you I had it," Josh protested.

"*And I determined that you did not, so I took appropriate action to protect you and the ship.*"

Josh took the controls and began to turn back toward the engagement. "Women," he muttered.

"*I am only female because you chose this voice for me.*"

"*Are you okay?*" Nikolas asked over comms.

"I'm fine," Josh assured him.

"*You're clear.*"

"Thanks," Josh replied. He glanced at his tactical

display, which was still connected to the Aurora's systems via his AICC node. "Shit. They've jumped."

"*About a minute ago,*" Nikolas confirmed. "*Talisha, Allet, and Tika went after them.*"

"Did they transmit their track data?"

"*Of course they did,*" Nikolas replied.

"Then let's go."

"*You're down an engine, Josh, and you can't even land to change into another service frame.*"

"Aurora, Dragon One, requesting hot swap."

———————

"The Traverna jumped!" Laza reported from the Aurora's sensor station.

"Dragon Three reports she has a track," Sima announced. "Three, Four, Seven, and Eight are going after them."

"Shit," Aiden cursed. The situation was rapidly spinning out of control, and the Traverna was gone, taking Nathan, Jessica, Vladimir, and Doctor Barra with her.

The incoming weapons fire suddenly stopped.

"All contacts are jumping!" Laza announced. "They didn't even wait to recover their drones."

"What are the drones doing?" Aiden wondered.

"They've gone dormant."

"Aurora, feel free to take those drones out, just in case they decide to act on their own."

"*Understood.*"

"Captain," Sima called, "Dragon One has suffered damage to one of his main engines. He's requesting a hot swap so that he and Dragon Two can join the pursuit."

"That's our last spare, right?" Aiden said.

"My link with Dragon One indicates that I can still remotely pilot his service frame back to ship for repairs," Aurora reported. *"Shall I dispatch the last service frame for the hot swap?"*

"Do it," Aiden confirmed. "The last Dragon pilot we want to be without right now is Josh."

The Traverna was a simple ship, with a single long corridor running from the flight deck at the bow of the ship all the way to the engineering section at its stern. But while it was quick to get from one end to the other, it also made one part of the ship hard to defend from the other. The hatches at every major bulkhead along the way were the only natural defensive positions, and poor ones at that. A well-armed assault force with proper personal shields, stunners, and hatch-popping charges could sweep the Traverna in minutes, immobilizing everyone on board.

Jessica had two things going for her at this point. First, the Dragons had managed to keep most of the boarding shuttles from getting their assault teams on board. The second advantage was that she had Vladimir at the aft end, and he was not your average, nerdy engineer.

Jessica was more aggressive than their invaders, and she had spent seven years training with the Ghatazhak, so there was a good chance she was better trained than any of her combatants, and she knew it.

She paused momentarily at the first hatch, peeking around it before continuing aft as quickly as possible. She could already hear weapons fire echoing from the far end of the corridor, likely from Vladimir fiercely defending his position, which was impressive since he hadn't come aboard with a weapon himself.

Two more hatches down, her peek revealed Dr Barra running toward her in a panic. "Doctor Barra!" she yelled.

The overhead suddenly blew apart, followed by a rush of air as the interior pressure dropped slightly. The impact nearly knocked Jessica off her feet, but she knew what it was.

Doctor Barra, however, did not. The crash caused her to stumble forward awkwardly, ending up prone on the deck. Four armed men suddenly dropped through the opening blown through the overhead, drawing their weapons as they landed.

Jessica wasted no time. She fired twice, causing two men to fall to the side but without injury, their personal shields protecting them from her precisely placed weapons fire. She charged forward, holstering her weapon and drawing her combat knife as she ran toward the two intruders turning to take aim at her. As the first man brought his weapon to bear, she dropped to her knees with her knife arm outstretched, sliding along the deck toward him. Her knife, having very little kinetic energy with which to react to the man's personal shield, penetrated it easily, allowing her to drive it into his groin just left of his manhood. The man immediately dropped his weapon, his instinct to protect his genitals overcoming his sense of mission.

Jessica quickly withdrew her knife, then spun around to her right, driving her blade through the second man's shield and stabbing him in the left thigh before he could get his weapon pointed at her.

With those two preoccupied momentarily, Jessica turned her attention to the first two men, who were getting back on their feet. One fired, his shot streaking so close to Jessica's left ear that she could feel the heat and hear the sizzle as the energy singed her hair. She dropped and rolled toward the man, her entire body passing easily through the bottom of his personal shield where it met the deck. Now on her back, her sidearm was again in her hand, firing upward at the man's unprotected left buttocks. The man cried out in pain, his left hand going to the burning flesh in his butt. Jessica reached up and grabbed the control pack to the man's personal shield from his belt, disabling it.

She jumped to her feet, pulling the wounded man's weapon and firing at the two men she had previously wounded, both of whom were now on the deck, writhing in pain. Her shots were placed at the edges of their shields, where they met the floor. The bolts of energy ricocheted off the deck, tagging the men and injuring them further, but still not killing them.

The last man, the one who had just returned to his feet and had yet to be injured, drove himself into Jessica with all his weight, driving her into the wall and knocking the wind out of her. What he didn't know was that the Ghatazhak regularly trained in that precise state, having no breath in their lungs. Jessica drove both her fists into the sides of the man's head just below his helmet, striking the lower portions of his ears. The man stumbled backward, momentarily stunned. This bought Jessica just enough time to draw another breath, refilling her lungs. The man drew his saber, a murderous look on his face.

"Really?" Jessica said.

He lunged at her, swinging his saber up and over, then downward toward Jessica's head. In one swift move, Jessica drew her combat blade again, bringing it up to parry the attack, deflecting it just enough to miss her head while still allowing the man's kinetic energy to carry his blade downward, pulling his own body with it.

Another, smaller blade magically appeared in Jessica's left hand, finding its way through the man's personal shield and into his abdomen just right of his mid-line, where she gave it a twist and then an inward pull, making sure that she sliced open his large intestine and his descending aorta before withdrawing the weapon. The man dropped, blood spewing from his gaping wound. But so far, he was the only attacker who was completely incapacitated.

Doctor Barra looked on in horror. Never had she witnessed such violence...and from someone she *knew*.

Jessica wasted no time dispatching the next man, easily penetrating his personal shield with her slow-moving blade, then slicing open his carotid artery. "Get to the flight deck!" she ordered the doctor as she moved to execute the next wounded man.

"What about you?"

"I'm headed aft to help Vlad," Jessica replied as she moved to the last man, taking his life without hesitation or remorse.

Kayci stared as blood gushed from the gaping neck wound on the last man. Every instinct in her was telling her to rush to the man's aid. Even with just the most basic medical tools, she could have closed that wound and saved his life, but...

"GO!" Jessica demanded as another explosion

from further down the long corridor aft of them rocked the ship, and Jessica ran toward it.

Kayci did the opposite, turning and running forward, not looking back at the faces of the dead and dying.

———————

Talisha's Dragon came out of its jump only a few hundred kilometers away from both the Traverna and the two ships that had originally attacked her.

"Hell yeah!" she exclaimed in disbelief. "Nice job, Leta!"

"*They did not bother to conceal their jump signatures,*" her AI replied. "*However, if we continue to pursue them, they may.*"

"Stench, you with me?" Talisha called over comms as she glanced at her tactical display, spotting a single blue icon directly behind her.

"*I've got your six, boss!*" Evan replied. "*Let's go get 'em!*"

Talisha rolled left, pushing her nose over onto an intercept heading, dialing up a short jump at the same time. As soon as she finished her turn, she moved her thumb to the jump button on her flight control stick. "Weapons hot, Leta," she instructed. "If it's not a friendly, kill it."

"*Understood.*"

"*Three, Seven,*" Allet called as Talisha pressed her jump button. A second later, the contacts that had been a few hundred kilometers away were now only a few hundred meters directly in front of her and approaching fast. A quick glance out of her forward windows revealed that two boarding pods had already attached themselves to the Traverna, and two more had just been launched from one of the assault ships.

"Kusya, try to force those assault ships away from the Traverna," Talisha instructed as she opened fire on the two assault pods on their way to the cargo ship. "Traverna, Dragon Three. Four Dragons are still with you, sir. We'll keep any more breach pods from reaching you, but we can't do anything about the two that are already attached. Not without opening your hull to space."

———————

"Jesus," Josh exclaimed, looking straight up. Just outside, their only reserve Dragon service frame pulled into position, inverted, directly above Josh's wounded fighter. "Fucking weird to see one of these things without a cockpit in it."

"*Stand by for transfer,*" his AI warned.

"Let's do it," Josh insisted, impatient after already having been out of action for two whole minutes.

"*Initiating transfer.*"

All of Josh's displays suddenly went dead as his AI disconnected his cockpit module from the damaged service frame. Next came the familiar 'clunks' as the four retaining clamps holding his cockpit in place disengaged. His cockpit began to rise smoothly out of its service frame, completely exiting the frame two seconds later. Tiny attitude thrusters fired, causing his cockpit to roll to the left. A few seconds later they fired again but on the opposite side, arresting his roll exactly one hundred and eighty degrees later.

Josh sat patiently watching out his forward windows as his cockpit slowly descended into its new service frame.

"*Contact with frame eleven,*" his AI reported.

Three seconds later, the clunks returned, this time securing him into his new fighter service frame. His displays lit up again as his AI connected his cockpit module with service frame eleven.

"*Conducting quick-checks,*" his AI reported.

"Come on!"

"*That was pretty cool to watch,*" Nikolas commented over comms.

"Tell me you have the Traverna's current coordinates," Josh asked his AI.

"*Affirmative. Quick-checks complete. Successful mating. Service frame eleven is ready for full operation.*"

"Fuck yeah!" Josh declared as he shoved his throttles forward and immediately rolled toward the heading for the Traverna's new position. "Let's get back at it, Remo!"

"*Right behind you, boss,*" Nikolas replied.

"We can get in there and protect them!" Kit insisted, challenging Aiden directly on the Aurora's bridge.

"They've already jumped again," Aiden replied. "And the moment your shuttle jumps in, they'll deploy those drones and blast you to hell before you get anywhere *near* that ship."

"We're willing to take that chance," Kit argued.

"I know you are, Kit, but I'm not," Aiden insisted. "Besides, short of you and your men, the three most capable defenders we have are already on board that ship. The best we can do is to keep any more boarding pods from reaching them."

"Can we at least take out those assault ships?"

"They're too well shielded. We'd have to empty out all our ordnance bays to do so. Besides, we've already lost ten percent of our jump emitters. We can't afford to go toe-to-toe with them, not with our current armaments."

Kit looked down, frustrated.

"I'm sorry, Kit," Aiden said, sharing the lieutenant's feeling of helplessness. "I know you want to help."

"No, you're right. You made the right call, Aiden." He took a deep breath. "If the Dragons can keep those breach pods away, Jess will do the rest."

———

"Shit!" Talisha exclaimed as she came out of the next jump in pursuit of the Traverna and was immediately met with heavy weapons fire from the two assault ships. She jinked her fighter wildly, jumping ahead two kilometers just to get out of their field of fire. "Coming about!" she announced as she entered a hard turn to port. Her tactical display suddenly lit up as dozens of icons began appearing, pouring out of the two icons representing the assault ships. "Kusya, you gotta get those assault ships out of here!"

"*I'm working on it!*" Kusya replied over comms.

———

Kayci reached the Traverna's cockpit, slightly out of breath from her jog down the long corridor as well as her encounter with the enemy boarders.

Nathan glanced back at her, noticing the blood splattered across her chest and face. "Are you all right, Doc?"

"Yes...I think."

"*Traverna, Dragon Three! You've got a breach pod attached about ten meters aft of your flight deck! If they haven't already...*"

Another blast rocked the Traverna, this time occurring only a few meters behind Doctor Barra standing in the hatchway. The blast launched her forward, with Nathan barely catching her as he rose, preventing her from going face-first into the back of the copilot's seat. Debris flew everywhere, bouncing off the walls, ceiling, and deck, careening in all directions.

Nathan felt a sharp pain in his left shoulder, then in his right temple, as pieces of debris slammed into him. Kayci also felt a sudden, sharp pain across her back. Nathan dropped the doctor to one side, charging forward to meet the four men dropping from the ceiling. "Boarders!" he cried out over comm-sets as he charged. "Just aft of the flight deck!"

Josh came out of the jump a few kilometers away from the active engagement.

"*Holy crap, there are drones everywhere!*" Nikolas announced over comms.

"We gotta shake those ships off of them," Josh declared as he flipped his ship over and shoved his throttles all the way forward.

"*What are you doing, Josh?*" Nikolas asked.

"Kus, Hotdog," Josh called over comms, not bothering to answer his wingman. "Clear Heavy Two. I'm gonna try something."

"*Copy that,*" Allet replied. "*Watch out, Josh.*"

They've got mini-guns for close in. You can't get inside their defenses."

"Oh yeah?" Josh made some quick adjustments. "Sweetie, cancel all safeties."

"That is not advised," his AI warned.

"I didn't say it was."

"All safeties disengaged."

"Remo, I'm sending you my jump. Mirror me to starboard by two hundred meters. Do *not* follow me straight in."

"That's too close, Josh," Nikolas warned over comms.

"Close is what works."

"It would work better if I followed you in," Nikolas insisted.

"Negative," Josh reiterated. "If this doesn't work, I'll need you to cover my escape."

"This is a bad idea."

"Worse than jumping inside a main engine thrust port?" Josh asked as he pressed the jump button on his flight control stick.

Josh felt a sudden, violent bump, as if he had hit something big, then the assault ship appeared to his left so close that he felt as if he could reach out and touch it. His pulse instantly doubled as a massive dump of adrenaline hit his bloodstream. He toggled the missile select, choosing A-Sams. "Four of them, sweetie!" he commanded as he pressed and held the launch button.

————————

Four missiles dropped out of the Dragon's ventral weapons bay, but their main engines did not ignite. Instead, their maneuvering thrusters fired just enough to cause them to drift toward the enemy ship as the momentum imparted to them by their host continued to carry them forward.

Incoming weapons fire from the mini-guns Allct had warned of slammed into Josh's shields, lighting them up with dozens of tiny flashes of yellow light as the defensive barrier absorbed their energy.

Josh tapped his jump button again, waiting to feel the exit *bump* as he passed through the assault ship's shields. A second later, he jammed his throttles forward, going to full power.

Four explosions rocked the assault ship in rapid succession as the four anti-ship missiles detonated. The ship skidded to the left, her starboard hull torn open by the blasts. The ship, now badly damaged, immediately disengaged and turned away from the battle, seeking safety to lick its wounds.

"Holy crap!" Tika exclaimed over comms.

"Jesus, Josh," Talisha added. *"Are you insane?"*

"Hey, it worked, didn't it?" Josh defended.

As Jessica swung her blade at one of the boarder's faces, someone reached around and grabbed her from behind. Wrapping his armor-covered arm around her neck and pulling backward, he lifted her feet off the floor. Jessica immediately jabbed her blade backward over her right shoulder, catching the stranger in his right ear, causing him to release her. She dropped back to her feet, dropping down into a crouch just as the man in front of her swung his saber in a broad lateral arc, barely missing her head. She jabbed her knife forward into the man's left thigh, grabbing his second saber from his right hip with her left hand. She swung that saber to the outside, flipping her left wrist over and back as the tip of the blade arced around and then caught the man across his face, cutting him open across his left cheek. She then tucked low, diving forward between his legs and tumbling over once and returning to her feet. In a flash, she hurled her combat knife toward the third man four meters away. The blade was traveling slowly enough to pass through the man's personal shield, but not fast enough to penetrate the seam in his body armor, and it deflected harmlessly to the side.

The third man fired at her, and she dodged to her left just in time. Two more steps and she was within striking distance with her saber, but her opponent blocked her attempt to leap forward and spear him in the gut.

Jessica let her momentum carry her forward, ducking under the man's counterattack as she passed to his right. Again she tucked and rolled, picking up her combat knife in the process. After returning to her feet once more, she spun around, piercing its tip into the back of the man's calf and instantly withdrawing it. She came to a standing combat position before the man could turn to face her. When he did, he found her saber slicing across his neck, splaying his carotid wide open and sending blood spewing across her and the wall behind her. She took two steps, throwing her bodyweight into the man as his legs were giving out, sending him into the wounded boarder behind him. Both men toppled down, with the dead atop the wounded.

That bought her the time she needed to deal with the last two men, both of whom were now holding their sabers. For a moment, she wondered why they didn't just go for their sidearms and blast her, since she didn't have a personal shield. Either they didn't realize she was unprotected, or they just wanted to teach her a lesson, and a bloody one at that. Either way, it was a mistake, and it was one they'd never get a chance to repeat.

Nathan's only advantage was that a single blast from an energy weapon would blow out the cockpit windows and violently decompress the flight deck, along with the corridor behind it, where the boarders had just broken in. He charged forward, lunging at the nearest boarder before the man could pull his saber from its sheath.

Nathan's left hand went immediately to the man's left hand, which was in the process of pulling the saber, and then punched the man in the face with all his might. While the man was wearing protective combat armor, his face was not protected, and the blow drew blood from both his nose and his mouth.

The man was stunned at first but then regained his senses, butting his forehead into Nathan's, interrupting his assault. Nathan stumbled back, falling against the edge of the hatchway. He scrambled for something to grab to keep from falling, his left hand finding a small fire-bottle, which he pulled from its mount and swung toward his attacker, striking him on the right side of his head. The man fell to his left, his head striking a protruding soffit running along the port wall of the corridor, causing his neck to snap.

For a moment, Nathan was surprised, not expecting the blow to kill the man. But he didn't remain immobile, in shock, for long. He couldn't afford to. Three more men had dropped in along with the first and were turning to attack Nathan as well.

Nathan glanced about, spotting the dead man's saber laying under him. He dropped to his knees just as the next man pulled his own saber and, in the same motion, swung across where Nathan's head had been a moment ago. Nathan grabbed the handle of the saber, pulling the weapon out from under the dead man and swinging it around just in time to catch the second man's next attack and deflect it to the side. Nathan punched the man in the gut, causing him to double over, and then jumped back to his feet, stepping behind the man and toward the third attacker. He raised his saber above his head, turning it laterally and perpendicular to the third attacker's descending weapon, then raised his left foot up and jammed it into the man's abdomen, pushing him backward into the fourth intruder, causing them both to tumble backward.

But Nathan was unable to press the attack, as the man behind him was still a threat. Nathan spun around again just as the man lurched forward, angling the tip of his blade toward Nathan's torso. Nathan stepped to one side, knocking the man's saber in the opposite direction. This put Nathan's blade, now pointing downward as it parried the man's attack, at the mid-line of his opponent. Nathan slid his blade forward along his attacker's blade, leaning into him as his blade jumped off the hilt of the other man's saber. Nathan slashed upward, drawing the edge of his blade along the man's body armor. While the armor protected the man's torso, that protection ended at the base of his neck. Nathan's blade cut into the man's chin and lips, but instead of continuing upward, as soon as the tip of Nathan's saber cleared the upper edge of his opponent's chest armor, Nathan angled the tip inward, then drove it downward through the notch at the base of the man's neck, cutting into his both his trachea and esophagus.

The stranger's eyes widened with the realization that he was dead no matter what he did. Blood gushed from the gaping wound as he dropped to his knees, both hands grasping at his throat. But it was too late. Air and blood mixed, and quickly flooded the man's lungs, leaving him lying on the deck, drowning in his own fluids.

"Shit!" Allet exclaimed as warning lights began flashing red all over his console.

"*Kus!*" Tika called over comms. "*You're getting swarmed with drones! Get out of there!*"

"I can't maneuver!" Allet replied, frustrated. "They've done something to my systems!"

Nikolas followed Josh toward the next assault ship, which had already pulled away from the Traverna in order to maneuver and better defend itself. "Kusya! Charge your hull!"

"*What?*"

"Dump all your power into your outer hull! Do it now!"

"You have any idea what he's talking about?" Allet asked his AI.

"*I do,*" his AI replied. "*Channeling reactor power into outer hull.*"

The hull of Allet's Dragon fighter flashed with erratic webs of blue-white light as all the power from its main reactors was shunted into it. The energy leapt from the hull into the drones that had attached themselves to it. Unable to protect themselves from the massive amounts of power jumping from the hull into their bodies, the drones let go, falling away, some of them exploding in their own showers of sparks as a result of their systems being overloaded.

No one was more surprised than Allet. "It worked!" he exclaimed, laughing in relief as he regained control of his key systems. "How the hell did you come up with that?"

"*I know drones!*" Nikolas replied. "*Now jump the hell out of there. You've got about twenty of them headed your way!*"

"Jumping now!"

Vlad could hear the sounds of swords clanking together. There was a fierce battle happening on the other side of the hatch, and he had a pretty good idea of whom it involved.

The sounds suddenly stopped, followed by a thud.

Vladimir stopped what he was working on, moving closer to the hatch, listening. Three raps came on the hatch, startling him.

"*Open the hatch, you big oaf!*" Jessica's voice called from the other side of the hatch.

"Jessica?" Vladimir called back, surprised to hear her voice.

"*Nyet, eta kot Cosmos!*"

Vladimir opened the hatch. On the other side was Jessica, covered with blood splatter, a knife in her left hand, and a saber in her right. "That was *not* funny. By the way, when did you learn Russian?" Vlad looked to either side of her and behind her, spotting four men, all of them dead, and all of them covered in far more blood than her. "You are *so* sexy," he commented, looking at her again.

"Shut the fuck up," Jessica replied, stepping inside. "We gotta shake these guys," she continued. "The Dragons are getting swarmed by drones, and it's only a matter of time until they send more boarders than we can handle."

Vladimir closed the hatch. "*Nyet.*"

"*Nyet? Nyet shto?*" Jessica asked.

"We jump, they follow. They read our jump signature and calculate our jump range. We'll never lose them."

"I assume you have a plan?"

"*Konyeshna,*" Vladimir replied, heading back to the panel he had opened. "We need a decoy jump."

"A what?"

"A big flash of jump energy, followed by the *real* jump a tenth of a second later," Vladimir explained as he continued rewiring the circuit. "All I have to do is…"

"Don't bother explaining how," Jessica insisted. "Just tell me how I can help."

The engagement had started as well as a sword fight in a cramped space could. In the first thirty seconds, he had managed to defeat two of the four men and knock the other two off their feet. But now, both were upright and coming at him with fury in their eyes.

The attacker to Nathan's left lunged forward, attempting to skewer him, but Nathan moved to his right just enough to get out of the way. Now against the starboard bulkhead and unable to get his blade up in time to parry the descending saber of the second attacker, Nathan chose to bend down and throw himself into the man's abdomen, sending both himself and his attacker tumbling to the deck.

"Fucking hell!" Josh exclaimed as he jinked his fighter about, trying to prevent the drones that were chasing him from attaching to his hull. "What are you doing back there, Reems! These things are all over me!"

"*I'm working on it!*"

"Well work faster!" Josh insisted. "There's another breach pod about to latch onto the Traverna, and I can't get a shot off while I'm dodging drones!"

"*Shut down your shields!*" Nikolas instructed.

"What? Are you nuts?"

"Do it now!"

Josh put his fighter into a rapid roll. "You heard him, sweetie."

"*Shutting down shields.*"

"What? No 'that action is not recommended?'"

"*I am connected to Ensign Sorenson's AI, so I am aware of what he is attempting to do.*"

Several energy blasts slammed into Josh's fighter, causing it to rock violently while it continued to roll.

"Niko!" Josh yelled. Suddenly the incoming fire ceased, and the icons representing the drones that had been swarming around him began drifting aimlessly away from center. "What the hell?"

"*You're clear!*" Nikolas exclaimed with excitement.

Josh applied counterthrust and stopped his roll, then turned toward the Traverna. "What did you do?"

"*Doesn't matter,*" Nikolas replied. "*It isn't going to work a second time.*"

"Shit, he's attaching," Josh said as he looked out the front windows. He pushed his fighter into a dive, pulling out and skimming along the top of the Traverna. Ahead of him, the breach pod was attaching itself to the cargo ship's hull. Josh opened fire, blasting the breach pod and blowing off its top half. Four bodies were violently ejected, one of which bounced off the nose of his fighter. "Damn!" he chuckled. "What are the odds of *that* happening twice in one lifetime!"

The ship shook and the lights went out. Nathan felt his body begin floating up off the deck. Emergency lighting switched on a moment later, just in time for Nathan to see the second man's saber jabbing toward him. He reached out and grabbed the man's sword hand, pulling it as hard as he could. Half of the energy of the pull brought the man forward, and the other half caused Nathan to accelerate past him in the opposite direction. Realizing what was about to happen, the man tried to move his blade to the side as he floated toward his cohort. Instead of accidentally stabbing him, he instead sliced open his comrade's face, sending globs of blood floating out in all directions.

The lights came back on, as did the gravity, and both Nathan and the only uninjured attacker fell back to the floor. Nathan scrambled back to his feet, spinning around just in time to parry the now even angrier man's strike, its force nearly knocking the blade from Nathan's hand.

"*Nathan!*" Vladimir called over comm-sets. "*Jump the ship! Jump the ship!*"

"I'm a little busy!" Nathan replied as he continued countering the last attacker's attacks.

———

Jessica looked at Vladimir. "That didn't sound good."

The ship shook again as more energy blasts slammed into the hull. The lights flickered again, but the gravity held.

"If we don't jump now, we're not going to be able to jump at all!" Vladimir exclaimed.

"Kayci!" Jessica called over comm-sets. "Are you on the flight deck?"

———

Kayci was crouched down behind the copilot's

seat, watching in horror as Nathan battled the last two boarders in the corridor outside the cockpit.

"*Where's Nathan?*" Jessica called over Kayci's comm-set.

"In the corridor," Kayci replied. "He's fighting them."

"*Then you've got to jump the ship, Doc.*"

"What? I don't know how!"

"*Go to the pilot's seat,*" Jessica instructed. "*The one on the left.*"

Kayci started to rise but ducked back down again at the sound of clanking swords.

"*Hurry, Doc!*" Jessica urged as the ship shook from incoming weapons fire. "*We're running out of time!*"

"Oh God," Kayci said as she moved over to the pilot's seat. "What do I do?"

"*Find the console that says Jump Nav Com,*" Jessica instructed.

Kayci searched for the console.

"*It should be in the center, or maybe the center pedestal.*"

"You don't know?"

"*It'll have a display with a lot of numbers on it. Range settings, course data, speed, that kind of stuff.*"

Kayci looked down at the center pedestal, spotting something that fit the description just below the throttles. "I think I found it."

"*Find the jump button and push it!*" Jessica urged. "*Hurry!*"

"*You have to push it and hold it for at least three seconds!*" Vladimir added.

"Don't I have to enter something first?" Kayci asked, afraid to do something wrong.

"*Just push the damned button!*" Jessica yelled.

Kayci looked over the console but didn't find a button labeled 'jump'. "There is no 'jump' button, only an 'execute' button."

"*PUSH THAT!*"

Kayci did so, holding it in. The cockpit flashed blue-white, then flashed again. Kayci removed her finger and looked around. The incoming weapons fire had ceased, as had the clanking of swords. "I did it!" She exclaimed. "I think."

"*Great! Now go help Nathan! I'm on my way!*" Jessica replied.

Kayci turned to get out of her seat, unsure of how she was going to be of any help in a sword fight. She stopped, breathless as she spotted Nathan standing in the hatchway, blood covering the front of him, spurting from several wounds on his chest and shoulder. "Oh my God. Are you alright?"

"I've been better," Nathan admitted, stumbling forward into the cockpit and practically falling into one of the side station seats.

———

Josh immediately jumped in pursuit of the Traverna, but when he came out of the jump, there were no contacts. "What the hell? Sweetie, are you sure of the range?"

"*The Traverna should be here,*" his AI insisted.

Two more icons appeared, then several others as the rest of the Dragons joined him.

"*Where are they?*" Talisha asked over comms.

"I don't know," Josh replied. "But they sure as hell ain't here." He thought for a moment. "Search pattern Delta Three, starting back at the last engagement area. Slider left, Kusya right. I'll go up center. Let's go, people. We've gotta find them before the bad guys do."

"*Speaking of,*" his AI said. "*One heavy, directly astern. Ten kilometers and closing.*"

"Everyone, one light year forward, then we double back."

"Dragons report they've lost the Traverna," Sima announced from the Aurora's comm-station.

"What?" Aiden exclaimed. "When you say lost…"

"They have lost contact," Sima explained. "It jumped, and they followed based on her jump energy signature, but she wasn't where they expected. They've started a search pattern."

"Whoever was attacking will be searching as well," Kit pointed out.

"Lieutenant, split your team between the Seiiki and the Mirai," Aiden instructed. "And come loaded for bear."

"You got it," Kit agreed, turning to exit.

"Loki, you take the Seiiki, Erica will take the Mirai."

"I will?" Erica said.

"Would you rather stay here and take the conn?" Aiden asked.

"I'll take the Mirai," Erica agreed, also heading out.

"We'll find them," Loki promised before following Erica out.

Aiden sighed, turning to Sima. "Contact Captain Taylor. Update her on the situation and tell her we need shuttles and pilots."

CHAPTER THREE

"What happened to you?" Vladimir asked after stepping into the Traverna's cockpit.

"Men with swords," Nathan explained while Doctor Barra did her best to patch him up with the cargo ship's meager medical supplies.

Vladimir looked at Jessica, then back at Nathan. "Guess you need more training."

Nathan just glared at him.

"We have a problem," Vladimir said.

"Ya think?"

"No, I mean a *big* problem. We're leaking air," Vladimir explained. "Lots of it."

"Can you fix it?" Jessica asked.

"Not before we suffocate," Vladimir replied. "We're leaking in at least five places I've identified so far, and the pressure shields on the breach boxes are battery-powered, so they won't last long."

"How long?" Nathan asked.

"Minutes? Hours? I have no way of knowing," Vladimir admitted. "We need to get off this ship."

Nathan sighed, rising.

"I'm not finished yet," Doctor Barra warned.

Nathan ignored her, going to the pilot's seat and punching in some commands on the center console. "Can we jump again?" he asked Vladimir.

"*Da.*"

"How far?"

"This ship is a series jumper, so we can make ten-light-year jumps indefinitely."

"We only need to make three," Nathan said, pointing at the navigational display. "That will put us within escape pod range of the Nishida system."

"What's there?" Jessica asked.

"As far as I know, nothing. But this thing shows that the fourth and fifth planets are habitable," Nathan explained.

"Are there any settlements there?" Kayci asked.

"Not according to these charts," Nathan replied. "But we don't know how up to date they are. But if it's classified as habitable, that means it has breathable air and liquid water."

"But we'd be stranded," Kayci pointed out.

"Better than being dead," Jessica opined.

"Maybe we can seal ourselves up in one compartment to buy us time to fix the ship?" Kayci suggested.

"I can't fix this ship without the Aurora," Vladimir told her.

"But they'll come looking for us, right?"

"Yes they will," Nathan assured her.

"About that," Vladimir said. "I sort of masked our jump."

Nathan looked at him. "Huh?"

"I masked our *real* jump with a fake one. Anyone analyzing our jump flash will only see the fake one, so they'll be looking in the wrong place."

"But sooner or later, they *will* find us," Jessica stated. "They know our heading, so..."

"Yes, eventually *someone* will find us," Nathan agreed. "The question is, who?"

"We have two escape pods," Jessica stated.

"So?" Nathan asked, not sure where she was heading.

"So we cold-launch the one *we're* in and hot-launch the empty one. With any luck, they won't even *detect* the cold-launched pod."

"Assuming they find us," Kayci said.

"They'll find us," Nathan insisted.

"How can you be sure?"

"Those weren't pirates," Nathan explained. "They were too well trained and too well equipped."

"*And* they came *back* after getting their butts kicked once before," Jessica added. "They were after something, and I'm betting it's that girl in cold storage back there."

"That was my thought as well," Nathan agreed.

"If we're evacuating, we're going to have to wake her up," Doctor Barra warned.

"How long will that take?" Nathan asked.

"Not long, but don't forget, we still don't know what's wrong with her."

"What makes you think something is wrong with her?" Vladimir asked.

"She's in medical SA," Kayci reminded him.

"So she might have some deadly disease or something?" Vladimir asked.

"If that were the case, I would expect that information to be in the SA unit's medical logs or at least have a warning placard on the outside," Kayci explained. "But there's nothing."

"So if we wake her, we could be exposing ourselves to some deadly pathogen," Nathan stated.

"I don't believe that to be the case," Doctor Barra stated. "There doesn't appear to be *anything* wrong with her, at least not that I can detect."

"But all her metabolic functions are greatly slowed in SA, right?" Jessica clarified.

"Yes, but not completely halted. I can't be certain of course, but if she did have some disease, there would be at least *some* minor abnormalities in her scans. And she has *none*. I mean, her scans are so perfect that they're hard to believe."

"But if she does have a contagious disease, we'd be exposing the entire planet to it," Jessica pointed out.

"But if I'm right, and she doesn't have any disease, and we don't wake her and bring her with us, she'll die."

"More likely, she'll end up in the hands of the guys who just attacked us," Jessica argued.

"Actually, she *will* die," Vladimir corrected. "She's running on batteries, remember? And I don't have a way to connect her to the ship's power grid, not without the Aurora's fabricators."

Nathan sighed. "Wake her, Doc. I'll start plotting the jumps."

"Just so you know, there's a slim chance that just *waking* her could kill her."

"I thought you said you couldn't find anything wrong with her?"

"I can't," Kayci agreed, "but that doesn't mean there *isn't* anything wrong with her."

"Well not much choice I suppose. Vlad, move all the survival supplies from one pod into the pod we'll be taking," Nathan instructed. "There's no telling what kind of conditions we'll be facing."

"I'll take care of it," Vladimir promised.

"Jess..."

"Round up all weapons and personal shields from the dead guys," Jessica said for him.

"After that, search the ship for anything that might be of help to us. Cargo areas, crew quarters, everywhere."

"How long do we have?" Jessica asked.

"I can complete three jumps in a few minutes," Nathan replied. "So as soon as Doctor Barra has our mystery lady awake, we should go."

"I'm on it," Jessica promised, heading out at once.

Nathan turned back to the navigation console to begin plotting the first jump. After a moment, he realized that Kayci was still standing behind him. He turned to her. "Something on your mind, Doc?"

"Is it always this wild?"

"If you're talking about life aboard the Aurora, then this is actually fairly calm."

"Not the answer I was hoping for," Kayci said, turning to exit.

"Not the answer I wanted to give either," Nathan said to himself.

* * *

"*You made the right call,*" Cameron assured Aiden over vid-comm. "*The Aurora is the base of operations, and when they locate the Traverna, there is a good chance they're going to need her for the rescue. Better to lick your wounds and prepare for the next engagement, and let your Dragons and shuttles do the searching.*"

"Yeah, but it's a lot harder than I thought it would be," Aiden admitted.

"*It doesn't get any easier.*"

"Not the answer I was hoping for."

"*I'll send all our shuttles and pilots to help with the search. Would you like me to send engineers as well?*"

"Our damage isn't that bad," Aiden replied. "We can handle the repairs."

"*Well don't be afraid to ask the Norleandar to come to your aid if needed. They're only a few jumps away.*"

"I know."

"*The shuttles should be there in about a day and a half,*" Cameron told him. "*Until then, try to use your recon drones as much as possible, and don't let your Dragon pilots wear themselves out. They'll fly twenty-four seven if you let them, especially Josh."*

"Yeah, I've already ordered them to fly twelve-hour rotations."

"Twelves? That's not too much?"

"I was asking for eights, but Josh insisted on around-the-clock patrols, taking a few hours off whenever a ship needed to recycle," Aiden explained. "Did you know that they catnap in their fighters during patrols?"

"I heard something about that, yes," Cameron replied.

"Anyway, Aurora's coordinating the search to maximize efficiency, and each Dragon is flying with two recon drones that are constantly jumping around them to widen their search ranges, so that should help."

"Once the shuttles reach you, we should start searching habitable planets and moons that would be in range of the Traverna's escape pods. You might want to check with her captain about their range."

"I did. She doesn't know. Her engineer is in and out, so as soon as Doctor Chen says it's safe, she's going to give him something to wake him up long enough for us to interrogate him."

"Interrogate him?" Cameron asked.

"Pirates don't come back and try again after getting shut down. Someone wanted whatever was on that ship, and I have a sneaking suspicion it had something to do with that girl in SA they found."

"What girl in SA?" Cameron inquired.

"Nathan didn't tell you?"

"No he didn't."

"They were carrying a young woman in a medical

SA pod, tucked in under their main reactor to hide her from sensors. The captain didn't know anything about her, and neither did her engineer."

"*Could either of them be lying?*"

"If they are, we'll find out."

"*Has Laza assessed the damage to the Traverna?*" Cameron asked.

"Yes. She thinks it's minimal. They were able to jump, so we know they still have main power, even if they don't have maneuvering or main propulsion. She's still studying the scans just in case she missed something."

"*Well, we'll find them,*" Cameron assured him.

"We *should* have *already* found them," Aiden insisted.

* * *

Nathan entered the bay outside the reactor room where Vladimir had repositioned the medical SA pod. "How's it going?" he asked Doctor Barra as he entered.

"Aren't you supposed to be in the cockpit?"

"I've already completed all three jumps, so there's nothing left for me to do up there," Nathan replied. "How much longer until she's awake?"

"A few minutes I think," Kayci answered.

"You think?"

"This pod is like nothing I've ever seen. In fact, I think it's a prototype."

"What makes you say that?" Nathan asked.

"Regardless of who built them, SA pods are a collection of components built by a variety of companies. The average *medical* SA pod is assembled from components from over three hundred different manufacturers."

"They teach you that in med-school?"

"Actually my son told me that."

"Isn't he like *six*?"

"Only in years," Kayci quipped. "Anyway, *this* pod's components don't have *any* manufacturer markings. Best I can tell, every component is fabricated from scratch."

"And that is meaningful why?" Nathan wondered.

"Only a handful of companies have that kind of fabrication capability. The big ones like SilTek, Annapolaris, and Gangess."

"So you think this pod was *stolen*?"

"That would explain why someone came after it, wouldn't it?"

"Maybe," Nathan admitted. "But it doesn't explain why someone is *in* a stolen prototype. Is there anything else unusual about it?"

"Only that it's got a really large data core."

"Maybe it's an extended-use SA pod?" Nathan suggested.

"Those usually have more robust power systems, complete with their own miniature fusion reactors."

"Jasher?"

"Yup," Kayci confirmed. "There's something else. This panel here. I have no idea what any of these readings are for."

"They're not medical readings?" Nathan asked.

"If they are, they're not like any *I've* ever seen."

A warning indicator flashed on the pod's control panel.

"She should be waking up any moment now," Kayci announced as she activated the opening cycle.

The clear lid lifted slightly, then slid slowly down toward the foot of the unit, stopping once the occupant was exposed down to her knees.

"She certainly looks healthy enough," Vladimir said as he and Jessica joined them.

"You guys get all the supplies moved over?" Nathan asked.

"All we could fit," Jessica assured him. "There's barely enough room for us now."

"She is exaggerating," Vladimir insisted. "I did the math on the weight and distribution."

"The patient's metabolic functions are back to normal," Doctor Barra announced. "We can move her anytime you like."

"Shouldn't she be awake first?" Nathan wondered.

"I figured since we're pressed for time, it would be better if I kept her sedated," Kayci explained. "We have no idea under what circumstances she was put into medical SA. We may have a lot of explaining to do once she is fully conscious."

"Good thinking," Nathan agreed.

"Which one of you is going to carry her to the escape pod?" Jessica asked.

Nathan looked at Vladimir.

"What?"

"I can make it an order."

"Of course," Vladimir droned. "Leave it to the big, strong Russian," he mumbled as he scooped up the unconscious woman with both arms and lifted her out of the SA pod.

* * *

"Starting scans for grid one seven five," Talisha announced over comms as the blue-white light from her jump faded.

"*We should've found them by now,*" Allet insisted.

"*Assuming we interpreted their jump energy expenditure accurately,*" Nikolas added. "*And that they didn't jump again, or change course and jump again, or somehow hide their jump flash..."*

"We get the point," Talisha said, cutting him off.

———————

Josh began scans of the next sector of his search route, just like the rest of the Dragons. While the AICC nodes gave them live comms regardless of the distance between them, it also meant more comms traffic. Sometimes, Josh missed the solitude of being out of comms range, especially when he flew solo. It gave him time to think and to relax in an environment that was more like home to him than any other: the cockpit of an extremely fast space fighter.

But at times like this, it was the last place he wanted to be. Blindly searching the frigid black depths of space for one of only two men who had ever had any faith in him. Even his stepfather, Marcus, didn't have as much faith in Josh as Nathan had shown. Josh was determined to find him no matter the cost and would stay in his fighter until his leader was safe again.

"I've got a contact," Talisha reported over subspace comms. *"A pair of raiders, just like the ones that attacked the Traverna."*

"Show me Dragon Three's tactical, sweetie," Josh instructed his AI. A second later, what Talisha saw on her tactical display now appeared on Josh's. "Looks like they don't have a target," Josh decided.

"Agreed," Talisha replied. *"I think they're searching just like us."*

"Have they spotted you?"

"I don't believe so. We went cold and dead the second they showed up on sensors."

"Shadow them, Talisha," Josh instructed. "But do *not* let them spot you, and do *not* engage them *unless* they find the Traverna and take hostile action."

"I'd rather just blow them out of the sky and be done with them," Talisha replied.

"Normally I'd agree with you," Josh told her. "But right now we need to concentrate on finding our people."

"What about the search grid?" Talisha questioned. *"We can't scan if we're running cold and dead."*

"Let me worry about that," Josh replied. "You just keep your eyes on those assholes. And if they go weapons hot, you blast the shit outta them!"

"Copy that."

"Aurora, Dragon One. Launch Dragons Five and Six, and Nine and Ten," Josh instructed. "Five and Six will take Three and Four's search tasks. Nine and Ten will search along the same heading as the new raider contacts, keeping one light year ahead of them, just in case they know something we don't."

"Understood," the Aurora's AI replied.

"Talisha, Nine and Ten will take their jump cues from you. Every time those raiders jump, they jump."

"Got it."

"If they've got a better trail than we do, we do *not* want them finding the Traverna before us," Josh stated.

"I'm just about dry," Allet reported.

"You and Doom RTB and recycle. Take a couple hours and rest," Josh ordered. "Remo, you go with them."

"You're going to fly alone?" Nikolas asked.

"It won't be the first time," Josh assured him.

"I'll recycle and come right back," Nikolas promised.

"Negative," Josh countered. "You take a couple hours down time as well. I need rested pilots if we go hot again."

"*What about you?*" Nikolas questioned.

"I never get tired," Josh replied. "Now RTB your ass."

"*Aye, sir,*" Nikolas confirmed. "*But I'm sleeping in my bird in the launch tube, just in case.*"

Josh smiled. Nikolas had come a long way in the last two months.

* * *

"I demand to be present during questioning," Captain Helder insisted outside of her engineer's recovery room in the Aurora's medical department.

"Your presence might influence his answers," Aiden reasoned with her.

"He's my crew. He's my responsibility," Tap argued, standing her ground. "Either I'm in there with you, or you don't question him...*period.*"

Aiden turned to face the Traverna's captain squarely, meeting her eyes with the most confident and assertive look he could muster. Confrontation had never been his thing, but the stakes were high. "My people are in danger because of you and your ship."

"I had nothing to do with..."

"But you are her captain, which makes everything that happened on that ship while under your command *your* responsibility. And *your ship* has been attacked twice in less than a day, and by an entity far better equipped than your average pirate. I intend to find out *why*. Now you can either wait out here *willingly*, or I can throw your ass in the brig."

"Under what authority?" she challenged.

Aiden just laughed. "Seriously?" He snapped his fingers, and an armed crewmen stepped forward.

"You wouldn't dare," she challenged, calling his bluff.

"I don't have time for this," Aiden replied, nodding to the crewmen. "Lock her ass up."

"Ma'am, if you'll come with me," the crewman said politely.

"I will not."

The crewman looked at Aiden. "Shall I stun her, sir?"

Aiden looked back at Captain Helder. "Your call, lady."

Tap stared at him for a moment, then backed down, turning to the armed crewman. "Lead the way."

"After you," the crewman insisted, wanting to keep her in front of him.

Aiden watched them leave, then turned back to Doctor Chen.

"I didn't know you had that in you," Doctor Chen commented.

"Neither did I," Aiden admitted as he tapped his comm-set. "Sima, send another armed guard to meet up with Specialist Periman and Captain Helder on their way to the brig from medical."

"*Aye, sir.*"

Aiden looked at Doctor Chen again. "Don't want to underestimate her."

"The patient is awake whenever you're ready," Doctor Chen commented.

Aiden straightened his uniform and stepped into the patient's room. "Mister Townsend, I'm Captain Walsh, acting commander of the Aurora. I'd like to ask you a few questions if you feel up to it."

Remi looked at Aiden, then at Doctor Chen, who had followed him in. "I suppose I can."

"What do you know about the girl in the medical SA pod tucked under the Traverna's main reactor?"

"Nothing really."

"But you *knew* of her presence?"

Remi's eyes shifted nervously between Aiden and the doctor. "Uh, yes."

"How did she end up on the Traverna?" Aiden questioned.

"Iros arranged it."

"The loader?"

"Yeah. He said we could make enough money to pay off the Traverna's mortgage and still have a tidy sum in our pockets."

"Did he say who she was?"

"He said he didn't know."

"Who asked him to arrange her transport?" Aiden asked.

"Some guy at the spaceport," Remi replied. "That's what he told me anyway."

"And you just *agreed* to this?"

"It was a *lot* of credits, and Tap really needed it. They were going to repossess her ship."

"Did you even ask why she was in a *medical* SA pod? Like what was wrong with her?"

"Iros said it was the only SA pod available. He swore there was nothing wrong with her."

"Then why bother putting her in SA at all?" Aiden challenged. "Why not just bring her in with the passengers?"

"Iros said people were hunting for her."

"The authorities?"

"No, just some very scary people. The kind of people you didn't want to cross."

"Did he say who was funding this woman's escape?"

"I don't think he knew."

"How well did you know Iros?"

"He had just signed on. Seemed nice enough though. He was eager to learn, to help out."

"And you just agreed to this deal with a guy you just met?"

"Tap needed the credits. And if she lost the ship, I would've lost my *home*." He looked at Aiden. "Am I in trouble?"

"With us? No," Aiden assured him. "But I'm pretty sure whoever is hunting that woman isn't too happy with you."

"You gotta protect me...I mean us," Remi pleaded. "The captain...she didn't know anything about this. She *never* would've agreed to take such a risk, not even to save her own ship. You gotta believe me."

"I believe you," Aiden assured him, hoping to ease his nerves. "Do you have *any* idea...any *guess* as to who attacked the Traverna?"

Remi's gaze shifted back and forth again. "Maybe corporate?"

"Corporate?" Aiden wondered.

"You know, corporate security types?"

"What makes you say that?"

"The pod had no markings on it," Remi explained. "Nothing to indicate who built it. When was the last time you saw a piece of tech that didn't have a company name or logo emblazoned on the side? I think that pod was a *prototype.*"

"And you think someone *stole* it from its maker?"

"It makes sense," Remi defended. "Only corporations can afford the number of credits they were offering us to smuggle her out."

"Smuggle *her* or smuggle *it*?" Aiden questioned.

"Maybe both?" Doctor Chen suggested.

Aiden looked at her, thinking. Then he turned back to Remi. "Thank you, Mister Townsend. We'll talk more later." Aiden turned and left the room, followed by Doctor Chen.

"That was easier than I thought," Aiden admitted once they were in the corridor.

"I mixed a little sorbatex into his meta-boost."

Aiden looked at her, chuckling. "And here I thought I was looking at a whole new career as an interrogator."

* * *

Jessica joined Nathan in the Traverna's cockpit after helping Vladimir and Doctor Barra move the unconscious young woman from the SA pod and secure her inside the escape pod.

"Everything ready back there?" Nathan asked as he entered final instructions into the cargo ship's auto-flight systems.

"Sleeping Beauty's all strapped in, and Vlad is getting the good doctor mentally ready for the experience."

Nathan looked at her. "It didn't occur to me that she hasn't been escape pod trained like the rest of us."

"Well if she can survive getting shot at by boarders and watching me slaughter the fuckers, then she can survive a ride down in an escape pod," Jessica insisted. "What are you doing?"

"Just finishing up flight instructions," Nathan explained.

"Why?"

"I programmed a series of distress calls to play periodically after we leave to make it look as if we never left. Then I instructed the auto-flight system to attempt a crash landing on the other planet."

"I thought this bucket was too busted up to fly?"

"It's grav-lift systems are still functional," Nathan told her. "It just doesn't have any main propulsion or maneuvering."

"Do you actually think it will make it down in one piece?" Jessica wondered.

"God no," Nathan chuckled. "I just want it to *look* like we tried."

"I'm impressed," Jessica decided. "We might make a covert operator out of you yet."

"Never happen," Nathan replied. "Too much lying. I wouldn't be able to keep my stories straight."

"It is a gift."

Nathan finished the last entry, breathing out a sigh. "I feel bad that we can't save the ship. After all, it *is* Captain Helder's only source of income."

"It's mortgaged," Jessica reminded him. "Which means it's insured as well."

"You don't know anything about spacecraft insurance, do you?"

"No I don't, and I'm proud of it."

"The mortgage company will probably be paid off, but Captain Helder will be left with nothing unless she's been paying on a supplemental policy, which I doubt."

"Don't really care," Jessica replied.

"You really are heartless, aren't you?" Nathan commented.

"It's not that I'm heartless, it's just that a person only has so much emotion to give. I save mine for people I care about."

"Well let's get this over with," Nathan said, rising from his seat.

* * *

Laza continued staring at the sensor displays, just as she had been for the last few hours.

"You're going to go cross-eyed," Aiden warned.

"Pardon?"

"Something my grandmother used to say when I spent too much time staring at my view screen in my room," Aiden explained. "Maybe you need to take a break?"

"I cannot," Laza replied, returning her attention to her screens.

"You've been staring at the same data for hours, Ensign."

"There is a subtle variation at the very end of their jump flash," Laza explained.

Aiden leaned down, looking more closely. "I don't see it."

"Here," she said, pointing. "Jump flashes have a standard decay rate. All flashes, regardless of the luminosity of the original flash, still decay at the same rate. From the moment of the jump, all the way down to zero luminosity...the same rate. But this flash's decay rate sort of *pauses* for a few milliseconds, only a fraction of a second *after* the initial flash. The only reason I noticed it was because I ran a comparison between the flash that *we* recorded and the flash that each of our *Dragons* recorded. The delay only takes place from Dragon Seven's perspective, and his AI tagged it as an instrumentation error."

"And you think it isn't?" Aiden questioned.

"Doctor Sorenson's father discovered superluminal transitions *because* he investigated an *instrumentation error* from the testing of multi-layered shielding."

"Good point," Aiden agreed. "So what do you think it means?"

"I'm not sure," she admitted. "It could just be emitter compensation. You know how our emitters can compensate for a neighboring emitter that is malfunctioning? But..."

"But what?"

"I've seen readings of emitter compensation before, and it didn't make the *entire* jump flash just *stop* decaying for a few milliseconds. The effect was more localized."

"The Traverna did take considerable damage in both attacks," Aiden reminded her.

"I have analyzed that damage, and none of it would explain this anomaly."

"Did you ask Doctor Sorenson about it?" Aiden suggested. "Maybe she has seen this before."

"I was about to do so."

"Very well. Don't let me hold you up," Aiden told her. "But I suggest you ask her in person."

Laza looked at him quizzically. "It would be faster to use comm-sets."

"Yes, but you need to get up and stretch your legs occasionally. And a few minutes away from studying that anomaly might make you think of something you hadn't thought of before."

"I don't see how."

"Humor me, Ensign," Aiden insisted.

"As you wish, sir," Laza agreed, rising to depart.

"You too, Sima," Aiden told his comms officer. "You've been at your console all day. Take a break. I'll watch the conn."

"Aye, sir."

* * *

Nathan was the last one into the escape pod,

activating the hatch controls before heading inside. The pod itself was designed to hold eight persons, so three of the seats had been loaded with supplies pulled from the other pod and covered with self-adjusting restraint netting. "How's our mystery lady?" Nathan asked the doctor as he climbed into his seat.

"Still out," Doctor Barra replied. "I wish I was."

"Piece of cake, Doc," Nathan promised as he buckled in and pulled down the small console from overhead, locking it into place in front of him.

Kayci watched as Nathan scanned the console as if looking for something. "You *do* know how to operate this thing, right?"

"I'll figure it out," Nathan assured her.

"Maybe there are instructions somewhere?"

"Escape pods are all pretty simple," Nathan replied. "I just need to figure out how to initiate a cold release."

"What's a cold release?"

"No explosive launch systems," Vladimir explained.

"Why would you *want* an explosive launch?"

"When the ship you're escaping from is about to blow up," Jessica said.

"In this case, we want to fall away slowly, without any emissions that would alert anyone picking up our old light that we ejected."

"Old light?" Kayci asked.

"When looking at emissions from far away, you see what was happening in the past," Vladimir explained. "Just like light from a star a hundred light years away is one hundred years old. Old light."

"How do you guys keep these things straight?"

"We don't," Nathan admitted. "Ah, found it. Hang on."

Nathan pressed the button, and the pod jolted. There was a sliding sound, and then they were free floating.

Kayci's long hair began to float up beside her head. "Oh my God. Are we in zero gravity?"

"Yes, and we're going to be for a few hours," Nathan warned.

"You could've told me."

"Sorry."

"A few hours?" Kayci wondered. "Don't escape pods jump?"

"Old light," Nathan repeated.

"Of course."

"We'll be cold-coasting all the way to atmospheric interface," Nathan explained. "At that point, I'll fire things up, jump us past atmo-interface, and then deploy the chutes to ride them down."

"Chutes?"

"Parachutes."

Kayci looked nervous. "Maybe it would be better if you just didn't tell me *how* all this works."

* * *

It had been a week since Captain Scott had issued his warning. General Gogol had every unit she could spare searching for both the Aurora and the two gates he had stolen. At this point, Oliana didn't much *care* about the gates, despite the representative from SilTek's constant nagging for their recovery. She wanted the Aurora, and more specifically, its arrogant, rogue captain. Crimes against the Alliance were rare, and crimes of his magnitude were unheard of; hence the Alliance's decision to keep knowledge of these crimes out of the public's awareness. But that could only work for so long. And when the truth finally came out, she needed to have Captain Nathan Scott and all his cohorts either in custody or *proven* dead.

Commander Denkin, her right-hand man, burst into her office, a comm-pad in hand. "We just received a communiqué from a Genstar agent."

"The corporate security firm?"

"Elliot Nada. He's one of our reservists. Pretty high up in their intelligence chain. He's in charge of security for one of Biodyne's top-secret R&D projects. Apparently it is something that is being heavily funded by the highest levels of the upper council."

"Some sort of black-ops tech then?"

"The blackest according to Elliot."

"Why is he contacting us?" Oliana wondered.

"Their only prototype was stolen about a week ago. Nada says it was an inside job. Their retrieval corps traced it to a small cargo jumper running passengers and light cargo from the fringe out to the frontier. A ship called the Traverna."

"I'm still waiting for the part I care about," Oliana warned, growing impatient.

"It gets better," Commander Denkin assured her. "They caught up with her and boarded her, but someone intervened before they were able to retrieve their property."

That piqued her interest.

Commander Denkin smiled. "The Aurora. Genstar regrouped and came back. The Aurora was still there. In the battle, the Traverna managed to escape. They followed her jump trail, but she wasn't where her jump flash indicated, and her trail went cold. They're starting a full-length back trace, but with the number of units they have available, it will take weeks."

"Divert all our forces currently searching for those gates to that back trace," Oliana instructed. "If we find the Traverna, we find the Aurora. I can feel it."

"Immediately, General," the commander acknowledged, turning to depart.

General Gogol pressed her intercom. "Captain Hyam, ready the Maturo. I want to be wheels up in ten minutes."

"*Destination?*" Captain Hyam inquired.

"Get that from Commander Denkin."

"*Yes, sir.*"

Oliana smiled as she rose from her seat and grabbed her jacket. Captain Scott's incurable habit of coming to everyone's aid, regardless of the risk, would be his undoing.

CHAPTER FOUR

"That planet is getting awfully close," Kayci commented, watching from one of the escape pod's portholes.

"We've got a problem," Nathan stated.

"Don't tell me the jump system is damaged," Jessica said.

"It's fine," Vladimir insisted. "I checked it myself."

"He's right, it's fine," Nathan confirmed. "Passive just picked up a jump flash. About ten thousand clicks away. Not very big. Maybe a cargo ship..."

"Maybe a gunship," Jessica added.

"Maybe."

"Are there any settlements here?" Jessica asked.

"Nothing listed on the charts, but we don't know how current they are," Nathan explained. "Besides, there may be unregistered settlements."

"How likely are *unregistered* settlements to get cargo ship traffic?" Jessica wondered.

"I wouldn't think very likely," Nathan admitted. "Unless it's their own ship."

"What settlements have their own ship?" Vladimir asked.

"I've read about settlements in the fringe that contract smaller ships to make multiple runs to establish the settlement," Kayci stated.

"It could also be a cargo ship's first trip to establish a settlement," Nathan postulated.

"On the same planet we're going to?" Jessica asked. "What are the odds?"

"Not much different than the odds of them going to the other planet, I suppose."

"Maybe we'd better jump down and haul ass away

from this thing," Jessica suggested. "It'll be like a big flashing neon sign, especially if we're using any of its systems."

"I've got a better idea," Nathan said. "We hot-ride our way down instead of jumping."

"Nathan," Vladimir interrupted. "I don't think this thing was built for full atmospheric transitions."

"Well it has shields, so..."

"Those shields are designed to protect us from debris and such," Vladimir reminded him. "Not from the heat of atmospheric interface."

"Can't we beef them up? Channel some more power into them or something?"

"Wrong kind of shields I'm afraid."

"Come on, Vlad, you're Mister Whiz-Fix-it," Jessica declared. "Work some magic."

"It's an *emergency escape pod*, Jessica. It isn't designed to be *fixed* from inside."

"If I wait until the very last second, like right before we burn up, our plasma wake *should* hide us from anyone's sensors."

"*Should?*" Kayci questioned, not feeling terribly excited about the idea.

"It will," Nathan assured her.

"It will look like we burned up," Vladimir realized.

"That's what I'm hoping."

* * *

"That is curious," Abby admitted, studying Laza's sensor logs.

"At first I thought it was a sensor error. A misread. Occasionally Aurora gets it wrong at first, but even after analyzing all the sensor logs from all the Dragons, she still couldn't offer anything other than 'unexplained energy fluctuation in target's jump flash,'" Laza explained.

"Did Commander Kamenetskiy's reports help at all?"

"He found nothing about the Traverna's jump drive that stood out. Only that it was a more recent model than most others we've encountered out here."

"What are the differences?" Abby questioned.

"Only that the older jump drives, which many fringe ships are still using, are technically capable of long-range jumps; they've just been altered to limit their range to ten light years, as you already know. Newer ships, especially ones built *in* Alliance space, *cannot* jump more than ten light years even if they wanted to. So that rules out Captain Scott deciding to long-jump to lose his pursuers long enough to escape."

"Is it possible that Commander Kamenetskiy found a way to long-jump?"

"Based on his reports, no."

"Well he *is* awfully clever."

"Indeed he is," Laza agreed. "But even if they *did* long-jump, that doesn't explain the energy fluctuation."

"What if he double-jumped?"

"Double-jumped?"

"Two jumps occurring so close together that they appear to be a single jump flash," Abby explained. "It's an old trick Josh developed when flying the Falcon to disguise his jump range. A double jump of one light year each would look like a single jump of one light year."

"That maneuver isn't in the tactical database," Laza said.

"Josh tends to keep many of his tricks to himself," Abby explained. "It's how he keeps *ahead* of other pilots."

"Then how do you know about it?"

"My son flies his wing, remember?"

"And he discusses tactical strategies with you?"

"He tells me *everything*," Abby said, almost complaining.

"And that bothers you?"

"There are some things a son does that his mother does *not* need to know."

"Of course."

"How long was the Traverna's jump flash?"

"Five light years," Laza replied.

"Is she a series jumper?"

"Limited. She can handle single-light-year jumps in series, but to a maximum of twenty jumps before she needs to spend an hour recharging her jump banks."

"And they've found no trace of her at five light years?"

"Correct."

"Then we should be searching *ten* light years out," Abby insisted. "But tell them to be careful. Josh came up with that maneuver over five hundred years ago. It's a pretty safe bet that others know of it by now."

* * *

General Gogol entered the bridge of the Zhulati flagship, Maturo, as it came out of its final jump.

"Sensor contact," the Maturo's sensor officer reported. "It's the Genstar ship Trela."

"Comms," Captain Hyam called. "Contact the Trela and inform them that all Genstar forces currently searching for the Traverna are now under Zhulati command."

"Aye, sir."

"You don't really believe they're going to just

accept Zhulati command authority," General Gogol commented.

"Of course not," Captain Hyam chuckled. "Isn't that why you're here?"

General Gogol smiled.

"Sir, I have Captain Ning, commander of the Trela, on comms."

"Pipe him through," Captain Hyam instructed.

The comms officer nodded at him.

"This is Captain Hyam of the Maturo," the captain announced.

"This is Captain Ning of the Trela," the other captain replied over comms. *"On what grounds are you assuming command authority over my forces?"*

"May I?" General Gogol asked Captain Hyam.

"Be my guest."

General Gogol stepped forward, speaking toward the microphone built into the captain's command chair. "Under section seventeen subsection five of the Alliance Interstellar Maritime Code."

"Section seventeen point five refers to acts of war against the Alliance. I hardly see how the Traverna has committed such an act."

"It is not the Traverna that has committed the act," General Gogol explained. "Just as it is not *your* place to question the command authority of the Zhulati."

"To whom am I speaking?" Captain Ning demanded.

"General Oliana Gogol. Supreme commander of all Zhulati forces. The only person who can implement seventeen point five *without* consent of the Alliance Senate. Now do you yield command of your forces, or do I have to send Zhulati boarding teams to take your ships by force?"

After a pause, the Trela's captain responded.

"You do realize that we have our own security forces, many of whom are former military themselves."

"Captain Ning," General Gogol said, changing her tone from steadfast military leader to negotiator. "Your goal is to find the Traverna and retrieve Genstar property. Property that is largely funded by the Zhulati I might add. My goal is to find the ship that defended the Traverna, allowing her to escape your grasp. Therefore, our goals are closely aligned."

"But not identical."

"No, they are not," General Gogol agreed. "The question you must ask is: do they differ enough to be worth dying for?"

"You wouldn't dare."

General Gogol looked to Captain Hyam.

"Tactical, lock all weapons on the Trela...full power...and prepare to open fire."

"Locking all weapons onto the Trela at full power, aye," the tactical officer confirmed.

"Trela is raising shields," the sensor officer reported.

"Their shields are no match for our main guns," the tactical officer pointed out.

"They know that," Captain Hyam replied, looking to General Gogol.

"Captain Ning," the general began. "If you do not lower your shields and comply, I will lay waste to your vessel and locate the Traverna and her protector without you, satisfying the needs of both Genstar *and* the Alliance." After a pause, she added, "The choice is yours."

"All weapons are locked on the Trela," the tactical officer reported. "Main guns are fully charged and ready to fire."

Captain Hyam said nothing, confident that the

captain of the Trela would yield. A moment later, he did.

"*General Gogol*," Captain Ning called over comms. "*The Trela is at your disposal.*"

"Thank you, Captain Ning. I shall transmit new orders shortly. Please stand by."

"Power down all weapons," Captain Hyam instructed.

"Powering down all weapons."

Captain Hyam looked at General Gogol. "How did you know?"

"The most important thing the people know about the Zhulati is that we answer to no one. Not even the Alliance Senate. Captain Ning had no other course of action available."

This was only the second time that Captain Hyam had flown with the general. "Would you really have destroyed the Trela?" he asked.

"Without batting an eyelash," the general replied.

* * *

The escape pod shook violently as it fell uncontrolled through the thickening atmosphere. There was a sudden mechanical sound, like something separating from the main body of the pod, followed by a jolt.

Alerted and a bit concerned by the sudden jolt, Nathan glanced at Vladimir. That's when he noticed that his engineer was doing something on his control panel. "What the hell are you doing?" Nathan demanded, yelling over the din of reentry.

"I'm jettisoning things," Vladimir yelled back.

"Why?" Nathan demanded in dismay.

"To make it look like we're breaking up!" Vladimir replied as if it were obvious.

"You could've warned me!"

"Why else would I be doing it?"

"You might want to look at hull integrity!" Jessica warned.

Doctor Barra was already scared to death, and Jessica's last comment hadn't helped.

"It's at forty percent and falling fast!" Vladimir reported, glancing at the display. "In thirty seconds, I won't be able to guarantee that the jump system will still work!"

"Just a few more seconds!" Nathan insisted.

"Not a good idea, Nathan," Vladimir argued.

"It's got to look like we burned up!" Nathan argued.

"Oh God!" Kayci exclaimed, losing control of her emotions.

Jessica reached over to Nathan's console and activated the jump-down command.

"What the hell are you doing?" Nathan barked, surprised by her actions.

The jump flash washed over them, and they were thrown against their shoulder restraints as the escape pod's parachutes suddenly deployed.

A moment later, once the jolt had subsided and the pod had settled into a stable, non-life-threatening descent, Jessica replied. "I'd rather be alive and hunted than dead and buried."

"I was about to activate the jump-down..."

"Then what are you complaining about?"

"Twenty seconds to impact," Vladimir warned. "It's going to be rough."

"Firing the landing thrusters," Nathan replied, reaching for the thruster control panel.

"Don't bother," Vladimir told him. "They were damaged during atmo-interface."

"Nice plan, skipper," Jessica scolded.

"Everyone, brace!" Nathan shouted.

A second later, they hit. The impact was accompanied by the ear-splitting sound of the pod's bottom being crushed, just as it was designed to do. While it prevented their deaths, it did not absorb all the impact's kinetic energy, the rest of which was transferred into their seats and bodies. The pod rolled over onto its side, and for a moment, it felt as if it would settle in place. But it did not. It continued rolling, picking up momentum and rolling over again and again. Finally, it slammed into something more solid than the pod itself, coming to a stop. Smoke from shorted circuits began to rise, causing them to cough. Nathan activated the main hatch jettison, sending it flying and allowing the building smoke to escape. "Everyone out!" Nathan ordered, unbuckling his restraints and nearly falling onto Doctor Barra next to him.

* * *

Aiden had never gotten used to walking out onto the flight deck with nothing more than the nearly transparent, pale blue pressure shield that covered an Expedition-class ship's flight deck. The dramatic drop in temperature when passing from the hangar bay airlock out onto the flight deck only served to remind him how potentially exposed one was when protected only by a pressure shield.

Nevertheless, no one was aware of Captain Walsh's aversion to being on the open flight deck. Being a captain didn't make one's fears suddenly disappear. But it did make those of lesser rank assume that the captain had no such fears. And Aiden hid his aversions well, strolling out to meet the six shuttles that had just made the thirty-eight-hour journey from Libertara to assist in the Aurora's search for the Traverna.

To Aiden's surprise, Cameron came down the ramp of the Leonid. "Why didn't you tell me you were coming?" Aiden asked as she approached.

"It was a last-minute decision," Cameron admitted, "and I didn't want to inhibit your command."

"You worry too much," Aiden chuckled. "I'm not that sensitive...trust me."

"It wasn't actually my idea," Cameron admitted as she and Aiden headed back toward the hangar bay. "Robert pulled rank on me, insisting that I *belonged* here with all of you." She looked at him as they walked. "I hope you don't mind."

"Are you kidding?" Aiden chucked. "I haven't slept a wink since the last engagement."

"Any leads on the Traverna's whereabouts?" Cameron asked as they passed through the main airlock and into the Aurora's main hangar bay.

"Abby figured out the Traverna executed a double jump."

"You mean like two jumps, back-to-back?"

"Not exactly. Two jumps, the second jump only a fraction of a second after the first, so that it *looked* like a single jump."

"A deception?" Cameron realized.

"One that worked," Aiden admitted. "We were looking in the wrong area. Luckily, so were the bad guys."

"Any idea who the *bad guys* are?" Cameron asked.

"None," Aiden admitted. "They're not Alliance forces though, so that's a plus. I'm guessing it's a private security force hired by whoever built the medical SA pod the Traverna was smuggling."

"And the identity of the occupant?"

"The Traverna's captain wasn't aware of the pod, and the engineer didn't know much either. The crewman who arranged the whole thing was killed in the initial attack."

"Well now that we've got six more shuttles to help with the search, we have a much better chance of finding them," Cameron commented. "I don't suppose you've heard from them?"

"No such luck," Aiden replied. "The Traverna's subspace comm-array was damaged in the initial attack, so once they jumped away..."

"If Nathan could contact us, he would have," Cameron surmised. "Without any evidence of the Traverna's destruction, we have to assume he's gone dark, probably in order to shake pursuit."

"He won't get far," Aiden opined. "The Traverna took quite a bit of damage. I'm surprised they were able to get under way at all, let alone pull off a double jump like that."

"Yeah, Vlad has a habit of pulling off the impossible, just like Nathan."

"A difficult duo to track," Aiden opined.

"We just have to think like Nathan," Cameron stated. "That's why Robert insisted I take command."

"He was right," Aiden agreed. "No one knows Nathan better than you."

* * *

"Just because I'm the biggest and strongest of us doesn't mean none of you need to help," Vladimir complained as he carried the still unconscious mystery woman from the crashed escape pod over to their makeshift campsite.

"Jesus, Vlad, she probably weighs all of forty kilos," Jessica teased as she hauled survival supplies over.

"We're going to have to pack all of this up to travel you know," Nathan warned. "If someone figures out our deception, we want to be as far away from this pod as possible."

"What if our people figure it out?" Doctor Barra asked as she helped Vladimir lay the woman down on the ground.

"They'll hail us," Nathan stated, pointing at the comm-set hanging on his left ear.

"We need to find higher ground. Scope out the area before we decide which way to go."

"Aren't you forgetting about something?" Doctor Barra said, pointing to the woman she was examining.

"Can she walk?" Jessica asked.

"Not while she's unconscious," Kayci retorted with a hint of sarcasm.

"You're going to have to wake her, Doc," Nathan said.

"I don't know if that's a good idea."

"Someone is going to great lengths to retrieve her," Jessica stated. "We need to know who she is."

"I can't even figure out why she was in a medical SA pod," Doctor Barra pointed out. "Let's not forget she could still be infectious."

"Not much we can do about that now," Jessica stated.

"Jess and I will recon the immediate area," Nathan said. "You and Kayci get us ready to move. Round up all the survival gear we can easily carry. I want to move out as soon as Jess and I return."

"Got it," Vladimir assured him.

"What about the woman?" Kayci asked. "Should I wake her?"

"Not until we get back," Nathan instructed. He turned to Jessica. "Shall we?"

* * *

"Again?" Josh exclaimed as he and Nikolas completed yet another jump. "That's three in a row. Ever since we followed your mom's search recommendations, we're finding search drones at every waypoint."

"*These ones are different,*" Nikolas stated.

"They look the same to me," Josh insisted.

"*Ensign Sorenson is correct,*" Josh's AI said. "*These are not the same type of drones we encountered at the previous two waypoints.*"

"What's different about them?" Josh wondered, studying the tactical screen in his Dragon fighter's cockpit.

"*They're bigger for one,*" Nikolas told him.

"*They have more advanced power and propulsion systems, as well as better sensors,*" Josh's AI added. "*Also, they are armed.*"

"Armed?" Josh said, not liking where the conversation was going.

"*Missiles and plasma turrets,*" his AI explained. "*Not enough to destroy a Dragon fighter, but enough to make attacking them a poor option.*"

"Who do they belong to?" Josh wondered.

"*Their power signatures are very similar to the ones used by the ships the Scott encountered that identified themselves as Zhulati,*" his AI stated.

"The *Zhulati* are looking for the Traverna?"

"*It appears that way.*"

"*This is not good,*" Nikolas decided.

"You got that right," Josh said as he began shutting down systems. "Go dark until they leave, Remo. There's still a chance they haven't detected us yet."

"*They're just drones, Josh.*"

"That came from a ship, which may be nearby," Josh insisted. "And where there are drones, there are fighters."

"*If they find the Traverna before we do...*"

"I had the same thought," Josh agreed. "We'll wait until they leave, then we'll jump a light year ahead of them and continue searching."

"*And what if the Traverna is somewhere in that light year?*"

"We'll send a couple of our own drones to search that sector," Josh decided. "At least that way, if the Zhulati show up, the only thing we'll lose are a couple of drones instead of a Dragon fighter."

"*Never thought I'd see Josh Hayes run from a fight,*" Nikolas stated.

"Our mission is to find our people," Josh argued. "Besides, I have a feeling we'll being seeing the Zhulati again real soon."

* * *

Nathan and Jessica stood at the summit, staring down at a collection of buildings along the river that snaked its way from one end of the valley to the other.

"What are the chances?" Jessica said as she pulled out her handheld visual scanner to zoom in on the buildings.

"Actually better than you'd think," Nathan replied.

"How do you figure?" Jessica wondered as she continued scanning the valley.

"Well about ten percent of settlers seek out unsettled or lightly settled worlds, and there aren't as many hospitable worlds out there as people think."

"I thought there were like a million of them?"

"Yes, but they're spread all over the galaxy," Nathan pointed out.

"Still, what are the odds that we'd crash near one of the few settlements on *this* rock?" Jessica challenged.

"Also better than you'd think."

Jessica looked at him as if he were crazy.

"Small settlements almost always start along the equator. More temperate climate and less energy to get to and from orbit."

She looked at him again.

"Sorry, it's the pilot in me," Nathan said.

"It's the *dork* in you."

"Like you didn't already know that."

"Regardless, the odds are long," Jessica insisted.

"I'm getting the feeling I should just shut up and agree with you," Nathan muttered.

"It only took you what, five hundred years to figure that out?"

"Funny."

Jessica continued looking at the scanner screen as she aimed the device at the settlement below. "Houses, shops, light processing and manufacturing, and some cultivated plots. I'm picking up about a hundred or so people."

"Weapons?"

"Mostly low-power sidearms," Jessica replied. "A few long-range rifles, probably for hunting. No perimeter shields, not even any sensors or comms gear. In fact, the only power signature I can find is a small fusion reactor in what appears to be the manufacturing plant."

"The buildings don't have power?" Nathan asked, surprised.

"No, they're wired for power. They're just not using it. At least not enough for me to detect."

"This has *got* to be a new settlement," Nathan decided.

"Based on their ag plots, I'd say a year, two at the most. Assuming they planted right away. They don't always."

"Now who's a dork?"

"So I read the net," Jessica defended. "I am an intelligence officer, you know."

"An intelligence dork," Nathan muttered. "Should we go down and say hi?"

Jessica thought for a moment, sighing. "A settlement is the second place they'd look."

"The escape pod being the first?" Nathan assumed.

"A-firm," Jessica replied, looking at the settlement again. "If they agree to let us join them, we might be able to blend in, assuming they come looking for us."

"From what I've read, new settlements are not that open to uninvited guests," Nathan commented.

"Well if we are going to initiate contact, we should wait until morning." Jessica looked up at the sky, noticing that the sun had already fallen below the ridge on the far side of the valley. "We should head back. We're running out of light."

* * *

"If they are Zhulati, then things just got more complicated," Aiden commented as he, Cameron, and Laza studied the display on the Aurora's sensor console.

"Why would the Zhulati be interested in the Traverna?" Laza wondered.

"We can only hope that they are," Cameron said.

"You think they're looking for us," Aiden realized.

"I think we have to assume that." Cameron thought for a moment. "Although it could be both."

"The girl?" Aiden said.

"It *would* answer a lot of questions," Cameron agreed.

"And raises many more," Laza added.

"Indeed it does," Cameron concurred, tapping her comm-set. "Kit, Cameron."

"*Go ahead,*" Kit replied.

"Load your men up and rendezvous with each shuttle on their search patterns. I want one of you on each ship, ready for anything."

"*On our way,*" Kit acknowledged.

"What do you think is going to happen?" Aiden questioned.

"Nothing good I'm sure," Cameron sighed. "No matter what happens, I have a feeling we're going to need the Ghatazhak."

* * *

After securing and stabilizing the crashed escape pod, Vladimir had removed all the survival cargo, as well as several components he thought might be of use. The result was a considerable stockpile of goods which would be difficult to carry, assuming they were still planning on being mobile rather than setting up camp.

"How is she doing?" Vladimir asked Kayci as he sat down nearby to take a break.

"She's still out," the doctor replied, seeming surprised.

"I take it you didn't expect her to be?"

"Her last dose of semol was hours ago. Without the pod, she should have woken by now."

Vladimir leaned toward the sleeping mystery woman, examining her face. "She looks peaceful enough."

"Her scans are fine," Kayci stated. "She just isn't waking up."

"Can you give her something to bring her out?" Vladimir wondered.

"Yes, but I'm not sure it's safe. I mean, she's not behaving at all the way she should, so I'm reluctant to give her anything at this point, especially considering her vitals are all normal at the moment. Besides, the captain said to wait until they returned."

"Well I'm not carrying her all across this planet, that's for certain."

"I'll probably give her a stimulant once the captain and the lieutenant commander return," Kayci decided.

Vladimir glanced at the sky. "Shouldn't be long. They wouldn't stay out after dark."

"How can you be sure?"

"I've known them both for a long time," Vladimir explained.

"I keep forgetting about the history you all have together," Kayci said as she settled back against the tree next to their unconscious patient. "When did you all first meet?"

"We were all assigned to the original Aurora for her maiden flight."

"The infamous flight of the Aurora," Kayci stated.

"Nathan and I were cabinmates actually."

"What about Lieutenant Commander Nash?"

"Nathan already knew her so to speak. I didn't get to know her until a few weeks later, after we were tossed into the Pentaurus sector. Haven was the first away mission with her," Vladimir recalled. "We were all in a hell of a firefight together."

"Have you been in a lot of *firefights?*" Kayci asked.

"More than most engineers I'd imagine."

"You seemed quite calm in the face of imminent danger back on the Traverna."

"I was in the Russian infantry before joining the Earth Defense Force and becoming an engineer."

"That explains it," she replied with a sigh. "It never ceases to amaze me how some people can remain calm when fighting for their very lives."

"It's the training," Vladimir explained. "It kicks in, and your actions become instinctive. You ignore the danger and just deal with the situation as best you can."

"Do you *still* train for such things?"

"Not as much as I should, considering the ship I'm serving on," Vladimir chuckled.

"What about the captain and the lieutenant commander?"

"Nathan started training daily just after we time-shifted," Vladimir told her. "Jess, on the other hand, trains every spare moment. It's the Ghatazhak in her."

"What? Jessica was a Ghatazhak?"

"She trained with them for seven years. Lived and breathed it."

"That explains how frightening she can be."

"Oh she was frightening *long* before that," Vladimir chuckled. "If anything, the Ghatazhak made her *less* scary. More deadly but more self-disciplined."

"That makes sense," Kayci agreed. "I don't find the Ghatazhak at all frightening, which is surprising considering they are trained killers."

"They're not really," Vladimir defended. "I mean yes, they are quite adept at taking life, but not in the same way as other soldiers of their ilk."

"How so?"

"Most soldiers are just trained to kill the enemy any way they can," Vladimir explained. "The Ghatazhak only kill when killing is necessary to achieve their objective."

"Isn't that what all soldiers do?"

"Yes, but with the Ghatazhak, it is different. The difference is subtle I admit. But the more you witness them in action, the more you see it. They seem so detached from the horror that they inflict, and they get no joy from it."

"Who would get joy from killing?"

"In combat, adrenaline takes over and puts you into an altered state. The Ghatazhak do not experience this. Their demeanor barely changes during combat. And if it does, it is because they *choose* to let the change happen. And even then, that change is completely under their control. They can control their emotional state the same way you and I can control our voices."

"How is that even possible?" Kayci said, not really expecting a response.

"Training," Vladimir replied confidently. "Hours and hours of it. Every day, all day, for decades and decades. If they are not on a mission, they are training. And I'm not just talking about combat and weapons training and such, but constant studying as well."

"What kind of studying?"

"Ever since we got our AICC node connected to the Alliance net, they have been studying the last five hundred years of history that we missed."

"Why?" Kayci wondered.

"Because behaviors of the past influence those in the present," Vladimir stated. "At least that's what Lieutenant Vasya told me when I asked him the same question."

"He's right," a female voice stated.

Vladimir and Kayci both looked at the woman at the same time, but they were caught by surprise, especially Vladimir, who took the full force of her blow, knocking him unconscious.

Kayci froze, and in the next moment, the woman pulled Vladimir's side arm, taking aim at the doctor as the weapon charged.

"Don't move," the woman stated, a cold, dispassionate look in her eyes.

CHAPTER FIVE

Although all worlds hospitable to humans had their similarities, they also had their differences. Nathan likened them to the cities he had visited in his youth back on Earth. Each had its own ambiance. At first, it was unfamiliar and somewhat off-putting. But after time, it felt like an old coat that had been through the wash countless times and felt like a second skin when worn.

This world was not yet like an old coat. Every sound caught his attention. Every bird that flew by, every small creature that went scampering for cover as they approached, even the bugs on the foliage were an ever-present threat. Any of them could carry pathogens or venoms deadly to humans. As interesting as it was to explore an alien world for the first time, it was also horrifying, and it took great effort to remain calm and focused on the mission.

However, the discovery of a well-established settlement told them that this world was survivable, at least for those who knew its pitfalls.

At this point, their immediate mission was simply to return to their crash site and dig in for the night. As much as Jessica wanted to put some distance between them and the crash site, there was no way they were leaving the safety of the portable protective shield generator that was part of the escape pod's survival package. Especially in the dead of an alien night.

"Shouldn't we be there by now?" Nathan voiced as he followed Jessica through the forest.

Jessica stopped in her tracks, her entire body suddenly becoming motionless. Nathan also froze, having learned long ago to trust Jessica's instincts. Her hand moved slowly down to the butt of her sidearm.

"What is it?" Nathan whispered.

"The crash site is about seventy meters ahead," she whispered back.

"How do you know?"

Jessica pointed to a broken branch slightly ahead of them and on their left. "That's my marker."

"If the crash site is seventy meters away, why are we whispering?" Nathan wondered.

"The question is, why do we not hear Vlad's booming voice?"

Now Nathan's hand slid down to his sidearm.

"I'm going to circle left. You go straight in like nothing is wrong."

"I'm the bait?" Nathan protested, still whispering. "Why am I the bait?"

"I'm a better shot," Jessica said as she departed.

Nathan flipped the safety off on his sidearm but left it in its holster. "I've got to spend more time in the gun range," he mumbled as he headed carefully forward. As he advanced, his eyes darted left and right, looking for signs of danger. Jessica was rarely mistaken about such things, which meant he was walking right into danger.

After about ten steps, Nathan began to see glimpses of the crashed escape pod through the trees. Although the sun had set more than an hour ago, there was still plenty of light. Yet it seemed strange that Vladimir had not set up any portable lights.

As he grew closer, Nathan had to force himself not to appear apprehensive. He was supposed to be returning to the relative safety of the crash site and his people, not knowingly walking into danger.

"Doc!" Nathan called out as he stepped through the forest and into the small clearing that had been created by the pod's impact. The first thing he noticed was the look on her face. The second thing he noticed was that Vladimir was on the ground, unmoving. "Doc?"

Kayci tried not to look at the woman stepping out of the shadows to Nathan's right and slightly behind him, but failed. Nathan spun to his right, instinctively going for his sidearm, but froze when he too spotted the woman. She was holding her own blaster and appeared surprisingly confident about its use.

"Where is your friend?" the woman asked calmly as she took aim at Nathan's head.

"We got separated," Nathan lied.

"Unlikely," the woman said. She glanced about, but not as if looking blindly. Her head moved in exacting increments, and her eyes scanned each area of the forest around her in repetitive patterns, as if she were registering every tree and bush in her mind. After a moment, her focus returned to Nathan. "Tell the lieutenant commander to show herself, or I'll drop you where you stand."

"That would be a mistake," Nathan warned.

"I can live with it."

"No you can't," Jessica stated as she stepped out of the forest to their left, her own sidearm trained on the woman who was threatening Nathan's life. "You shoot him, I shoot you."

"But then your captain dies," the woman pointed out.

"I never liked him much," Jessica stated rather convincingly.

The woman glanced at Jessica, then back to Nathan. "If you miss…"

Jessica smiled. "I never miss."

"She's a Ghatazhak," Nathan told the woman.

"Nice try, Captain. The Ghatazhak died five hundred years ago."

"Not all of them."

"I don't have all day, lady," Jessica snarled.

Nathan looked into the woman's eyes. "We aren't your enemy," he assured her.

"If you knew me, you might be."

"Safe the weapon and drop it to the ground," Jessica instructed.

"If you kill me, she kills you, and then we'll never know," Nathan told her. "Besides, we *are* your best bet at survival."

"I could just kill you all and take your gear."

"Not gonna happen," Jessica said.

There was a confidence in Jessica's voice that registered in the woman's brain. The woman flipped her safety on, then lowered her weapon. "Very well," she said, sticking the gun in her belt. "But I'm keeping the gun."

"The hell you are," Jessica insisted, holding her aim steady.

Nathan shot a look at Jessica.

"Shit," Jessica grumbled, lowering her weapon and deactivating it as she re-holstered it in practiced fashion.

"Who are you people?" the woman asked.

"I'm Nathan. That's Jessica, and I assume you already met the doctor and my engineer."

"Not formally," the woman replied.

"Doc, is Vlad..."

"He's breathing," she replied, already tending to him.

"They referred to your rank as captain, and hers as lieutenant commander," the woman stated. "The only military I know of is the Alliance. Are you?"

"Alliance?" Nathan said. "We were a *long* time ago. We're now in the Free Fleet."

"Never heard of it."

"We're new to the area."

"The *area*?" The woman chuckled.

"It's a long story," Nathan stated. "And you are?"

"Breyanna," she replied. "Brey for short."

"Nice to meet you, Brey," Nathan said politely.

Breyanna looked at Jessica.

"Don't expect pleasantries from me," Jessica warned her.

"I expect you have a lot of questions," Nathan said. The last thing he needed was for Jessica's steely killer stare to spook the woman before they could convince her to trust them.

"Just one actually," Breyanna replied. "How did I get here?"

"You were in a medical SA pod," Nathan began. "On a cargo ship."

"You were being *smuggled* on a cargo ship," Jessica added. "A fact you're going to have to explain."

"I'm afraid I can't," Breyanna admitted.

"Can't or won't?" Jessica challenged.

"Why were you in a medical SA pod?" Doctor Barra asked as she injected something into Vladimir's neck. "What's wrong with you?"

"That's a long story as well," Breyanna stated.

"We appear to have time," Nathan said.

Vladimir began to wake. "What happened?"

"You got your ass handed to you by a girl," Jessica chuckled.

* * *

Josh entered the Aurora's medical department, pausing to look around. The main treatment ward was still full of injured and recovering passengers from the Traverna.

"Are you injured?" a woman asked.

Josh turned, spotting Martina. "Huh?"

"Do you need treatment?"

"Not exactly," Josh replied.

"Then why are you here?" she asked.

"Is the doc around?"

"She's in surgery," Martina replied as she returned to her tasks tending to the patients.

"Surgery? Who..."

"One of the passengers started bleeding internally," Martina explained. "She had to go in to stop the bleeding."

"Seriously? Why not just give them some more nanites?"

"The patient was crashing. Nanites wouldn't be able to stop the bleed fast enough."

"Damn."

"So why did you need to see her?"

Josh suddenly looked uneasy.

"You can tell me," Martina urged. "I am a med-tech."

"I heard you were a dodger."

"What's a dodger?"

"That's what we called law enforcement on Haven where I grew up," Josh explained.

"Well I was a trained and sworn med-tech before I was a *dodger,*" Martina told him. "Dumb name by the way."

"From what I hear, that was like…fifteen hundred years ago?"

"An oath's an oath isn't it?"

"As long as you believe in it I suppose."

"Well I still believe in mine," Martina assured him. She turned back to him. "Now are you going to tell me why you're here?"

Josh sighed. "Fine. I was hoping to get some stims from the doc."

"Stims?"

"Stimulants. Stay-awake pills?"

"Why?"

Josh pointed at the flight suit he was still wearing.

"Why not just take a nap?"

"We have to find the Traverna."

"Don't we have other pilots?"

"I'm the CAG."

"And CAGs can't take naps?"

"Are you going to give me the stims or what?" Josh demanded. "I'm kind of in a hurry."

"Stimulants aren't safe," Martina insisted as she headed for the supply room.

"I've taken them before without any problems," Josh insisted, following her.

"Having done something stupid before doesn't make it right."

"The *doc* gave them to me," Josh argued.

"And did she tell you they were safe?"

"Well…not exactly."

"I'm betting she felt the same way about giving them to you as I do," Martina insisted.

"But she gave them to me anyway," Josh countered. "And you know why? Because she knew the stakes, that's why. And she knew I was the best pilot we had. And you know what? I still am."

Martina pulled a small bottle out of her bag on the counter. "This is quana root." She opened the bottle and pulled out a piece about the size of her pinky. "Bite off a little, chew it a bit, then let it sit in your cheek until it dissolves. It will keep you awake but won't dull your senses like stimulants do."

"So it's like coffee then," Josh said, taking the root from her and sniffing it.

"Sort of, but better. No jitters." She snatched the root back from him. "On one condition though. First you take a nap."

"What?"

"One hour, that's all."

Josh rolled his eyes. "Fine," he replied, holding out his hand.

"Nope. There's an open bed over there. Lie down and take a nap, and I'll give this to you in an hour."

Josh turned and looked, noticing that it was the only open bed in the treatment ward. "Is that where the guy who went into surgery was?"

"Girl," Martina replied. "And yes. Don't worry, she'll be going to a critical-care suite after surgery."

Josh thought for a moment. He didn't much like being told what to do, especially by someone he outranked. But it was going to take at least thirty minutes for Marcus and his deckhands to turn his Dragon around and make it flight-ready again, so... "I'll see you in an hour," he sighed, heading for the empty bed.

Martina smiled. *That was easier than I thought.*

* * *

"I'd be more likely to believe you had you not claimed to have jumped *through* a singularity," Breyanna admitted.

"Why does everyone find that the hardest part to believe?" Nathan commented.

"Probably because we've always been told that nothing can survive inside a black hole," Doctor Barra said.

"No one knows for certain," Vladimir insisted. "I mean, the math says no, but math says nothing can go faster than the speed of light as well."

Nathan looked at his engineer, surprised.

"What?" Vladimir asked, noticing his expression.

"Nothing," Nathan said, turning his attention back to Breyanna. "I can't explain it. In fact, even Abby can't."

"Abby?" Breyanna wondered.

"Abigail Sorenson, the inventor of jump drive technology," Nathan explained.

"She's with you as well?" Breyanna asked, shaking her head in disbelief. "How many historical figures did you bring with you from the past?"

"I think that about covers everyone," Nathan assured her.

Breyanna thought for a moment. "Your story is so far-fetched, it seems too unlikely to be made up," she admitted. "I can come up with several cover stories for you that would be far more believable."

"It's been my experience that the *truth* is often the hardest thing to believe," Nathan stated.

"Especially when you work for him," Jessica joked, pointing to Nathan.

Breyanna sighed. "Honestly, a year ago I wouldn't have believed a word of it."

"But you do now?" Nathan surmised.

"I'm not sure," she admitted. "But my last six months have been nearly as unbelievable."

"Why?" Nathan asked.

After another sigh, Breyanna began her story. "Nearly a year ago, I was diagnosed with Jerrit's."

"Did you say *Jerrit's*?" Doctor Barra asked, her face turning pale.

"What's wrong?" Nathan asked Kayci.

"That isn't possible," Kayci insisted. "Jerrit's is very aggressive, and it's uncurable...*and* very contagious."

"But your med scans showed there was nothing wrong with her, right?" Jessica pointed out.

"That's why it isn't possible," Kayci explained. "Jerrit's is easy to detect, and it usually kills within six months of first onset. There's no way this woman has Jerrit's syndrome."

"How can you be so sure?"

"Because she'd have lesions and would have all but wasted away by now. She'd be nothing but skin and bones. This woman is in perfect health." Kayci looked at Breyanna, this time in a different light. "Are you telling me that someone *cured* your Jerrit's?"

"Not exactly," Breyanna replied. "In fact, the last time I closed my eyes, I did not expect to open them again."

"Then you were stage four?" Kayci seemed confused.

"What is it?" Nathan asked the doctor.

"Jerrit's is very rare and easy to detect. It's been around for centuries because no one bothers to develop a cure for it. There's no profit in it."

Nathan looked at Breyanna. "Something tells me there's more to your story."

Breyanna took a deep breath, letting it out slowly as she gazed up at the stars. Finally, her gaze came back down to Nathan. "Six months ago, I was contacted by a man who said he could save my life, but not without grave risk. He said I would be giving up everything. Family, friends, my career, even my identity. I would even *look* different."

"Sounds sketchy," Jessica mumbled.

"That's what I thought," Breyanna agreed. "But I was dying, so I had no choice."

"Nanites couldn't help?" Vladimir wondered.

"Jerrit's attacks every system in the body simultaneously. Even mega doses of the best nanites can't keep up with it. It's just too aggressive. The best they can do is to ease the pain. In fact, Jerrit's is one of the few conditions that qualifies for assisted euthanasia under Alliance law."

"That's what I was going to do until that guy showed up."

"Who was this guy?" Nathan asked.

"He never said," Breyanna replied. "I said yes, and he made all the arrangements. A few days later, I was moved to a facility on another world. I was told that when I woke, I'd be cured. But honestly, I didn't believe them. By that time, I was so far gone I could barely think straight."

"What happened when you woke?" Kayci asked.

"I heard you and him talking," Breyanna explained, pointing to Vladimir. "Sorry by the way."

"No problem," Vladimir replied.

"Well why did you attack them?" Jessica questioned.

"I honestly don't know," Breyanna admitted. "I was listening with my eyes closed for a while, and then...I just snapped. I can't explain it. I don't even know *how* I did it. I'm *not* a violent person, and he's *huge*. *Look* at him."

Nathan looked at Vladimir.

"She caught me by surprise," Vladimir defended. "I thought she was unconscious."

"I'm not buying it," Jessica said outright.

Nathan looked at her, surprised.

"She handled that weapon like a pro," Jessica explained. "Flipped the safety back on without even looking at it. *And* she was savvy enough to insist on holding onto it. She's got training."

"I swear I do not," Breyanna insisted.

"What were you before you got sick?" Nathan wondered.

"I was a forensic computer analyst."

"A what?" Nathan asked.

"She's a hacker hunter," Vladimir realized, a bit impressed.

"So a *computer geek* kicked your ass?" Jessica joked.

"She didn't *kick my ass,*" Vladimir argued.

"I analyzed comm-trails and back-traced illegal access attempts for a corporate cyber security firm."

"Captain," Doctor Barra interrupted. "Even if they completely cured her, there would be residual damage that I would have detected."

"Maybe she was cloned?" Jessica suggested.

"Jerrit's is genetic," Kayci explained. "If they cloned her, she'd just get it again in a few years."

"She's not a clone," Nathan insisted.

"How do you know?" Jessica challenged.

"It doesn't make any sense. They didn't ask for payment, and cloning is not cheap. Plus it's illegal in Alliance territory."

"She did say she was moved to another world."

"I'm pretty sure I was still in Alliance space," Breyanna stated. "Besides, I feel different...*very* different."

"How so?" Nathan wondered.

"Smaller for one. I was not a small gal. I was about one hundred and seventy-eight centimeters, and noticeably overweight. Kind of a side effect of the job."

"You're about one sixty-five and fifty-five kilos at most," Jessica told her.

"Are you serious?" Breyanna questioned, looking at her arms and torso. "My God, my boobs! They were a *lot* larger." She started to panic and reached for her hair. I had long hair as well," she exclaimed as she felt her short-cut hairstyle.

"Were you a blonde?" Jessica asked.

"Redhead."

"Not anymore."

"What the hell?" Breyanna exclaimed, starting to panic.

Jessica pulled her scanner from her belt and took an image, handing the device to Breyanna afterward.

Breyanna's mouth dropped open in astonishment. "Oh my God! What did they do to me?" She looked at the others. "This isn't me! Who am I?"

Nathan could see the fear and panic in Breyanna's face and stepped forward to console her. "Don't worry, we'll figure it out," he promised her, wrapping his arms around her as she began to sob. He looked at Jessica as the woman cried in his arms.

Jessica just shrugged, as perplexed as any of them.

* * *

General Gogol stared at the view screen on the briefing room wall. "And you believe that tiny spike represents a second jump?"

"I do," the Maturo's sensor officer replied. "If you remove the energy signature from the jump, what remains looks very much like the energy signature of another jump."

"But not *exactly*," General Gogol pointed out.

"No, but that could be because of the overlapping signature of the preceding jump."

"Assuming they were somehow able to execute a second jump even before the first one had occurred."

"I've spoken to our chief engineer, and he says it is *technically* possible, but very few people would be able to pull that off, especially in a ship like the Traverna. Even he did not believe he could do so."

"You're not convincing me," the general admitted.

"I'm not trying to, sir. I'm just reporting the possibilities based on my sensor readings."

"I don't suppose you have any way to verify your theory?"

"Unfortunately, none of the Genstar assets were actively scanning the Traverna at the time she jumped, and they never thought to take old light readings of her escape from multiple angles."

"Of course they didn't," General Gogol snarled. "Any guesses as to the distance of their second jump?"

"We originally estimated their first jump at seven light years but have not found them at that distance. The second spike, assuming it *is* a jump signature, would be between one to three light years."

"Then we go out to ten light years and start searching backwards," Captain Hyam suggested.

"Why ten?" the general questioned.

"That is the Traverna's maximum jump range."

"Let's start at twenty-two," the general insisted.

"General?" the captain questioned.

"The Traverna can series jump ten light years at a time. If they did two max-range jumps, that's twenty light years. And every ship's captain likes to keep an extra light year of jump range in reserve, just in case they jump into trouble," the general explained. "I'm betting the Traverna did so as well. Besides, if the Aurora is looking for her, and they came to the same two-jump hypothesis, they'll start just beyond the Traverna's max-jump range as well. With any luck, we'll come up behind them."

"As you wish, General," Captain Hyam replied.

General Gogol looked at the sensor officer. "Nice work, Lieutenant. If this leads us to the Aurora, you'll be a lieutenant commander before you know it."

* * *

The sun had set hours ago. Nathan sat on the ground, leaning against one of the trees that had been knocked over by their escape pod during their crash landing. Nathan's watch, still set to ship time, said it was only fifteen hundred hours. If he were on the Aurora right now, he'd be meeting Vlad for dinner in about an hour and then going to the gym for his evening training.

Jessica came over, making her way over the uneven, slightly sloped landscape by the waning light of the world's more prominent moon. "Hungry?" she asked, offering Nathan a ration pack.

"Thanks," Nathan replied, accepting the food packet. He opened it and tried to look inside. "I believe Neli was making Coran lasagna tonight." He reached into the bag, pulling out a nugget of food, popping it into his mouth. "Not exactly lasagna," he said as he grimaced, chewing.

"Did you buy any of that?" Jessica asked as she sat down on the ground next to him and opened her own food packet.

"Her story wasn't any more far-fetched than ours," Nathan said as he swallowed his food.

"There's more to it, that's for sure."

"You think she's holding something back?"

"Actually no."

Nathan looked at her. "Well that's a first."

"Her reaction when she saw herself on my scanner pad...even I couldn't have faked that."

"Then what are you thinking?"

"Doc says that medical SA pod was state of the art. That means it was expensive."

"So someone was willing to spend a lot of money saving her."

"The goal wasn't to *save* her," Jessica insisted. "They were just using her to test something. Something dangerous or illegal. Probably both."

"Whoever it was, they could afford to send a sizable force looking for her," Nathan stated. "Had to be corporate-level stuff."

"But why would they want to transfer someone into a *different* body?" Jessica argued. "If cloning is illegal, then surely cloning someone *else* and transferring someone into *that* body is illegal as well. Not that a big corporation would care."

"Yeah, but not that many people would have the kind of resources needed to afford that kind of service," Nathan said.

"That's what worries me," Jessica admitted. "If *my* suspicious mind can't come up with something, then whatever they *are* planning is *really* scary."

"Recommendations?" Nathan asked.

"Honestly, leave her here and get as far away from her as possible," Jessica suggested. "Hell I'd even activate the homing beacon on the pod just to make sure they find her."

"That's pretty harsh don't you think?"

"On the other hand, if we take her with us, we might learn more from her and eventually figure out what's *really* going on."

"Then you *do* think she's hiding something," Nathan surmised.

"She may not even *realize* she's hiding something."

Nathan looked at Jessica. There was something different about her tone, and it worried him. "What is it?"

"Like I said, she's got training. That means either she's lying..."

"Or?" Nathan asked, fearing the answer.

"Or she's some kind of weapon."

Nathan sighed. "I was afraid you'd say something like that."

"If she *is*, then we should probably know *that* as well."

"What are you thinking?" Nathan asked.

"What if she's some kind of prototype?"

"Prototype for what?" Nathan challenged. "If you're making a weapon, why move someone's consciousness into a different body?"

"I don't have all the answers, Nathan. Just the questions. But if someone *is* developing a kind of deep-cover agent slash weapon, there's a pretty good chance they'll eventually try to use it against us. Better to find out now."

Nathan leaned back, sighing. "I've got to stop being such a good samaritan."

"Fat chance."

* * *

The alert indicator began beeping and flashing over Nikolas's tactical display but stopped a moment later.

"*Miss me?*" Josh asked over comms.

"What took you so long?" Nikolas asked.

"*Medical made me take a nap.*"

"Oh you poor thing."

"*It was that fifteen-hundred-year-old gal they've got working there. She wouldn't give me the stims, but she gave me some root to chew on that's supposed to do the same thing.*"

"Why did she make you take a nap?" Nikolas wondered.

"*Probably to demonstrate her authority over me,*" Josh complained. "*Doc Chen never would've done that.*"

"I suspect Doc Chen knows you a bit better."

"*Damn right. I don't suppose you found anything?*"

"Nothing."

"*Well I have an idea,*" Josh told him.

"I'm afraid to ask."

"*Everyone is assuming the Traverna's first jump was five light years, and that her second jump was five or less than five, right?*"

"Because she's got a ten-light-year max."

"*Yeah, but she can jump ten light years at a time for about twenty jumps before she has to do a recharge layover.*"

"Because her charging system can't keep up with max-range jumps forever. It starts to fall off."

"*That's right. If she doesn't, she'll only jump nine light years, then eight, then seven, and so on, until she can't jump at all.*"

"What's your point?" Nikolas wondered.

"*What if she jumped ten light years both times?*"

"But her first jump signature indicated a five light year jump," Nikolas reminded him.

"*But what if they were wrong?*" Josh said. "*What

if the second jump event somehow altered the energy signature of the first one?"

"Seems unlikely."

"Maybe. But maybe that's why that double-jump trick was so good at shaking a tail."

"Did you run this idea past my mom?"

"Damn right I did," Josh replied. *"She said theoretically that might be true, but she had no idea how you could do two max-range jumps only a split second apart, at least from an engineering standpoint."*

"But she's not an engineer," Nikolas stated, seeing where Josh was going.

"And Vlad is," Josh replied over comms. *"And probably one of the best. If anyone could pull off a double max-range jump all within the same second, it's him."*

"So we're changing our search pattern?"

"Hell yes."

"Did you get permission?"

"I don't need permission," Josh insisted. *"I'm the CAG, remember?"*

* * *

General Gogol wasted no time getting to the bridge after being hailed moments ago. "Report?" she beckoned as she entered.

"Your hunch paid off, General," Captain Hyam announced. "Our search drones have picked up the Traverna's jump trail. She came out of her double-jump nineteen point three light years from her departure point. They were stationary for about fifteen minutes before jumping another ten light years. I've taken the liberty of sending the majority of our drones to that area."

"If they jumped again that soon, then the damage

to their jump systems must have been minimal," the general decided.

"The Genstar commander was certain the Traverna's propulsion and maneuvering were inoperable at the time they jumped away. He also stated there were several hull breaches that had not sealed up automatically."

"Which means they would want off the ship as soon as possible," the general added. "Show me their jump plot."

Captain Hyam looked to his tactical officer, who immediately activated a holographic display of the area of space in question in the middle of the bridge. "The last engagement was here," the captain stated, pointing to the red icon floating in the air amongst the stars. "Our drones detected them again here," he added, pointing to the orange icon halfway across the holographic projection.

"Show me all habitable systems along that heading," the General instructed. A moment later, several of the stars became encircled in green, one of them directly along the Traverna's course.

"The Nishida system," the tactical officer reported. "Two hospitable worlds, one of which has a thriving colony."

"That's only three jumps," the general realized. "That's where they'll be."

"It could be a ruse," the captain warned. "If they managed to get maneuvering restored, they could have changed course. I would advise that we continue searching along their original course, focusing first on the ten-light-year jump points. It should be easy to verify their arrivals and departures and confirm that Nishida *is* their destination."

"Agreed," the general replied. "But I want this

ship in the Nishida system as soon as possible. If they *are* there, I do not want them to get away."

"We can be there in a few minutes," Captain Hyam promised.

General Gogol smiled. She could feel that she was close. She would have Nathan Scott and the Aurora, *and* the missing Genstar package. Once she did, her place in history as the greatest Zhulati commander in Alliance history would be assured.

* * *

Aiden and Cameron had been taking four-hour shifts on the Aurora's bridge since her arrival. The nap she had just awakened from was the first real rest she had taken since she had left Libertara. She never could sleep worth a damn on those shuttles. The beds and staterooms were just too small. After a decade of command and the accommodations that accompanied it, she had become spoiled.

Cameron often wondered how Nathan managed to sleep on the Voss. Even the captain's quarters on that ship were small. Not quite as cramped as those on a shuttle, but still more compact than Cameron found comfortable.

Despite the fact of them being identical, walking onto the Aurora's bridge was different than walking onto the Celestia's, especially now that she was shut down for overhaul on Libertara. The Aurora's bridge was alive. Every display was active, and they weren't just showing simulated data like most of the Celestia's bridge displays. The Aurora was in space in every sense of the word. Even when the Celestia had been in transit, she still hadn't felt as alive.

"Good morning, sir," Aiden greeted when he noticed Cameron's entrance.

"Anything to report?" Cameron asked as she glanced about.

"Just a few more passing contacts with recon drones," Aiden replied. "Whoever is searching for them is pulling out all the stops."

Cameron looked up at one of the overhead view screens. "Someone's off grid."

Aiden glanced up as well. "Josh and Nikolas. Josh does that from time to time. He likes to follow hunches."

"He's leaving a whole sector uncovered."

"He'll double-back once he's done following his gut," Aiden assured her. "He always does."

"We can't afford that kind of inefficiency," Cameron insisted. "Especially now." She turned to the comm-station. "Get Josh on the line."

"Yes, sir," Ensign Dass acknowledged.

"He won't answer," Aiden said under his breath.

"I know," Cameron replied, also in a low voice.

A confused look came across Aiden's face. "Then why?"

"To remind him that he still has to answer to those above him." Cameron smiled, turning toward Aiden. "It keeps him from getting *too far* out of line."

Aiden didn't look convinced.

"Trust me," Cameron told him. "I've been trying to maintain control over Josh for a *long* time."

"Have you ever?" Aiden asked.

"No. But I'll be damned if I'm going to give up now."

"Dragons One and Two aren't answering, sir," the comms officer reported.

"Keep hailing them every few minutes," Cameron instructed. "They'll answer as soon as Josh realizes his hunch isn't panning out," she told Aiden. "And

141

Josh will offer some lame excuse, like he thought he detected something jumping away on whatever heading he decided to chase. He may go off to chase hunches from time to time, but he always comes back."

"I'm afraid to ask what happens when he doesn't," Aiden admitted.

"Well that usually means he was right and has therefore saved the day."

"Or he got killed."

"Josh doesn't believe in getting killed," Cameron joked.

* * *

The night had been far shorter than any of them had hoped, lasting only six hours. Still, it had been enough to get a few hours of sleep for most of them.

Not for Nathan however. Something made sleep impossible for him. It might have been the unusual noises coming from the darkness or the strangely lavender hue of the nighttime skies. Most likely it was their predicament in general. Only a few meters away was a woman they did not know, who obviously had significant combat training and had easily taken down the largest of them. That woman was either lying or believed the lies she had told were the truth. Either way, neither he nor Jessica slept well that night.

Daybreak had been a welcoming event for him. Despite how quickly it had come, the dawn of a new day filled him with renewed energy. There was something about a real dawn that could not be simulated by a ship's environmental system. Nor could its effects on the human body and mind. A new day meant new possibilities. On board, everything followed a set routine. Their environment was completely controlled. The only surprises came from outside their controlled environment, and even those could be controlled by simply jumping away. On a world, especially an unfamiliar one, everything was new. Even a tree, which there always seemed to be plenty of on hospitable worlds, was new, despite its familiarity. A simple hike down the side of a mountain was an incredible adventure.

"I still don't understand why we didn't just stay put," Kayci commented as they made their way down the mountainside toward the settlement that Nathan and Jessica had spotted the night before.

"Five people and a crashed escape pod off all by themselves are much easier to spot from orbit than five people mixed in with a hundred others," Jessica explained.

"But if we mix in with them, aren't we putting them at risk?" Kayci stated.

"We're just going to stop in and say hello," Nathan told her.

"And then what?" Kayci asked.

"One step at a time, Doc."

"I thought you had some grand plan."

"Not this time," Nathan admitted.

"We should limit contact with the locals," Jessica suggested. "We have no idea if they can be trusted."

"Then why are we headed there?" Kayci wondered.

"Even if we don't make contact, just being in the general vicinity of that settlement will look less suspicious on someone's sensors," Vladimir said. "They might think we're just a small group of them off hunting or something."

"We might even be lucky enough to find a barn or a warehouse to hide in for a while," Nathan said. "If we're *really* lucky, they'll have regular cargo service, and we can get off this rock."

Nathan doubled his pace to catch up to Jessica at the head of the line. "We *do* need to make contact with them," he told her, keeping his voice low enough that the others couldn't hear him.

"I don't like it," Jessica argued. "If they're the only settlement on this world, they won't exactly be welcoming."

"How often do you see only one settlement on a world?"

"Even if there are others, they'd still be suspicious."

"Then what do you suggest?"

"We grab one of the locals and question them," Jessica suggested.

"A little aggressive don't you think?"

"Not really."

"And after we interrogate them?" Nathan asked. "Then what? Kill them?"

"We buy their silence," Jessica replied.

"With what?" Nathan wondered. "We don't have any credits on us."

"Medical supplies, blasters, food packs...I'm sure we've got something of value."

"And of course, there's the fear that you'll come back and kill them in their sleep if they say anything."

"That too," Jessica agreed.

* * *

"*They're still hailing us,*" Nikolas said over comms.

"And we're still ignoring them," Josh replied as he adjusted the range on his sensors.

"*We're going to get in trouble.*"

"But we're not in trouble *yet.*"

"*I don't know. Dass sounds really irritated.*"

"She's a comms officer who isn't being answered," Josh chuckled. "Of course she sounds irritated."

"How long are we gonna follow this hunch of yours?"

"Until we find something, or until Cam gets on comms and yells at us herself," Josh explained. *"That's* when we're in trouble. Right now, she's just reminding us that she's in charge."

"I keep forgetting who I'm flying with."

Josh continued to fiddle with his sensors. They had been on this waypoint for nearly a minute and still hadn't picked up anything. It was beginning to look like his hunch was wrong, which was something Josh wasn't very good at admitting.

"Maybe we're just too late," Nikolas suggested. *"By now, we'd have to be about thirty light hours out to see their flash. It could be so weak we'd miss it."*

"We should be able to detect an arrival flash from at least thirty-five light years, and you know it."

"Under ideal circumstances, yes."

"Just give it another minute," Josh insisted.

"Another minute and we're not going to be able to make up our missed search quadrants," Nikolas argued.

Josh sighed. "Fine," he said, punching a new course into his nav-com.

"I have a contact," Josh's AI announced. *"It appears to be a jump flash. Bearing one two five. Twenty-eight down relative, thirty-two light hours. Recommend we jump out one light minute from target to verify."*

"You got 'em too, Remo?" Josh asked.

"I do," Nikolas confirmed. *"Looks like a jump flash to me."*

"That's gotta be them," Josh insisted.

"*We can't be sure,*" Nikolas reminded him.

"I'm sure," Josh replied. "Aurora, Dragon One. We've picked up their trail. Transmitting sensor data to you now." Josh couldn't contain himself. "Hot damn!" he exclaimed. "We're back in the game, Remo!"

"*Let's go get 'em!*" Nikolas replied with equal excitement.

CHAPTER SIX

"Captain," Laza called from the Aurora's sensor station. "You might want to look at this."

Cameron moved away from the tactical station to Laza's station, looking over her shoulder at the sensor displays. "What are we looking at?"

"As you know, during our search efforts we spotted a number of drones that appear to also be searching for the Traverna. At first, they were all of the same basic design, so we attributed them to whomever was originally trying to capture the Traverna. Just a few hours ago, we began detecting different drones, ones that matched those known to be in use by the Zhulati."

"The Alliance's special ops force," Cameron remembered.

"Precisely. But a few minutes ago, we picked up a third type of drone." Laza called the image up on one of her displays.

Cameron's eyes widened. "Please tell me I'm wrong, but that looks a lot like..."

"A Dusahn drone," Laza confirmed. "The Aurora's identification database made a positive ID, and I recognize many of its attributes as being based on ancient Jung technologies."

"But we defeated the Dusahn," Cameron said. "They were disbanded, and all of their ships and technology were either dismantled or repurposed."

"I am not saying this *is* a drone being operated by the Dusahn," Laza corrected. "It has been highly modified, but the basic structure and flight systems are of Dusahn design. Whoever is operating this drone has access to Dusahn technology."

"I need to make a call," Cameron said, turning to depart.

* * *

"Since arriving in the Nishida system, the Traverna has done nothing," the Maturo's sensor officer summarized. "She essentially cold-coasted with almost no emissions until she launched an escape pod as she passed the planet Antoli."

"Antoli?" General Gogol questioned.

"One of two hospitable worlds in the Nishida system. It has a colony of around five thousand, with regular transport service."

"What about the other world?" the general wondered.

"Nishida Five has not yet been settled. At least not that we know of," the sensor officer explained.

"What is the Traverna doing now?"

"She is essentially dead stick. Very low power signature and almost no life support. There are no life signs aboard."

"What about the package?"

"With such low power readings, we cannot tell if they took the package with them or left it behind. Not without sending a boarding team."

"Send them," the general said, turning to Captain Hyam. "And send a team to do orbital scans of Nishida Five. If there are any humans detected on that world, I want to know about them."

"Yes, General," the captain confirmed. "And what about Antoli?"

"We'll send a full assault team to that escape pod's landing site. It's only been about seven hours since they would have landed, so they can't have gone far."

"There's one other thing," the sensor officer

added. "We've detected reconnaissance drones of an unusual type in the system."

"What kind of type?" the general asked.

"At their core, they are similar to an old Dusahn drone, but they have been highly modified."

"Privateers?" Captain Hyam suggested.

"Using Dusahn drones?" the sensor officer said. "More likely it's resistance."

"The resistance can't afford to bribe an insider at Genstar," Captain Hyam insisted. "More likely it was another corporation and the resistance found out about it."

"Or another corporation arranged it and then paid the resistance to pick up the package once it was outside of Alliance space," the sensor officer postulated.

"Everything points to Captain Scott and the Aurora," General Gogol reminded them.

"But how would *he* get someone on the inside at Genstar?" Captain Hyam questioned.

"Someone has been bankrolling them," the general insisted.

"One of the corporations?" the sensor office wondered.

"Possibly," the general agreed. "And when we find out who, we'll take them down as well."

"Regardless, these new, or should I say *old,* drones could complicate things," Captain Hyam warned.

"We've got the Traverna's trail now," the general stated. "Recall all other drones and dispatch armed drone escorts. If we encounter any other search drones or ships, we take them out. That should bring the Aurora to the Nishida system, where we will be waiting for them."

* * *

Josh came out of his stealth jump a few light minutes behind the Traverna's estimated position in the Nishida system. The moment he arrived, his AI shut down all systems and switched to battery power. A cold-coast meant exactly that. Every system went cold. Power, propulsion, maneuvering, active sensors, even life support was down to absolute minimums. Within seconds, his Dragon's emissions dropped so low as to make her practically invisible against the background radiation that filled space. Only the most adept sensor officers controlling the best sensor equipment available could detect him, and even then, only with a bit of luck.

"*Running in full stealth mode,*" his AI said in a low voice, as if to underline their current running state. "*Attempting to locate the Traverna using passive sensors.*"

Josh had a love-hate relationship with cold-coasting. Having everything turned off made him extremely vulnerable to attack, with nothing more than his docking thrusters, which required almost no power to operate, to adjust his attitude. If he was detected, it would take him nearly thirty seconds to spin up his reactors enough to raise his shields, and another thirty to reach full power and become a fully operational fighter again.

On the other hand, most cold-coast missions allowed him some time to relax. As small and cramped as a Dragon cockpit was, the modifications made to the space behind the pilot's seat made them practically luxurious compared to most fighters. Josh could have something to eat, watch a few vid-flicks, and maybe even get in a nap. His AI monitored the passive sensors, collecting every emission possible for later analysis. And in the event of a sudden threat detection, she would notify him and have the spin-up cycle started before he could even comprehend the danger.

Unfortunately, this was not one of those cold-coast missions. If they had detected the Traverna's double-jump, so could the enemy, whoever they were. He would not be the only person searching the Nishida system, and that made it impossible for him to relax.

Josh glanced at his sensor display, ensuring that his wingman did not show up on his sensors. Nikolas would have jumped in two light-minutes behind him, at his four o'clock and a few degrees below him. Under normal circumstances, they would communicate using direct-beam laser comms. Their tightly focused emissions were nearly undetectable from anywhere other than close range. But these were not normal circumstances, and Josh had opted for complete comms silence. Even their AICC nodes were shut down. Josh was completely cut off from the Aurora and the rest of the Dragons and shuttles still searching other sectors, on the off chance that what they detected was not the Traverna. He simply had to trust that his wingman was in position, ready to spring into action should something go amiss.

Even though he could not prove that the contact *was* the Traverna, it had been enough to keep Cameron from chewing his butt when Josh finally came up on comms to report it. Once again, one of Josh's wild hunches had paid off.

Josh often wondered how he had managed to be so lucky through most of his life. As a toddler, he and his mother had been sold to the Haven Syndicate to pay off debts that his mother had been unable to pay. As *unlucky* as that was, if it had not happened, they never would have been taken in by Marcus. It had been Marcus's indulgences that had allowed him to spend so much time on flight simulation games and discover his gift for flying. Had they not been on Haven, he never would have been able to pilot a mining harvester as a teenager, putting the skills he had learned in the simulator to good use. His piloting skills had promoted his mother off the sorting line. Unfortunately, it had been too late to prevent the disease that prolonged exposure to the raw materials harvested from Haven's rings caused in many, including his mother.

Despite his unbelievable natural talent for piloting, it was his time with Loki as his copilot that had made Josh a *real* pilot. Loki had taught him all the procedures of flying and space navigation. Subsequently, his time served under Captain Scott had honed his skills beyond his wildest dreams.

As much as Josh hated to admit it, his formal flight training at the Earth Defense Force Fleet Academy had really polished him up. For years, Loki had insisted that he needed to *understand* why pilots did the things they did, repeating that *instinct,* while a blessing, just wasn't enough. Josh had thought him crazy at the time but had realized the truth during his formal training.

Still, that training had not resulted in what many had hoped for. It never turned Josh into the type of by-the-book pilot that many had wanted him to be. In fact, Nathan was the only one who had ever understood the way Josh flew. Most likely because Nathan, although a far more disciplined pilot, flew much the same way...by instinct. *That* was why *finding* him was more important to Josh than any other pilot. Nathan was not only his friend but was also the *only* captain who would *let* Josh fly the way he flew best.

"*I have contacts,*" his AI reported.

"Already?"

"*One Zhulati heavy cruiser in orbit above the fourth planet, a flight of four Zhulati fighters at two nine five mark one five, two million kilometers out, and several recon drones at varying ranges.*"

"What about the Traverna?" Josh asked.

"*Nothing yet.*"

"*Additional contacts at two zero two mark three five one, approaching the fifth planet. Two Zhulati assault shuttles.*"

"Pretty good indicator that we're in the right place, I'd say," Josh chuckled.

"*Agreed.*"

Josh had to fight the urge to activate the tight-beam comms that allowed him to brag to his wingman. He loved a good dogfight, but experience had taught him to avoid one whenever possible. Getting detected by Zhulati fighters would guarantee a fight, and because he was cold-coasting, they had the advantage.

"*More contacts,*" his AI reported. "*Descending through the atmosphere of the fourth planet.*"

"Shit," Josh cursed. "Power up, sweetie."

Recon was over.

* * *

"You see anyone?" Nathan questioned Jessica as they peered out from the edge of the forest at the nearby homestead.

"No one," Jessica replied. "Wait..."

In the distance, an elderly man wearing work clothing came out of his house and headed toward the barn near them.

"One old guy. Looks like he's headed for the barn," she added. She turned to look back at the others. "Stay here but keep your eyes on the back door of the barn."

Vladimir nodded.

"We wait for him to go inside, then I head to the front while you sneak in the back," Jessica instructed Nathan.

"Shouldn't *you* sneak in the back?" Nathan suggested.

"I'm less threatening," she said as she removed her gun belt and handed it to Vladimir. "Especially with that scraggly hair of yours."

"Aren't you going to need this?" Vladimir asked, accepting her gun belt.

"Not for this guy I won't."

"What if there are more people already *in* the barn?" Nathan asked.

"That's why you're *sneaking* in through the back." Jessica didn't wait for Nathan's approval, since the man had already disappeared behind the barn. "Don't fuck up," she warned Nathan as she headed out.

Nathan rolled his eyes, following her out.

Jessica ran to the front edge and peeked discretely around the corner, spotting the old man as he entered. She stepped out, the open door now shielding her from view from the house beyond, following him in.

Inside, the old man was heading for a workbench. Jessica appeared in the doorway, her hair now down around her shoulders and her jacket unzipped enough to reveal her chest beneath her T-shirt. "Excuse me, sir," she said in a soft and sultry voice that she rarely used.

The old man turned, surprised to see her. "Who are you?"

"My name is Jessica. I hope I didn't startle you."

"How'd you...? Why'd you sneak up on me?"

"I didn't mean to," she lied. "I saw you walking toward the barn and called to you, but I guess you didn't hear me."

The old man looked her over, already suspicious. "Where'd you come from?"

"My escape pod crashed up in the hills," Jessica told him. "I saw the smoke from your settlement and thought I might find transport."

"You just continue on into town, lady," the old man said dismissively as he turned back toward his workbench. "Ain't no transports here."

"Not gonna happen, old man," Jessica said, her voice changing to a more threatening tone. She closed the barn door behind her and turned back to the old man. "Answer a few questions, and we'll be on our way," she told him.

The old man turned to look back at Jessica, who was now walking toward him. He picked up a small sledgehammer from the work bench and headed toward her. "I told you to leave."

"That's far enough!" Nathan yelled from the other end of the barn, behind the old man.

The old man spun his head toward Nathan, spotting the blaster in Nathan's hand.

"Drop the hammer!" Nathan added.

The old man complied.

"You could have waited," Jessica complained. "I didn't even get a chance to have some fun," she added, looking back at the old man and winking.

"Leave him alone, Jess," Nathan groaned, moving

closer. "No one's going to hurt you, sir," he assured the old man as he neared.

"You sure about that?" he asked, eyeing Jessica.

"Jess, be nice," Nathan instructed. "Go signal the others while this gentleman and I have a little chat."

"I should be the one interrogating him," Jessica argued.

"We're here to ask for help, not to interrogate," Nathan insisted. "Now go."

Jessica rolled her eyes and headed for the back of the barn to signal Vladimir and the others.

The old man waited for Jessica to get out of earshot before speaking again. "You sure you can control that one?"

"*Manage*, yes," Nathan chuckled as he holstered his weapon. "*Control?* Well that's a whole other problem."

"I'll bet."

"Connor Tuplo," Nathan said, offering his hand to the old man.

"Gillis Paparo," the old man replied, cautiously shaking Nathan's hand. "Is what she said true? You guys crash nearby?"

"Up in the hills to the south," Nathan explained. "Just the other side of the ridge. Sometime yesterday afternoon."

"My first guess would be that you're settlers on your way to Antoli, but something tells me I'd be wrong."

"It's a long story," Nathan assured him. "I was hoping your little settlement had regular transport service."

"Not since this place was established."

"How long ago was that?" Nathan wondered.

"Two of *our* years ago. Not sure how many standard Alliance years that would be."

"What do you do when you need something? Or if someone decides they don't like it here?"

"Never comes up. People are here because they want to be."

"What if there was an emergency?" Nathan asked.

"Then I guess we'd call Antoli and ask for help," the old man stated.

"Then you have interplanetary comms?"

"We've got all kinds of comms," the old man chuckled. "Just because we live simply doesn't mean we're completely backwards."

"Any chance Antoli has an AICC node?"

"What's an AICC node?" Gillis asked.

"It gives you real-time comms to pretty much anywhere in the galaxy," Nathan explained.

"I've got something that allows me to call my son on Juris Prime. Is that what you're talking about?"

"That depends. Is Juris Prime in this system?"

The old man threw an odd glance at Nathan. "Juris Prime is in the *Juris* system, about fifteen hundred light years from here. This rock is so far out in the fringe that my son insisted I buy the damned thing. He can't really afford to travel out here to visit, especially considering how long it takes to get here."

"*That* would be an AICC node," Nathan told him. "I don't suppose you'd let us use it to call for a ride."

The old man surveyed him again. "Who are you going to call?"

"That's another long story," Nathan said, realizing just how often he seemed to be repeating that to people ever since they had jumped ahead in time.

* * *

"*Dusahn?*" Jakome said, equally surprised. "*That doesn't seem possible.*"

Cameron stood next to the desk in the captain's ready room, facing the view screen currently filled with Jakome's image. "I was hoping you might know something about it."

"*There was an incident involving an attempted theft of a Dusahn ship,*" he said as he entered something into his terminal. "*Ah yes, here it is. About ten years after the Aurora's disappearance. Someone tried to steal a Dusahn cruiser from one of the storage docks in the Takaran system. But something went wrong, and the hijacked ship lost control and collided with the dock. The dock was heavily damaged, but the ship they were trying to steal exploded.*"

"Exploded? Why would it explode?"

"*The belief was that its reactor had become unstable. Possibly because of the collision, or perhaps because they had to bypass some of its safeties in order to start it quickly enough to escape. There were no survivors, and the ship was obliterated.*"

"Did they ever verify the wreckage?" Cameron wondered.

"*There wasn't much left, and some of it could have been from the dock itself,*" Jakome explained. "*Curious that you should encounter this ship now, assuming it is the same ship.*"

Cameron sighed.

"*What is it?*" Jakome wondered.

"If it isn't, then we've got *another* problem to deal with," Cameron said.

"*You don't think it's really the Dusahn, do you?*"

"Stranger things have happened," Cameron replied.

* * *

"Nice little place you've got here," Nathan said as Gillis led them to his home.

"Damn prefab," the old man grumbled. "I was planning to replace it with an honest-to-God log cabin that I built myself, but I couldn't afford the tools to mill my own logs. Maybe in a few years."

"How do you earn a living out here?" Nathan wondered.

"I raise sheep. Berkers. I've got about fifty of them grazing out back. I sell or trade their wool and meat to town folk."

"You do well?"

"I barely get by," the old man laughed as he led them inside. "Takes time to build up a herd. Plus I'm gonna need to ship product over to Antoli if I *really* want to make a profit."

"They don't have any sheep on Antoli?" Vladimir asked, following them in.

"I'm going to stay out here and keep watch," Jessica stated.

Nathan nodded in agreement, holding the door open for Kayci and Breyanna.

"Something about the grass on Antoli. Wrecks their digestive system. Same for dollag," Gillis explained. "That's one of the reasons this rock was settled. To provide products from ruminants that can't thrive on Antoli."

"Makes sense," Nathan agreed. "So where's your comm-unit?"

"Over there," the old man replied, pointing to a desk in the corner. "Don't ask me how to use it though. I just answer when it beeps. Means my boy is calling."

"I'm pretty sure we can figure it out," Nathan assured him. "Vlad?"

"Who are we going to call?" Vlad asked under his breath.

"Uh, the ship?"

"We can't," Vladimir stated. "Not without an encryption key. It's a secure network, remember?"

"Well can't you hack it?"

"That would take forever! Besides, the best I could do is blast them with text messages and hope they notice."

"How long?"

"You're talking about hacking a split-level, side-shifting, randomized ten-K encryption algorithm. Do you know how many key combinations there are?"

"Eight hundred and fifty-seven trillion to the eighth power," Breyanna stated as if it were common knowledge.

Nathan and Vladimir both stared in awe at Breyanna, as did Gillis.

"Who's the math whiz?" the old man asked.

"We don't really know," Nathan mumbled. He looked at Vladimir. "Is she right?"

"I have no idea," Vladimir admitted.

"I can hack it for you," Breyanna told them.

"How long?" Nathan asked, still in shock.

"Less than an hour I'd guess."

"That's impossible," Vladimir insisted.

"Please," Breyanna said, moving between them and going over to the comm-unit on the desk. "I was hacking split-level, side-shifting randomized algorithms while I was still in diapers." She pulled out the keyboard and began typing furiously. "Talk about *old school.* No one's used that kind of encryption in like what, five hundred years?"

"Either of you understand what the hell that woman is talking about?" Gillis wondered.

"Don't look at me," Nathan insisted.

Vladimir said nothing; instead he moved over to peek over Breyanna's shoulder. His eyes widened as he watched the code she was inputting stream across the screen in row after row. "Why are you randomizing the hack?"

"I'm not," Breyanna said, almost laughing. "That's to find the randomization pattern. Computers can't *really* randomize. Everybody knows *that*."

"Of course."

"That should do it," she said, standing up and turning to face them. "You just have to enter the address of the target node and press enter. In less than an hour, you should be able to connect and make your call."

"Wait; you just wrote a program?" Vladimir asked in amazement. "In less than a minute?"

"I can type *really* fast," she boasted. "Even faster than usual in this body...for some reason."

"Is she right?" Nathan asked Vladimir. "Is this going to work?"

"I have no idea," Vladimir admitted.

* * *

"Where the hell are they going in such a hurry?" Josh asked no one. Luckily, his AI never learned to recognize a rhetorical question.

"*There is an escape pod on the surface, approximately fifty kilometers, bearing zero zero five,*" his AI reported.

"Oh really? Is it squawking?"

"*Negative. But I am detecting four life signs nearby.*"

"Bingo," Josh spouted. "Sweetie, relay the location to the Aurora. Niko, I think we found them, but we need to get these assault shuttles out of the way."

"*Lead the way*," Nikolas replied.

Josh quickly dialed up his jump range, knowing that whatever he selected would automatically be sent to Nikolas's Dragon so that he would follow. He adjusted his heading slightly downward, just in case, and pressed the jump button on his flight control stick once, jamming his throttles to full power at the same time. A split second later, the two shuttles were directly ahead.

Josh rolled slightly left. "I got left," he called over comms.

"*I got right*," Nikolas replied.

Josh opened fire, sending streams of red-orange plasma streaking toward the target from both of his forward turrets and his main plasma torpedo cannons. On an unshielded ship, it was enough fire power to blast a hole big enough for him to fly through. But all it did was make these shuttles' shields flash brightly with the impacts as they absorbed the energy.

His target immediately opened fire with its own defensive turrets, which were much more formidable than he had expected. Josh's shields also flashed with the incoming impacts, rocking his fighter violently in the process.

Nikolas's eyes widened as he was pelted with energy cannon fire. "Damn!" he exclaimed. "What kind of shuttles are these?"

"*Zhulati*," his AI replied. "*And our weapons are having minimal effect on their shields. Meanwhile, our shield strength is quickly decreasing.*"

"*Launching two!*" Josh announced over comms.

Nikolas glanced down at his tactical display as a pair of small triangular icons left the icon representing Josh's fighter, heading rapidly toward the shuttle he was targeting. He quickly followed suit, selecting ship busters and launching two of his own. "Launching two!" Nikolas announced. "Those are Zhulati shuttles, Josh!"

"*Just means they're more fun to kill!*" Josh chuckled.

"Right."

"*New contacts,*" his AI reported. "*Zhulati fighters, directly behind us...*"

The shuttle Nikolas had just launched missiles at jumped away before their impact. His fighter shook as he took energy weapons fire astern from the newly arrived fighters.

"Shit!" Nikolas exclaimed as he took evasive action, rolling left and pulling up slightly before jumping ahead ten kilometers. "They've got fighter cover!" he warned Josh over comms as he started to come about.

Josh yanked his flight control stick left and right and forward and back in wild fashion, trying to avoid the hail of energy weapons fire the Zhulati fighters trailing him had unleashed. His ship rocked violently with each impact, causing him to bounce in his seat.

"No shit!" Josh replied to Nikolas. He glanced at his tactical display, noting that his wingman was ten kilometers ahead and coming about quickly. "How about you shake these fuckers from my tail, kid?"

"*On my way,*" Nikolas replied. "*Dive on my mark.*"

"Ready!"

"*Three......two......one......Mark!*"

Josh pushed his nose down just as a flash of blue-white light appeared less than five hundred meters in front of him. Nikolas's Dragon passed over him, its guns ablaze. Josh came about to the right as quickly as possible, bringing his nose back up in the process and coming to bear on the Zhulati fighter that broke right to avoid colliding with Josh's wingman. As his energy weapons lashed out at the jinking Zhulati fighter, Josh called to his AI. "Unleash four on that fucker!"

His AI didn't bother to confirm, launching four ship busters in rapid succession. "*Missiles away.*"

Josh didn't wait around to see if his missiles found their target, instead jumping forward a few kilometers just in case additional Zhulati fighters jumped in to reinforce the first two.

"*Target has jumped away,*" his AI reported. "*But it did take one missile strike to its starboard stern quarter. While it was probably not enough to destroy it, I would expect that shield section to be considerably weakened.*"

"He'll stay away until that shield section recharges," Josh opined. "Those Zhulati pilots aren't dumb."

"*By that logic, you are dumb,*" his AI said. "*You would immediately return to the fight.*"

Josh smiled. "Only because I know you'll protect me, sweetie."

* * *

"So if you don't mind me asking, why *did* you settle here?" Nathan asked the old man.

"I don't much like people, and I definitely don't like technology, so I just picked the furthest away, most tech-averse settlement I could find," Gillis explained.

"There are plenty of hospitable worlds out there. Why didn't you just settle one alone?"

"I'm anti-social, I'm not *crazy,*" the old man laughed. "Besides, my son insisted I be close to some sort of civilization, in case I got sick or something."

"Makes sense," Nathan opined.

"Not really, considering I've never been sick a day in my life, *and* settlement missions require everyone to be pumped full of health nanites. But since my kid is one of the few people I actually *like*, well, here I am."

"You ever get into town?" Nathan wondered.

"When I need supplies, which ain't often. I grow most of what I need. Mostly just need salt and such. You know, stuff I can't grow, gather, or make myself."

"What about when you need to sell your products?" Nathan asked.

"Herd's too small to do much selling at this point. Mostly I just trade with a few of my neighbors."

"But you plan to eventually, right?"

"That's the plan," Gillis replied. "But you never know. I may just keep it this way forever. Things are pretty good as is. Plenty of food and water. Don't really need much else."

"What do you do for entertainment?"

"Watch old vid-flicks on the holo. My son set me up with a subscription service over that comms doohickey. It's got about a million movies."

"I thought you didn't like technology?"

"I don't," the old man confirmed. "Doesn't mean I'm a luddite."

"It's my understanding that one can live with very little tech even on an Alliance world," Nathan stated.

"Yeah, but their worlds are so sterile. Everything has been landscaped and is in perfect condition. Hell even the weather is controlled on most Alliance worlds. Have you ever been to one of those so-called wildlife preserves? Even those have been crafted from the ground up. I mean, automated irrigation systems in a *wildlife preserve*? That ain't natural. And the livestock on Alliance worlds are pumped full of nanites. Did you know that when you're eating a dollag steak on an Alliance world, you're probably ingesting about a million dead nanites as well? This place, on the other hand, is about as real as it gets. Nothing is cut, trimmed, or manicured, outside of the town, that is. Even *in* town, most things are as they always were. The people here like it that way, and so do I. The weather does what it wants. The critters do what they want. And the *people* do what they want and suffer the consequences if they do wrong by others. Out here, it's the *natural* order. Not *Alliance* order. Out here, your life is what you make of it. What you have is determined by how much work you put in. Not by some group of stuffed suits who decide who gets what."

Nathan studied the old man, wondering if he was finished. "You feel better getting that all out?"

"A little bit."

"Good," Nathan chuckled. "For the record, I couldn't agree with you more."

"I know," the old man said. "Otherwise I wouldn't have let you in."

"What do you mean?" Nathan asked. "All you know is my name."

"I knew that when I saw you, Captain."

"Excuse me?"

"I was a history professor before I moved out here.

You're Nathan Scott, that's Vladimir Kamenetskiy, and that woman who wanted to interrogate me is Jessica Nash."

"Doesn't history state that those people died in battle over five hundred years ago?"

"History often states things that aren't true. Besides, I read the transcripts of Doctor Sorenson's testimony in front of the Alliance Science Academy board of regents. And believe me, those were not easy to find. As far as I'm concerned, you all were just *missing*. And I was right, because here you are." The old man chuckled to himself.

"What's so funny?" Nathan wondered.

"I can't wait until I get to rub this in Morgan Anson's face."

"I'd appreciate it if you didn't," Nathan said. "At least not for a while. We're still trying to get firmly established in this century."

"You're the ones who stole those ships, aren't you?"

"You *know* about that?"

"Word is already out about your return from the dead. Probably because you announced it so publicly back on Crowden after stomping out the Brodek clan."

"How do you know all of this?" Nathan wondered.

"I may use that comms thing to surf the free net on occasion."

"Not as *technology adverse* as you claim, huh?"

"Just because you can make a light come on automatically when you enter a room doesn't mean you should. It's about achieving a balance."

Nathan sighed. "Just how widespread *is* knowledge of our existence?"

"Well to the average 'man on the street' in Alliance

territory, probably not much. The Alliance has made sure their citizens believe it's all a big hoax dreamed up by junk journalists. They've even put out proof that the vid of your declaration on Crowden was faked."

"I guess I can stop using my Tuplo cover then," Nathan said.

Vladimir came running out onto the front porch. "It worked! We're hailing the Aurora now!"

* * *

Space was full of signals, most of them occurring naturally. A comms officer's job was to monitor the noise and identify actual comm-signals, especially ones meant for them. Most of the time, comms traffic came over preset channels, so it was easy. But there were thousands of ships that didn't use standard comm-channels, instead using old-style frequencies.

The Aurora used ten set comm-channels out of the standard set of one hundred used by ships in space. Any ship that *should* be communicating with them knew this and hailed on one of those ten channels. Those who didn't typically hailed on every known channel, and when nobody responded, they repeated the hailing process through all frequencies and bands.

It was a lot to monitor. The original Aurora had a comm-station with four operators. The current version used its AI to monitor all those possible channels, frequencies, and bands, alerting the comms officer when it found an incoming call.

The incoming call light began to flash, alerting Ensign Dass. "*Aurora, Dragon One!*" Josh called over comms. "*We found them! They're on the fifth planet in the Nishida system! Two Zhulati assault shuttles were on their way down to snatch them, but we ran them off! At least we thought we had. We're engaged with four Zhulati fighters at the moment. Recommend you send all Dragons here ASAP!"*

"Dragon One, Aurora," Ensign Dass replied. "Copy all. Stand by one."

"Order all Dragons and shuttles to the Nishida system," Cameron instructed.

"Aye, sir."

"Aurora, jump us to the Nishida system."

"Understood," the Aurora's AI acknowledged.

"Set general quarters," Cameron added.

Ensign Dass activated the all-call and pressed the general quarters button. The trim lighting on the bridge turned red, and the automated announcement echoed in the corridors throughout the ship. "General quarters, general quarters. All hands, man your battle stations. This is not a drill."

The incoming call light flashed again. Ensign Dass leaned in slightly, intently studying her display. "Uh, Captain?" she called. "We're being hailed over our AICC node, but it's not coming from one of *our* secure nodes."

"Who is it coming from?" Cameron wondered.

"Someone named Gillis Paparo?"

"How did they hack into our secure network?" Cameron asked.

"I have no idea, sir."

Cameron thought for a moment. "You can't be *located* using an AICC node, right?"

"That is my understanding," Ensign Dass confirmed.

Cameron sighed. "Very well. Put them through."

"Connected."

"Hello?" Cameron said.

After a moment, Nathan's voice was heard. *"Cam! Holy shit! It worked!"*

"Nathan?"

"Yes! It's me!"

"Confirmation code?" Cameron asked.

"Tango one seven five, alpha romeo two eight seven."

A wave of relief washed over Cameron. "Oh my God, Nathan. Are you alright? Are the others with you?"

"We're fine!" Nathan replied. *"We're all fine. We're on the fifth planet in the Nishida system! I'll get you the exact coordinates in a moment! Come get us!"*

"Everyone's already on their way," Cameron replied. "Josh and Nikolas have already engaged Zhulati fighters in that system, but over the *fourth* planet."

"Shit, I was hoping my little ruse would buy us some more time." Nathan said. *"Keep them fighting over that planet! In fact, send everyone except for one shuttle there. We need the diversion while you slip one shuttle in to pick us up!"*

"Understood," Cameron replied. "We're on our way!"

"All shuttles and Dragons are on their way to the Nishida system," Ensign Dass reported.

"Get me Captain Walsh on the Mirai," Cameron instructed.

"On course for the Nishida system," the Aurora's AI announced. *"Shields are up, weapons are hot. We're ready to jump."*

"Take us in," Cameron instructed her AI.

"Jumping."

"Captain Walsh is on the line, sir."

"Aiden, Cam," Cameron called out as the jump flash washed over the bridge.

"*We are now in the Nishida system,*" Aurora reported.

"I need you to go covert and head for the fifth planet in the Nishida system. The captain and the others are there, but we're engaged with the Zhulati over the *fourth* planet. We'll act as a diversion to keep them focused on *that* world."

"*I'll jump in on the far side, using the fifth planet as a cover,*" Aiden replied over comms.

"Good idea. Stay covert as long as possible. Pickup coordinates are incoming," Cameron assured him.

"Got them!" Ensign Dass reported. "Sending them to the Mirai."

"Contacts!" Laza reported. "Multiple Zhulati fighters and assault shuttles, and one heavy cruiser, all over the fourth planet. Our Dragons and shuttles are jumping in all over the place. They're engaging!"

"Sima, have one of the shuttles go down as if they're trying to get to the escape pod landing site," Cameron instructed.

"I'm on it," Ensign Dass replied.

"This diversion isn't going to work for long," Cameron stated. "At this point, it's all about speed."

* * *

"Captain!" the Maturo's sensor officer shouted from his station. "It's the Aurora! Bearing two five two. Range, two hundred million kilometers and closing fast."

"You were right," Captain Hyam congratulated General Gogol.

"Jump away," the general ordered.

"What?" Captain Hyam couldn't believe what he was hearing.

"I want to surprise them from behind and take out their main propulsion and jump systems before they can get away."

"Of course, General," Captain Hyam acknowledged.

"And notify the Genstar ship," the general added. "We'll need them to help block her way."

CHAPTER SEVEN

"Whoa!" Josh exclaimed as five small ships suddenly jumped in directly in front of him. "What the fuck are those?" he asked, pushing the nose of his fighter down slightly and rolling to the right to avoid colliding with one of the unknown ships.

"Too small to be manned," Nickolas said over comms. *"Too maneuverable as well."*

"Combat drones," Josh's AI reported as the ship rocked from incoming weapons fire. *"They're on our six. Firing aft turrets."*

Josh continued jinking his Dragon fighter about, trying to be as difficult a target as possible. "I hate drones."

"More just jumped in behind me," Nikolas reported. *"Maybe we should jump clear and get a better angle?"*

"We're a diversion, remember? Follow me," Josh said as he pushed his nose down and jammed his throttles to their forward stops.

———————

"What are you doing, Josh?" Nikolas called out anxiously, maneuvering to follow him.

"We have to buzz the evac site before the shuttles get here to make sure it's safe."

"You're taking it kind of far, aren't you?"

"They can outmaneuver us, but they can't outrun us," Josh replied.

Nikolas leveled off behind Josh, skimming the treetops. "I hate drones," he muttered to himself.

———————

Lorelei's shuttle came out of the jump already

deep in the atmosphere of Antoli. She had never jumped from space directly into the atmosphere of a world before, and even though the Leonid's inertial dampening fields buffered most of the deceleration forces, she could still feel the sudden change in her ship's forward speed.

Not only had she never jumped into an atmosphere before, but she most definitely had never jumped in so close to the surface. Although the Leonid's AI would never let the ship crash, a planet suddenly appearing so close up in the windows, when only a moment ago they were in space, was jarring.

"*Damn!*" Desmond exclaimed over comms, having jumped in just behind her. "*That'll get your heart pumping!*"

"What the hell are you doing, Des? They said *one* shuttle!"

"*No way I was letting you have all the fun!*"

The tactical display contact light began flashing.

"We've got contacts all over the place!" Lorelei realized, glancing at her display.

"*Just let your AI manage your defenses and act like we're coming in for an evac.*"

"This is *not* what I signed up for," Lorelei mumbled to herself.

"*Way more fun than flying survey missions over Libertara.*"

Multiple icons suddenly appeared on Lorelei's tactical display, all of them moving toward her. Her shuttle shook violently.

"*We are under attack,*" her AI reported. "*Engaging all defense turrets.*"

"This is *not* my idea of fun!" Lorelei exclaimed.

"*Inbound shuttles,*" Josh called over comms.

"We'll be there in thirty seconds. Buzz the LZ once and then jump ahead ten clicks before coming about."

"Coming about?" Lorelei exclaimed. "Why the hell would we come about? And why only ten kilometers?"

"We're a diversion!" Josh yelled. *"Now do as I say, or you'll get your ass blown off!"*

Lorelei took a deep breath as her shuttle was shaken by incoming energy weapons fire. "Copy that," she replied.

"You've got this, Lorelei," Desmond said encouragingly over comms.

Lorelei pulled herself together, then guided her shuttle even lower, accelerating at the same time. "Try to keep up, Des," she replied confidently.

———

"Dragon One reports six Dragons and two shuttles are now engaged over the LZ on Antoli," Ensign Dass reported from the Aurora's comm-station.

"Two?" Cameron replied. "I only ordered one shuttle for the diversion."

"Josh reports two," Sima explained. "The Leonid *and* Haley."

"Desmond," Cameron realized.

"Zhulati cruiser has jumped away," Laza reported.

"What?" Cameron suddenly became suspicious.

"Based on their last course, they may be headed for the Traverna," Laza suggested.

"No way," Cameron disagreed. "Not with forces in play."

"If they are after the woman in the pod, it would make sense."

"Maybe. But keep an eye on our six just in case,"

Cameron instructed. "Aurora, head us toward Antoli. We have to sell this."

"*Understood*," the Aurora's AI acknowledged.

"Dragon One reports all Dragons are now in play over Antoli. They're meeting heavy resistance. Drones, manned fighters, and assault shuttles."

"New contact!" Laza reported. "Directly ahead! One point five kilometers! Same course and speed!"

"The Zhulati cruiser?" Cameron asked.

"Negative. Same ship that attacked the Traverna. She's blocking our jump path."

"Ready stern guns. Weapons free."

"*Stern guns ready. Acknowledged weapons free,*" Aurora answered.

"Forward target is firing," Laza warned. "Guns only," she added as the Aurora's forward shields lit up.

"*Returning fire,*" the Aurora's AI reported as red-orange bolts of plasma streaked toward the forward target from various angles.

"Very little effect on their stern shields," Laza warned.

"Aurora, ready forward torpedoes," Cameron instructed.

"Contact astern!" Laza interrupted. "It's the Zhulati cruiser again!"

"*Firing stern guns,*" Aurora reported. "*Forward tubes ready.*"

"Multiple contacts," Laza added. "Ten, twenty... I'm losing count!"

"What are they?" Cameron demanded as the Aurora shook from incoming energy weapons fire from both nose and stern.

"Mines!" Laza realized. "They're mines, Captain! Eighty and still counting!"

"Aurora! Evasive!"

"*Translating upward,*" Aurora replied.

"They're moving with us!" Laza realized.

"Damn it!"

"*Stern shields are down fifty percent,*" Aurora reported. "*Forward shields at sixty-five percent.*"

"The Zhulati ships' weapons are more powerful, as are their shields," Laza reported.

"*Aft tubes are ready as well,*" Aurora stated.

"Launch all tubes and get us out of here!" Cameron ordered.

"*Launching all fore and aft torpedoes,*" Aurora acknowledged.

"Incoming torpedoes," the Maturo's sensor officer reported.

"Point-defenses have activated," the tactical officer added.

General Gogol watched quietly. Captain Hyam was an accomplished officer, having served for nearly three decades. He was known to be a difficult man to work for, constantly drilling his crew and demanding near perfection. It had paid off, as his crew was handling the attack with very little direction from the captain.

"Inbounds destroyed," the tactical officer reported as calmly as if it *had* been a drill.

"Continue targeting aft shields," Captain Hyam instructed, equally as calm. "As soon as they fail, neutralize her main drive. I want her dead in the water but *intact.*"

"Aye, sir," the tactical officer acknowledged.

"Incoming message from Genstar," the comms

officer announced. He spun around to look at the
general and his captain. "They've located the package
contents. She's on the *fifth* planet, not the fourth."

"She's awake?"

"They've transmitted surface coordinates," the
comms officer added.

"Launch two more assault teams to the fifth
planet, and back them up with as many fighters as
we have left," General Gogol ordered.

"Should we pull forces from Antoli?" Captain
Hyam inquired.

"Not yet," the general replied with a wry smile.
"With any luck, it will be a few minutes before they
realize they're looking on the wrong world."

"We have no more assault teams," Captain Hyam
pointed out. "We'll have to redirect the ones about to
board the Traverna."

"That's fine," General Gogol replied. "That ship's
not going anywhere."

"As you wish."

"Just get me the Aurora," the general added.

———————

"Three jumps, each one coming out closer to the
surface than the last, will get us around this rock,
close enough to the evac point that we can slip in
before they notice us," Aiden explained.

"Sounds dangerous," Erica commented as she
watched Aiden enter the parameters into the Mirai's
jump control computers.

"Better than jumping straight in. At least this
way, we get a chance to eyeball the LZ on the way
in."

A warning light flashed and beeped over the tactical display.

"Multiple contacts," Erica reported. "Drones and fighters. Just jumped into orbit, evenly spaced."

"They're taking positions to cover the entire planet from orbit," Aiden realized.

"A few of them are turning toward us," Erica warned. "They just... Shit! They're right on us! One click to port, two clicks astern. They're locking weapons on us!"

"Time to go!" Aiden decided, pressing the jump button.

A split second later, they were in the atmosphere, a few thousand meters above the surface, their AI automatically adjusting their course and speed for the next jump in the series that Aiden had outlined.

"We're still going?" Erica realized in disbelief.

"They would for us," Aiden replied calmly.

Erica understood. "That's the job," she said, more to herself than to Aiden.

"That's the job," Aiden repeated.

***

"They got through," Breyanna told Jessica as she approached her outside in front of the old man's prefab home.

"So quickly?" Jessica wondered. "I thought it was supposed to take hours?"

"I guess their security measures weren't as good as they thought."

"I would've loved to have seen Vlad's face when he realized that," Jessica chuckled as she scanned the area for unwanted guests.

"I felt a little guilty, to be honest," Breyanna

admitted. "He just stood there with his mouth open, staring at the screen in disbelief."

"He needs to be taken down a notch every once in a while," Jessica told her. "Keeps his enormous ego in check."

"Well he is five hundred years behind the times."

"We may have a position for you once we get back to the ship," Jessica told her.

"I thought you didn't trust me."

"Don't take it personally," Jessica told her. "I don't trust anyone. It's part of the job."

Breyanna suddenly began staring at the sky, squinting.

"What is it?" Jessica asked, seeing nothing but clear skies in all directions.

"Two shuttles headed this way," Breyanna told her. "You don't see them?"

Jessica also squinted but still saw nothing. She pulled out her hand scanner and pointed it in the direction she was looking. "Nothing. Are you sure?"

"I can see them; they're descending. How can you not see them?"

"You must have *really* good eyesight."

"Not that I remember," Breyanna insisted.

"Come on," Jessica told her. "Let's get inside."

"Then you believe me?"

"No, but if you're *not* hallucinating, we need to be inside."

"New contacts!" Laza reported from the Aurora's sensor station as the ship shook from the incoming energy weapons fire. "It's those drones! The ones similar to Dusahn recon drones!"

"*Aft shields are down to twenty percent,*" the Aurora's AI warned. "*Forward shields are at thirty percent. Estimate aft shield failure in one minute.*"

"The new contacts are gone!" Laza announced.

"*Captain, I am unable to find a clear jump path,*" the AI reported. "*The mines are able to maneuver more quickly, and their number has grown to several hundred.*"

"Can we jump *through* them?" Cameron asked.

"If doing so triggers their warheads, we don't know what the effect would be, especially if one detonation triggers the others."

"*Aft shields at eighteen percent,*" Aurora updated.

"Load nukes into the aft tubes, maximum yield, and launch when ready," Cameron ordered.

"*Even if they reach the target and disable their forward shields, we will not be able to inflict enough damage before our aft shields fail, at which point they will target our main propulsion.*"

"You believe they plan to board us?" Cameron realized.

"*Analysis indicates that it would be advantageous for the Alliance to capture, charge, and convict those whom history blames for the great war.*"

"Aurora, on my mark, channel all available power to the forward shields and jump us ahead ten light minutes."

"Captain, Laza was right," Abby said from her station. "It's too risky."

"We die now, or we die at a public execution later," Cameron replied. "At least if we jump, we have a chance."

"A very *small* chance," Abby pointed out.

Jessica came charging into the old man's home, with Breyanna right behind her.

Nathan spun around. "What's wrong?"

Two claps of thunder sounded, as if lightning had struck just outside. For a second, the room filled with blue-white light.

"Please tell me those are our shuttles," Doctor Barra pleaded.

Jessica turned around and looked out the window. Outside, two hovering shuttles drifted slowly apart as men clad in combat armor and carrying heavy assault rifles dropped the few meters to the ground.

Nathan ran to the window, looking out as well. "Vlad, tell Cam our situation just became desperate. And tell our ride they're headed for a hot LZ."

Two more thunderous claps sounded from behind the house.

"We're being surrounded," Jessica realized.

The old man walked over to the closet, pulling out a large-bore plasma hunting rifle, similar to the boomers carried by the Ta'Akar five centuries ago.

"What the hell is that for?" Jessica wondered.

"Hunting," Gillis replied.

"What the hell do you hunt? Elephants?"

"There are some big-ass predators on this little world," the old man grumbled, heading for the front door.

"Where are you..." Jessica was unable to finish her sentence.

Gillis walked right out onto the front porch and opened fire, sending four enormous blasts of energy toward the troops on the left. As he fired, the troops fired back, peppering the front of the house.

Jessica charged out, activating the personal shield she always wore as she stepped in front of the old man, protecting him from the incoming blasts of energy. "Are you fucking stupid!" she hollered, shoving the old man back through the door.

Meanwhile, Nathan busted out one of the windows and opened fire.

"Vlad, take Breyanna with you and cover the back!" Jessica instructed. "We gotta hold them off until help arrives!" she added, turning and breaking a second window with her elbow.

"Those open, you know!" the old man told her.

"Shut up and start shooting, old man!" Jessica replied.

The Mirai came out of its low-level jump series less than a kilometer from the evac coordinates. As soon as they arrived, their threat warning flashed and their shields were lit up by energy weapons fire.

"Jesus!" Erica exclaimed as the shuttle bounced and shook. "Four fighters to port, two more directly ahead!"

"*Mirai, Aurora,*" Sima called over comms. "*Hot LZ! Hot LZ! Package is under fire!*"

"A little late," Aiden said.

"I've got three buildings dead ahead," Erica announced. "One of them has six life signs and is surrounded by troops. They are under fire."

Several jump flashes appeared in front of them, accompanied by six combat drones, all of them opening fire.

"Son of a bitch!" Aiden exclaimed, pulling back on his flight control stick to bring up his nose, and pushing his throttle forward to climb. "I'm jumping clear! We're going to need fighter cover to get in there!"

"Aurora, Mirai!" Erica called over comms. "LZ is too hot! We're not getting in without fighter cover!"

"*Aft shields are down to five percent,*" Aurora warned. "*Failure in thirty seconds.*"

"It's now or never," Cameron sighed. "Aurora..."

"New contact!" Laza reported.

The violent shaking of incoming fire suddenly ceased. Cameron looked around, unsure of what was going on. "What happened? Why did they stop firing?"

"It's a Dusahn warship!" Laza added, excitedly. "It's engaging both targets! They're both breaking off to maneuver!"

Cameron glanced at the tactical display on the overhead view screen. "Aurora! Hard to port and translate down and left at the same time! And target the mines along the edge! I want a clear jump line ASAP!"

"*Executing,*" Aurora acknowledged.

"Who the hell is operating that ship?" Cameron wondered.

"*Aurora to all Dragons and shuttles,*" Sima called over comms. "*All units are to rally on fifth world at transmitted coordinates. Captain Walsh on the Mirai has operational command for that area. Be advised, there may be multiple hostiles from different forces to defend against.*"

"Shit," Josh cursed as he came out of his turn

and opened fire on one of the fleeing Zhulati combat drones. "I guess the diversion's over huh?" He rolled off the contact just as it jumped away, then pulled his nose up toward the sky. "We're outta here, Remo."

"*What's our new target?*" Nikolas asked.

"If it shoots at us, shoot back," Josh replied.

Cameron breathed a sigh of relief as the Aurora came out of her escape jump. "Hard about," she instructed the ship's AI. "I want to jump back in five hundred kilometers from the battle."

"*Coming about, sharply,*" the AI replied.

"Sima, update Nathan about that Dusahn ship," Cameron ordered.

"I've lost contact with the captain," Sima replied. "His connection is no longer active."

"Can you call him back?"

"I'll try."

Cameron tapped a button on the comm-console on the arm of the command chair. "Dragon Leader, Aurora Actual."

"*Go for Dragon Leader,*" Josh replied promptly.

"Josh, we've lost contact with Nathan, and a Dusahn warship just joined the party."

"*Did you say a Dusahn warship?*" Josh asked.

"Affirmative."

"*So we're fighting three different hostiles now?*"

"Unknown. The Dusahn saved our ass, but I can't be sure if that was their intent. So watch out."

"*Great. Thanks.*"

"*Turn complete,*" Aurora announced. "*Ready for return jump.*"

"Execute," Cameron instructed.

"*Jumping.*"

"Let's update our tactical picture quickly," Cameron told Laza. "I want to be able to jump again on a moment's notice."

The jump flash faded, and the various view screens arranged along the overhead forward of the command chair refreshed, their contents repainting.

"I'm picking up a lot of debris," Laza reported. "The Dusahn ship is still engaged with the Zhulati cruiser, but the Zhulati's shields are rapidly draining. The Dusahn ship is launching dozens of smaller vessels. Combat drones and small shuttles. They're headed for the fifth world."

"Sima, warn all units they have multiple inbounds, but do *not* engage anything that doesn't shoot at *them* first," Cameron instructed.

"Josh is *not* going to like that," Sima commented.

———————

Josh jumped in ten meters above the surface of the fifth planet in the Nishida system. What seemed like a leisurely speed in space felt like a bat out of hell this close to the ground, but it was something Josh had gotten used to long ago. And with his AI backstopping him, he could be even more reckless than before and still survive. AIs made bad pilots good, and good pilots great. In Josh's case, it made him more insane than anyone could have imagined.

Josh pushed his fighter even lower, staying just high enough that he wouldn't kick up any dust. He had a clear line down the valley where the pickup coordinates were located, following the river that had carved it.

"*I'm picking up twelve bad guys surrounding a*

building with six people inside," Talisha reported over comms. *"There's a hell of a firefight going on down there."*

"Dragons Seven and Eight are approaching the LZ from the south," Allet announced.

"One and Two are coming in low from the north," Josh announced as he skimmed the river, his main thrust kicking up a spray of water behind him.

"Four shuttles and about twenty drones are approaching from the east," Allet added.

Josh glanced at his tactical display, his eyes immediately reverting back to his front view. All ten Dragons were in the immediate area, and three of their shuttles had just jumped into orbit and were maneuvering to jump down to the engagement area.

"Dragon Leader, Mirai Actual," Aiden called over comms. *"I can't get in there. The LZ is too damned hot. If you guys can clear out half of those clowns on the ground, I might be able to drop in and use our shields to pick them up."*

"Has anyone even verified our people are *there?"* Josh asked.

"Negative," Aiden replied. *"They're no longer on comms either."*

"I guess that's my job," Josh said. "Niko, you keep those drones off my ass. I'm going to try to spot our people. Everyone else, pick a target and let 'em have it."

"I thought we were only to shoot if shot at?" Tricia reminded him.

"Fuck that!" Josh exclaimed. "If they're not ours, shoot 'em! That's an order!"

"Five seconds to LZ," Josh's AI warned.

Josh flipped his fighter over so that he was flying backwards and jammed his throttles to full power.

"*What the hell, Josh!*" Nikolas exclaimed. "*We're in atmo! You can't fly that way!*"

"Oh yeah? Watch me!" Josh replied as he advanced his grav-lift controls to keep him from falling into the river a few meters below.

"*You're insane!*" Nikolas yelled over comms.

Besides flying backwards, he was also inverted, so a glance upward had him looking at the river rushing beneath him. "You might be right about that one," Josh declared as he yanked his throttles back to idle and flipped over so he was flying nose-first again. "Damn!" he exclaimed as he eased his throttles forward just enough to maintain his new, much slower, airspeed. He peered out his forward windows, spotting the firefight on the ground. Three pairs of heavily armed men were exchanging fire with whomever was inside what looked like one of those prefab homes that were so common on newly settled worlds. Josh pulled his throttles back to idle then twisted his joystick to the right, keeping his nose pointed at the enemy soldiers. He squeezed the trigger, holding it in and sending a stream of plasma torpedoes at the nearest pair. "You've got the others, sweetie!"

Josh's AI understood and immediately locked their ventral guns onto the other two pairs of soldiers, also opening fire.

Outside, the ground exploded wherever his Dragon's incoming energy weapons struck. The two men Josh had fired upon disappeared in a fiery burst of red-orange plasma and dirt. A glance toward the others showed one of them turning around to fire at Josh's Dragon, while the other three dove for cover to avoid being incinerated.

"That fucking scattered them!" Talisha exclaimed over comms.

Josh ceased fire as the house slid in from his left, not wanting to blow it apart and kill the very people they were trying to rescue. "Zoom forward window, factor of ten," he instructed his AI. The view suddenly enlarged, with the front face of the home filling the window. A familiar face glanced out the window, shaking a fist victoriously at him. "It's them!" Josh exclaimed. "I've got eyes on Jess!" he added as his fighter continued sideways, passing the house. He twisted his joystick to the right again, bringing his nose back around so that he was flying backwards again. This time, he spotted Vladimir firing through a broken window. "Eyes on Vlad as well!" Josh added, twisting his joystick some more to bring his nose back around to forward. "You might be able to make it in now!" he told Aiden as he jammed his throttles forward again and pulled his nose up to gain altitude.

"Mirai is going in," Aiden announced over comms.

"Those drones are already moving back into position," Erica warned.

"Our shields can handle the drones," Aiden told her as their shuttle jumped from high and far to low and close to the LZ. He dropped the ship lower, barely clearing the treetops.

More red icons began appearing on the tactical display while alert lights flashed and alarms sounded.

"Shuttles are back!" Erica announced, a slight panic in her voice.

The ship rocked as energy weapons fire struck their dorsal shields.

"Somebody wanna get those shuttles off our back!" Aiden demanded.

"We're trying," Tricia replied over comms. *"Their shields are like nothing I've ever seen on a shuttle!"*

"DRONES!" Erica shouted, pointing out the forward window.

Aiden glanced up, quickly pulling the Mirai's nose up and jamming his main throttles all the way forward. "Fuck!" he cursed, pressing his jump button to escape. "It's still too hot!"

———————

An explosion rocked the entire house as smoke and debris came flying out into the main room where Nathan, Jessica, and the old man were firing from the windows.

"Breach!" Jessica yelled, turning and firing into the cloud of smoke.

Both Nathan and Gillis also turned to engage whoever was coming through the breach in the east room.

"Stay on the front!" Jessica insisted as she advanced toward the breached room, shooting into the smoke. "They're trying to distract us!"

Nathan and the old man returned to the windows, opening fire as two more shuttles came to a low hover about twenty meters away, with more soldiers dropping out of them.

"We've got more landing in back!" Vladimir bellowed from the back room.

Jessica charged into the kitchen, barely able to see anything through the smoke. The only thing she could see was light coming through the hole in the wall. A shadow appeared and she opened fire, hearing a body hit the ground. Someone fired through the hole, barely missing Jessica, who had dropped to the floor. She fired again from down low, dropping the second man before getting up and scrambling to the side.

Another shadowy figure appeared, stepping inside and firing toward where Jessica had been a moment ago. She didn't move, remaining silent and motionless, using the cover of the smoke that hadn't yet dissipated.

Two more men followed, but only the lead man was firing. Jessica waited, making sure no more were entering, then opened fire, dropping all three. She then moved quickly to the hole, peeked around, and dropped two more soldiers waiting outside. "You Zhulati suck!" she yelled, drawing fire from those still under cover in the distance. A quick peek outside as the fire poured in was all she needed to identify their positions. The incoming fire stopped, and she remained motionless, listening to the sounds of the ongoing firefight from the main room where Nathan and the old man were blasting away.

A few more seconds and she stepped out, firing four shots, two to the left and two to the right, dropping all four soldiers with single shots. "Jesus. What kind of dumbass spec-ops troops don't use personal shields?" She stood there a moment, waiting to see if anyone else popped their head up. But just as she felt like they might be getting the upper hand, another shuttle jumped in only a few meters above the ground, and six heavily armored men jumped to the ground. "We've got a problem!" she yelled as she opened fire on the new arrivals, then dove to the side as the Zhulati troops returned her fire ten-fold.

"Six Zhulati shuttles are landing troops," Laza reported from the Aurora's sensor station. "Our Dragons are not having much effect on their shields, but the Zhulati shuttles' weapons quickly drain the shields on *our* shuttles."

"Aurora, can we go down to help?" Cameron asked the ship's AI.

"*Negative,*" Aurora replied. "*Grav-lift systems are offline. We've lost too many grav-lift emitters on the port side, and our thrusters aren't powerful enough to compensate. We'd flip over.*"

Cameron pressed the comms button again. "Josh, you've got to keep those shuttles off the Mirai so they can pick up our people."

"*We're trying!*" Josh assured her.

Heavily armed Zhulati entered through the hole in the kitchen wall, firing through the opening into the main room.

Jessica dove through the doorway, just as the bolts of energy whizzed past her. "NATHAN!"

Nathan spun around, firing like crazy in the direction of the incoming fire as Zhulati energy bolts barely missed him, slamming into the wall all around. One of the bolts ricocheted off the metal door and grazed the old man's shoulder, knocking him off his feet and causing him to drop his own weapon.

"Gillis!" Nathan yelled, but he couldn't help him.

He had to continue firing in the direction of the kitchen.

"Nathan!" Jessica yelled as she continued firing. "Front! Front!"

Nathan spun back around, moving to the window Gillis had been shooting from in order to get out of the line of fire coming from the kitchen. Six Zhulati soldiers, far more heavily armored than the original combatants, were moving toward him in a line. He opened fire, but these soldiers were protected by energy shields. "They're shielded!"

"Vlad!" Jessica yelled as she fired. "How many you got back there?"

"*Too many!*" Vlad yelled back.

"How's the doc?" Nathan yelled.

"I'm okay!" Doctor Barra squeaked.

Nathan looked around but didn't see the doctor anywhere. He gave up and continued firing at the advancing line of Zhulati, despite the fact that it wasn't slowing them down. "This isn't working!" he yelled back at Jessica.

An energy blast struck Jessica's left shoulder, knocking her back. "Shit!" she yelled, holding her arm. "My arm's numb! They're firing stunners now!"

"They want us alive!" Nathan realized. He turned to glance at Jessica but instead caught a stunner blast in the face, dropping him instantly.

"NATHAN!" Jessica yelled. She spun around and opened fire as she backpedaled toward Nathan. Then she too caught a blast in the face, falling.

Josh jumped into the center of the engagement area, turning hard to port and heading straight toward the nearest shuttle, opening fire with everything he had.

"*Ten seconds to collision,*" his AI warned.

"Override auto-protect!" Josh ordered.

"*That is not recommend...*"

"OVERRIDE!" Josh demanded.

"*Auto-protect, overridden,*" his AI acknowledged.

"Come on, fucker!" Josh yelled, holding course.

The pilot of the shuttle was the first to flinch, rolling and turning to starboard and then jumping ahead. Josh had no idea where the Zhulati shuttle had jumped to. He didn't care. All he cared about was that for the moment, it wasn't here.

"YES!" he exclaimed triumphantly. "Dragon Leader to all Dragons! Play chicken with them!"

———————

"*Just park it in a hover directly over the LZ, at three thousand meters,*" Kit yelled over the intercom.

"If I hover, we'll get our ass shot off," Aiden insisted. "Even at three thousand meters!"

"*Then don't hover! Just keep it under eight KPH!*"

"Pretty much the same thing!"

"*I just need a few seconds, then you can jump away. Look, if we don't get some boots on the ground, they're done for, and you know it!*"

Aiden looked at Erica, sighing. "Fine. How soon can you be ready?"

"*I'll be ready whenever you are!*" Kit insisted.

"This should be fun," Aiden said as he prepared to jump back into the fray.

———————

"Telemetry from our Dragons and shuttles

indicates a decrease in the firefight on the surface," Laza reported from the Aurora's sensor station. "Our people are about to be overrun."

"Aurora, can we jump into low orbit and loiter over the area long enough to put some suppression fire around our people to buy them some time?"

"Our ventral guns would only be usable for a few minutes," the Aurora's AI replied. *"It would also put our people at risk, as the accuracy of our weapons are negatively affected by atmosphere."*

"Captain," Sima called. "The Mirai and three other shuttles are preparing to drop their Ghatazhak operators into the LZ from an altitude of three thousand meters."

"Let me guess whose idea *that* was," Cameron muttered.

"Lieutenant Vasya's," Sima confirmed. "According to Captain Walsh."

"Have all our Dragons join them to provide cover just in case," Cameron instructed. She turned back to Laza. "Where's that Zhulati cruiser?"

"They've jumped to a new location about five hundred thousand kilometers from their last position," Laza reported. "The Dusahn ship is sticking with them. Estimate the Zhulati ship will lose shields in two minutes."

"Excellent," Cameron decided. At least something was working in their favor. "Aurora, jump us into low orbit in a position that will allow us to loiter over the LZ as long as possible."

"Understood."

"Now let's hope that Dusahn ship doesn't come gunning for *us* once they're done with the Zhulati," Cameron added.

———————

"Ten seconds," Aiden warned over Kit's helmet comms.

Kit was completely suited up in his heavy combat armor, complete with his jump-insertion rig. Attached to each thigh were heavy assault rifles, and on his forearms were double-barreled light cannons. Along with the assortment of grenades built into his abdomen and chest sections, he and all the other Ghatazhak were loaded for action.

"You guys ready?" Kit called over comms.

"Ready," the calls came from each of the other three Ghatazhak about to follow him down from their respective shuttles.

"Second squad will be one minute behind you," Chief Anson assured them.

"We'll try to leave you a few guys to play with," Kit joked as the cargo ramp began to deploy, opening the bay up to the atmosphere outside.

"Jumping in three......two......one..."

Blue-white light filled the cargo bay, dissipating a moment later.

"Go!" Aiden instructed over comms.

Kit walked out onto the level cargo ramp, stepping off the end and starting his fall toward the surface as three more jump flashes appeared behind them, with the other members of his squad following suit.

Kit only fell for a few seconds before his suit AI auto-jumped him to a point only a few meters above the surface, and about twenty meters behind the line of Zhulati who were advancing toward the house that Nathan and the others were defending. The Zhulati continued to fire, but only occasionally, just enough to keep whoever was inside from slowing their advance.

"Shit," Kit cursed to himself, realizing the gravity of the situation. The enemy was only seconds from breaching the building, at which point their only hope of rescuing their people would be when the Zhulati attempted to evacuate them. Kit broke into a jog toward the enemy, who was still not aware of his arrival.

The advancing Zhulati suddenly stopped, the sight of three jump flashes revealing single, armored, and armed combatants behind the other lines of Zhulati troops. One of the men turned around, realizing there was someone behind them, but it was too late.

Kit opened fire with both wrist cannons, first dropping the Zhulati soldier who had first turned around, then dropping the rest. Just as he had hoped, the enemy had channeled all of their suit power into their forward shields, expecting all the incoming fire to come from the front.

Six thunderous tearing sounds could be heard in the background as the other Ghatazhak also fired. Kit spun around, spotting four Zhulati shuttles coming in to drop off reinforcements, accompanied by two fighters that were already diving toward the LZ to blast them.

"Incoming!" Kit yelled, breaking into a run toward the house. "Get inside!"

Kayci was already checking on Nathan when Vladimir and Breyanna came charging into the main room from the back of the house.

Vladimir stopped in his tracks. *"Bozhe moi."*

"They're only stunned!" Kayci declared, moving to the side of the old man. "But he's not! He's badly injured! We have to get him to a medical facility!"

"Doctor, how are..." Vladimir was interrupted when the door burst open. He spun around and nearly opened fire before he recognized the Ghatazhak combat armor.

Breyanna did not. She fired, her energy blast bouncing off Kit's personal shield.

Not recognizing the woman, Kit instinctively returned fire, a stunner blast striking the woman squarely in the chest.

Breyanna was more than a little surprised and then even more so when she realized she was unharmed and still standing.

"Cease fire!" Vladimir demanded. "They're friendlies!"

Breyanna kept her weapon aimed at Kit. "But he shot me!"

"And you didn't fall!" Kit exclaimed. "What the fuck?" He looked at Vladimir. "Who the hell is she?" he demanded. "*What* the hell is she?"

Mori entered from the kitchen, both his hands pointed toward Breyanna, also not recognizing her and concerned that she was pointing a weapon at his cohorts.

"Everyone! Stop firing!" Vladimir demanded. "We're all on the same side!" He turned to Breyanna. "Lower your weapon, Breyanna."

"There are four more Zhulati shuttles landing out front *right* now," Kit warned. "And this time they won't make the mistake of channeling all their power into only their *forward* shields."

Breyanna reluctantly lowered her weapon but did not put it back in her belt.

Kit moved closer to Vladimir, looking down at Nathan and Jessica, both of whom still weren't moving. "Are they?"

"Doc says they're just stunned."

"Mori," Kit called. "Hit them with anti-stun, Jess first."

Jokay and Abdur entered, also from the kitchen side, having circled around after putting down the Zhulati troops originally in their way.

"They just dropped twenty-four heavies in front," Jokay reported. "They're fanning out as we speak."

"Let's keep them focused on us while second squad drops in to surprise them," Kit instructed. "Who is she?" Kit asked Vlad, leaning in closer to him.

"The girl in the SA pod," Vladimir replied.

Kit looked at Vladimir. "Seriously?" Kit shook his head. "That explains a lot."

"Really?" Vladimir replied. "Then maybe you can explain it to me."

* * *

"The second group of shuttles can't get into position to insert the rest of the Ghatazhak," Sima reported urgently from the Aurora's comms station.

"There are more than a hundred Zhulati combat drones over the LZ," Laza announced. "They've stacked about a dozen every five hundred meters. The moment one of our shuttles jumps in, they're attacked."

"What about our Dragons?" Cameron asked. "Can't they protect them?"

"They *are* trying," Laza assured the captain.

"But the moment they do, more drones *and* fighters appear and attack *them.*"

"Sima, tell them to keep trying," Cameron instructed. "We've got to get more boots on the ground before it's too late."

Another warning alarm sounded on Laza's console. "It may already *be* too late. There are now thirty Zhulati advancing on our people, and they have four more shuttles on approach to the LZ."

"Aurora! I need suppression fire on that LZ!" Cameron ordered.

"*Unable to comply,*" the Aurora's AI replied. "*There are too many friendlies jumping in and out of the line of fire.*"

"Damn it," Cameron cursed. After sighing, she said, "Sima, tell all our shuttles and Dragons to clear the area and stand by. And tell Kit to take cover."

"Captain!" Laza interrupted. "Eight Dusahn shuttles just jumped in over the LZ.

"Sima, belay that!" Cameron instructed. She turned to Laza. "What *kind* of shuttles, and what are they *doing?*"

"They're troop shuttles, sir," Laza replied. They're positioned around the outer perimeter of the LZ at about one thousand meters." Laza looked at Cameron. "I believe they're deploying troops."

Cameron's mind was racing. "What is that Dusahn warship doing?"

"Still slugging it out with the Zhulati cruiser," Laza replied. "Which is about to lose one of its port shield sections."

"They're still not targeting us?" Cameron asked.

"No sir. They're still ignoring us."

Cameron had a decision to make, but she had too

little information to rationalize any course of action. "Aurora, hold fire!" she ordered, going with her gut.

The eight Dusahn troop shuttles that had just jumped in began circling the engagement area below, jumping ahead by short distances every other second. In between each jump, a soldier stepped out, falling toward the surface as they disappeared in their own flashes of blue-white light.

In groups of eight, the soldiers in black, high-tech combat armor appeared behind blue-white flashes of light, only a meter above the ground. They landed in perfect combat stances, immediately opening fire with heavy assault rifles and shoulder mounted auto-blasters. Positioned in a circle around the Zhulati forces, their appearance forced the Zhulati to abandon their assault on the house and return fire on the new threat that was amassing behind their lines and all around them. With each passing second, another group of eight appeared with absolute precision, being placed perfectly around the compass. In less than fifteen seconds, eighty of the unknown soldiers had surrounded the Zhulati and were systematically mowing them down.

The sudden cessation of incoming fire caught Kit's attention, and he stood to see more clearly out the windows.

"What the hell's going on?" Nathan asked, finally

shaking off the effects of the stunner blast and struggling to get back on his feet.

Jessica was already standing, stepping carefully over next to Kit.

Kit watched as the firefight outside raged. But no one was shooting at them. Even more importantly, despite the incredible amount of firepower being pumped into the Zhulati lines, not a single bolt of energy was missing their targets and reaching their barely standing shelter.

"What the fuck?" Jessica wondered, seeing the same thing as Kit. "Who *are* these guys? Even the Zhulati don't shoot that well. Only..."

A blue-white flash of light appeared from overhead, just a few meters in front of the prefab home, followed by a thunderous tearing sound. A second later, ten soldiers appeared behind blue-white flashes of their own, dropping to combat stances on the ground. Their armor was flat black, with discrete touches of red trim reminiscent of the armor worn by the Dusahn long ago.

Nine of the soldiers turned toward the Zhulati lines, opening up and catching them from behind in a crossfire. The tenth man began walking toward the battered home, seemingly unconcerned with the firefight raging behind him. As he neared the front porch, his opaque helmet visor retracted upward, revealing the man's face and his stern, confident expression.

Jessica's eyes widened and her jaw dropped, as did Nathan's. "No way," she uttered in disbelief.

"Is that..." Nathan said.

Kit smiled broadly. "Rezhik!"

———

The Maturo's bridge was filled with the sound of alarms and urgent reports of catastrophic failures from all over the flagship of the Zhulati.

"Ground forces report they are surrounded," the comms officer reported. "They are caught in a crossfire and are losing forces rapidly."

"We've lost number eight port shield," the tactical officer warned. "Hull breaches, port side, section one five, deck three."

"Engineering reports loss of primary reactor," the comms officer added. "We're running on emergency power."

"We've lost power to weapons," the tactical officer added. "More shield failures are imminent."

Captain Hyam stepped in close to General Gogol, speaking in hushed tones. "If we do not disengage now, this ship *will* fall."

"We *had* them," General Gogol said, unable to accept the loss.

"We did, sir. But the situation has changed."

General Gogol thought for a moment, finally resigning herself to the inevitable. "Direct all forces to the rally point and get us out of here," she instructed.

"Helm! Jump us out of here, then head for rally point Delta Five!" the captain ordered. "Comms, send a signal to all forces to abort mission and flow to the rally point."

"Jumping!" the helmsman replied.

"Flowing all forces to rally point Delta Five," the comms officer acknowledged.

The jump flash washed over the Zhulati flagship's bridge, and the incoming fire that had shaken the ship to its core for the last five minutes stopped.

"Enjoy your brief respite, Captain Scott," the general said to herself.

"The Zhulati cruiser has jumped away," Laza reported from the Aurora's sensor station. "Their forces over the LZ are departing as well."

Cameron felt a wave of relief wash over her.

"The Dusahn forces have defeated the Zhulati ground forces and *are* advancing on the captain's position," Laza added. "However, they are not firing."

A jump flash filled the bridge with blue-white light, catching Cameron off guard. The main view screen was filled with the image of the Dusahn cruiser, now less than a kilometer away and directly in front of them over the fifth planet.

"Captain, Lieutenant Vasya is yelling something I can't quite make out," Ensign Dass reported. "I think he's saying '*Rezhik? It's Rezhik?*'"

"What?" Cameron couldn't believe what she was hearing.

"The Dusahn ship is hailing us," Sima added.

Cameron was still trying to add up all the pieces, but the answer she was getting wasn't making sense. "Put them through."

"*Aurora, this is the Atlantis,*" a familiar, male voice called over the speakers.

"It can't be," Cameron said.

"They're offering video," Sima told her.

Cameron gestured to her comms officer to accept the video. A moment later, the very face she had refused to believe would be there, *was* there. "Telles?"

In an uncharacteristic moment for the general,

a smile came across his stoic, chiseled face. "I am happy to see you, Captain Taylor."

"Not as happy as I am," Cameron replied, also smiling.

"It has been a long time."

"Not for us."

"Of course," Telles replied, his smile fading as his thoughts went back to the demands of the current situation. "Please recall your forces and prepare to get under way," the general instructed. "This is not yet over."

"We have people on the surface," Cameron stated, realizing the general was most likely aware of that.

"We will cover your evac, but we must move quickly," the general warned. "The Zhulati have called for reinforcements, which will arrive shortly," he added, ending the conversation abruptly.

Cameron slumped back in the command chair. "I did *not* see *that* coming."

CHAPTER EIGHT

"Mirai, Aurora. LZ is warm. Repeat, LZ is warm. Evac immediately."

"What?" Aiden couldn't believe what he was hearing. "Aurora, Mirai. What's going on? How did the LZ go from hot to warm so quickly?"

"The Dusahn ship is on our side," Sima explained. *"It's operated by the Ghatazhak. They're holding the LZ for us while we get our people out."*

"How is that even possible?" Erica wondered. "I thought our Ghatazhak were the only ones left."

"If you're going to fly for Captain Scott and the Free Fleet, you learn not to be surprised, even by the impossible," Aiden told her as he prepared the shuttle to jump back into the LZ.

―――――――――

The boot steps on the porch were followed by a knock on the front door.

Kit might have been eager to see his old friend, but Mori, Jokay, and Abdur were more cautious, each of them taking aim at the door as Kit opened it.

Captain Torren Rezhik entered, his entire helmet now retracted back into the collar of his combat armor. "Looks like you got yourself in over your head...again."

"Nah, we had them right where we wanted them," Kit insisted.

"Kit?" Mori prompted.

"Oh yeah," Kit replied. "Okay, what was the name of that wealthy socialite I hooked up with on Pentus Three?"

"Jaisa Fanella," Rezhik answered. "And you didn't

hook up with her. She shot you down cold. In fact, she laughed at you."

"I don't remember her *laughing* at me," Kit argued.

"Oh she did," Mori insisted, relaxing and lowering his weapon.

"Good to see you, Lieutenant Commander," Kit said, shaking Rezhik's hand.

"Good to see you as well, Lieutenant," Rezhik replied. "And it's *captain* now."

"*Captain,*" Kit replied. "How many of us survived?"

"There are eighty-eight of us left."

Kit was shocked. Both by how many had survived, as well as how many had been lost. "How..."

"We'll talk later," Rezhik told him, turning to Nathan. "Captain," he nodded.

"I can't tell you how happy I am to see you," Nathan said.

Jessica stepped forward and hugged him.

"Time is critical for multiple reasons," Rezhik said. "We have secured the LZ, and our ship has run the Zhulati cruiser off, but Zhulati reinforcements are on the way. It would be best if we left as soon as possible."

"Gladly," Nathan replied.

"Can you believe it!" Josh exclaimed as he brought his Dragon fighter around back toward the engagement area.

"*Did they say how many Ghatazhak are still alive?*" Nikolas asked.

"Well, if all those red dots on the surface scan are Ghatazhak instead of Zhulati, then it looks like *most* of them."

"Unbelievable."

*"*Dragon Leader to all Dragons. Perimeter cover positions. Ten-click radius, angels three. Remo and I will fly low cover."

After the rest of the Dragon pilots acknowledged their new orders, Nikolas spoke again. *"Josh, do you ever feel like we're characters in a really crazy sci-fi vid-flick?"*

"All the fucking time," Josh chuckled as he pushed his nose down slightly and pressed his jump button.

———

Kit led Nathan and the others out of the house, with Mori, Jokay, and Abdur at the rear, keeping an eye on Breyanna.

Captain Rezhik stood to the side of the door on the front porch as they passed. As Mori passed, the captain took him aside. "Is she the one?"

"That was in the SA pod?" Mori replied. "Yes."

"Keep a close eye on her," the captain urged. "She's why we're here."

"And here I thought it was for us," Mori joked.

"You guys were just a bonus," Rezhik replied with a wry smile.

Kit had to fight the urge to hug every Ghatazhak he saw outside. These were his brothers. These were the men he had trained with, fought alongside, and lived with since puberty. But the situation dictated restraint. They were still in a combat situation, and the Zhulati could jump back in just as quickly as the Ghatazhak had. Instead, he just exchanged smiles and nods with all the comrades he was able to make eye contact with as they made their way over to the Mirai, which had just set down.

Jessica felt the same as Kit. Although she had only spent seven years living and training with the Ghatazhak, she too had fought alongside them. In fact, the Ghatazhak had saved her from herself. They had taught her to control her anger and rage, turning what had been a negative into a positive. To put it simply, she owed them her life. "Hey, guys! Looking good!" was all she had time for as they crossed the short distance from Gillis's home to the Mirai twenty meters away.

"*We need to go,*" Aiden warned over Kit's comm-set. "*We've got incoming.*"

"Double-time it, people!" Kit instructed, pumping his fist in the air as a visual prompt.

At the same time, Captain Rezhik got the same message, as did the rest of the Ghatazhak on the surface. They immediately took up fire positions, preparing for the sudden arrival of the enemy.

Nathan and Vladimir carried the litter containing Gillis, with Doctor Barra practically jogging to keep up with the men's longer, faster strides. Jessica followed, with Breyanna and the other three members of Kit's squad close behind.

The group hit the ramp, continuing straight up into the Mirai's cargo bay.

Abdur was the last man to step on the ramp. "We're aboard!" he notified Aiden.

The ramp immediately began to rise. Two seconds later, the shuttle's grav-lift systems began humming, and the ship rose, climbing away. A few seconds later, its nose came up slightly as it began to accelerate forward, and then it disappeared in a blue-white flash.

The sky only a few hundred meters above their heads was suddenly filled with tiny flashes of light, followed by a cacophony of the thunderous tearing sounds that accompanied jumps into the atmosphere.

"Incoming!" Captain Rezhik yelled, dropping to the ground so that all his shield energy would automatically divert to covering his vulnerable backside. As he hit the ground, explosions detonated all around the battlefield as jump-enabled anti-personnel missiles struck.

———————

"The LZ is under attack," Laza warned from the Aurora's sensor station. "At least one hundred jump missiles have detonated all about the engagement area. Based on their lower yield, I believe they were anti-personnel weapons."

"What about the Mirai?" Cameron asked.

"They jumped away seconds before the attack."

"Sima, get me the Atlantis," Cameron ordered. A moment later, the image of General Telles on the bridge of the Atlantis appeared on the main view screen.

"*Captain,*" the general began, not waiting to hear what Cameron had to say. "*Jump away immediately. You are about to be attacked.*"

"General, your people are..."

"*We have things under control,*" the general assured her, ending the communication.

"New contacts," Laza reported. "Twenty-plus jump missiles. Five seconds to impact."

"Aurora..."

"*Jumping,*" the Aurora's AI reported as the jump flash washed over the bridge.

Cameron was a bit taken aback. She did not care for the ship's AI's tendency to act on its own if it perceived an immediate threat. However, she knew at least in this case, that action had saved the ship. "That was close," she said. "Where are we?"

"*Two light minutes from our previous position,*" Aurora reported. "*Shall I come about for a return jump?*"

"Negative," Cameron replied. "Stay put, but channel *all* available power into recharging our shields, starting with the weakest sections."

"*Understood.*"

"Sima, update all forces with our new position and order them to RTB ASAP," Cameron added. She turned back to Laza. "The Atlantis."

"We are two light minutes away," Laza reminded her.

"Right," she sighed. "Remind me to give them one of our AICC nodes...assuming they survive."

The Mirai came out of her jump in orbit over the fifth planet, turning toward the Aurora's new position two light minutes away.

Nathan entered the cockpit, with Jessica following him in.

"Damn good to see you guys," Nathan told Aiden and Erica.

"Good to see you too," Aiden replied. "We almost didn't make it in. If the Ghatazhak hadn't shown up, we'd still be trying."

"If they hadn't shown up, we'd all be prisoners," Jessica insisted.

"Where the hell did they come from?" Aiden wondered.

"I have no idea," Nathan replied. "But I'm sure it'll be a hell of a story." Nathan noticed something out the forward windows. "Is that it?"

"Mirai, zoom in on panel three," Aiden instructed.

The forward window immediately right of the center post changed focus, and the Dusahn cruiser appeared. It was under fire and was responding in kind.

"Zhulati gunships," Jessica said, recognizing the attacking ships.

"Considering the beating that ship gave the Zhulati cruiser, I doubt those gunships are going to be much of a threat."

"Anything is a threat if there are enough of them," Nathan commented. "Where's the Aurora?" he asked, looking out the other windows.

"She came under jump missile attack and had to jump out two light minutes," Aiden explained as the view through the number three window reverted to normal. "We're jumping out to her now."

"Good. The sooner we get out of here the better."

———

Only moments after the Mirai jumped away, the Ghatazhak shuttles appeared, jumping in only a few meters above the heads of the men waiting for them. They jumped in directly over each group of Ghatazhak spread all around the LZ.

As the shuttles descended, the Ghatazhak below them spread out just enough to provide the room the shuttles needed to land. Once they touched down, the troops boarded, and within less than half a minute of appearing, the shuttles began jumping away again.

Captain Rezhik was the last man to board, and his shuttle was the last to depart. As the commander of the Ghatazhak's expeditionary forces, he was the first man in and the last man out. It had been a long time since his troops had seen real action. Nevertheless, they had performed flawlessly, just as he had expected.

Captain Rezhik paused just beside his shuttle's open sides, scanning the area. It was littered with bodies and dropped weapons, all of which would end up in the hands of the locals once they came to investigate. The Zhulati did not waste time collecting their dead or recovering their technology. They were convinced that even with their weapons, no one could best the Zhulati.

Torren smiled as he stepped inside the shuttle. The Zhulati were wrong. They had been bested and with ease.

———

"The Mirai is on the deck," Sima announced from the Aurora's comm-station. "The Dragons and remaining shuttles are at rally point four, awaiting orders."

"Tell them to stay put; we'll come to them," Cameron instructed. "I want to be completely sure we've shaken the Zhulati before we try to cycle them in."

"Aye, sir," Sima replied.

"The Atlantis is still engaged over the fifth planet," Laza reported from the sensor station.

"The Zhulati cruiser returned?" Cameron assumed.

"Negative. They're engaged with twenty Zhulati gunships. They've deployed some kind of combat drones that are forming swarms around each gunship. Very small, very fast, and very maneuverable."

"Can the drones take out the gunships?" Cameron wondered.

"If given time, possibly," Laza replied. "But their weapons are not very powerful. I suspect their intention is to keep the gunships busy defending themselves, thus inhibiting their ability to conduct offensive operations."

"That won't work for long," Cameron insisted. "The commanders of those gunships will quickly figure out the drones aren't that big a threat and ignore them."

"The Atlantis *is* using it to their advantage," Laza reported. "They are targeting gunships that are completely defensive, easily taking them out. They have already reduced their numbers by half."

"Mirai is inside the bay," Sima reported. "Doctor Barra is requesting a medical rescue team."

"Did they say who's injured?" Cameron asked.

"Negative."

"Contacts," Laza announced. "Jump missiles inbound."

"Aurora, hard about into the incoming. All power to forward shields," Cameron ordered.

The Aurora's AI had anticipated the second part of her orders, based on the first, and had already rerouted all shield power to the forward shields as she came about hard to port.

"Those didn't come from the fifth planet," Cameron

stated as the ship shook from the incoming missile impacts.

"*Forward shields down to twenty percent,*" Aurora warned. "*Aft shields at thirty. Recommend escape jump.*"

"More contacts!" Laza warned. "To starboard! Three seconds!"

The Aurora's AI didn't wait for Cameron to order an escape jump. Its primary responsibility was to ensure the safety of the ship and her crew.

"Aurora!" Cameron began, but stopped midsentence when she realized her AI had already executed the order she was about to give. "Pos..."

"*One point five light minutes from last position. Still within the Nishida system. Recommend evasive jumps, or we will be attacked again.*"

Nathan walked briskly onto the bridge, with Jessica and Kit following close behind. "Aurora. Execute evasive pattern Delta Five Two."

Cameron turned to look at him. "I would have chosen Bravo One Five."

"Dragons and shuttles don't know that one," Nathan told her as he moved to the tactical console to determine the ship's current condition. "Sima, use a comm-drone to get a message to the Atlantis instructing them to meet us at the gate to Libertara. Point-to-point laser comms only."

"Aye, sir."

"Nathan, General Telles said this is not yet over."

"Telles is alive?" Jessica asked.

"He is."

"I'm sure he also said the Zhulati will have reinforcements on the way," Nathan said. "Gunships are fast series-jumpers. Larger ships will be following." He turned to Sima again. "Tell the Dragons and shuttles that we'll be taking them in on the fly during Delta Five Two, starting at the fourth jump in the series."

"Aye, sir," Sima replied.

"Marcus is reupping the Mirai. I'll jump to the Atlantis and meet with Telles and give him an AICC node while you get our forces out of here."

"You got it," Cameron agreed. "And by the way, Nathan, it's good to have you back. All of you."

Nathan smiled. "Thanks for not giving up on us."

CHAPTER NINE

"Captain," Breyanna called to Nathan as he and Jessica walked across the hangar bay toward the Mirai. "I demand to know why I'm being detained here."

"I don't know," Nathan replied. "Why are you being detained here?" He looked over to Kit.

"Telles wants her on the Atlantis," Kit replied. "He says all of this is about *her*, not *us.*"

"Who is Telles?" Breyanna demanded. "Why can't I stay here?"

"Look," Nathan began. "There is something special about you. Something that the Zhulati are willing to kill to retrieve."

"I'm a computer specialist," Breyanna pleaded. "Or at least I *was.*"

"A computer specialist who's unaffected by a stunner blast," Kit pointed out.

"They did something to you," Nathan said.

"Yeah, they gave me blonde hair!"

"Come on, let's go," Jessica insisted, pushing Breyanna toward the boarding ramp.

"I'm not going anywhere," Breyanna replied, knocking Jessica's hand away. Her body became tense, as if she expected to have to fight for her life at any moment.

Kit sensed her change in stance and drew his sidearm, as did Mori, Jokay, and Abdur.

Breyanna began to settle into a combat pose, a menacing look in her eyes. "Something tells me I can take you," she said ominously.

"All of us?" Jessica chuckled, pointing at Kit and

the others, all of whom had their weapons aimed at her.

"Stunners don't work on me," Breyanna reminded them.

"Mine isn't set to stun," Kit told her.

"Neither is mine," Mori added.

Breyanna locked eyes with each of the Ghatazhak, sensing no reluctance to mow her down if necessary.

"The only way any of *us* will cause *you* harm is if you *force* us to do so," Nathan told her.

Breyanna crouched a bit further, getting ready to strike.

"Please, Breyanna," Nathan begged. "These men are the most highly trained warriors in existence. They will try to spare your life when subduing you, but I cannot assure your safety *unless* you cooperate."

Breyanna shot him a confident look, one that was reminiscent of the very men she was about to face. "I can take them," she declared as if she were stating an indisputable fact.

Nathan stepped forward, slowly extending his right hand and putting it on her shoulder. "I believe you," he told her. He stared into her eyes, remaining calm. "Please come with us, so we can find out what they did to you."

Breyanna looked unconvinced.

"Tactically speaking, it would be better for you to make your move *inside* the shuttle, *after* we're already en route," Jessica suggested. "That way, you'd have a way to escape."

Breyanna began to relax, coming out of her combat stance. "Very well."

"You do realize that the shuttle's AI would never give you flight control," Nathan stated.

"I know," Breyanna replied, turning to head up the ramp.

Nathan looked at Jessica. "Really? Giving a potential attacker tactical advice?"

"Relax, Nathan. They've all got their blasters on full power."

Nathan looked at Kit.

"Yup," Kit acknowledged.

"Same here," Mori added.

Jokay and Abdur both shrugged, holstering their weapons as they headed up the ramp.

"Keep a close eye on her," Nathan suggested.

"She's not leaving the cargo bay," Kit assured him.

* * *

A subdued flash of blue-white light revealed the black and crimson Atlantis. Seconds after she came out of the jump, a series of jump flashes appeared all around her. With speed and precision, the incoming troop shuttles rotated around so they could back into their respective launch bays. It took them less than fifteen seconds to recover all ten of the shuttles, then the Atlantis jumped away.

At another point in the system five light minutes distant, another flash of light appeared from where the Atlantis had reappeared. This time, she was surrounded by more than one hundred tiny flashes of light as her drones arrived and found their respective docking ports. This too required only fifteen seconds to complete, despite the larger number of simultaneous recoveries taking place. When it was over, the Atlantis again disappeared in a flash of light.

A minute later, four Zhulati gunships jumped

in, expecting to surprise the Atlantis. They found nothing but empty space.

* * *

"Where are they?" Erica wondered, staring out the Mirai's forward windows.

"Are we at the right coordinates?" Nathan asked Aiden.

"Right where they told us to be," Aiden stated. "But according to their timetable, they won't be here for another…well, three……two……one…"

A flash of blue-white light filled their forward windows, translating into the Mirai's cockpit.

Nathan, just like the others, was slightly taken aback. Before them was the Atlantis, so close they could see the seams in her hull plating. He glanced down at the navigation display, then at the jump nav-com, which still displayed their last arrival coordinates. "Man, that is some precise jumping," he stated.

"*Mirai, Atlantis,*" a man's voice called over comms. "*Release controls to us and we'll bring you into bay three. Time is critical.*"

"Understood, Atlantis," Aiden replied. "Controls are yours."

The shuttle suddenly rolled sharply to starboard, diving and accelerating toward the Atlantis. It was an aggressive maneuver, especially for a shuttle, and for a moment, Aiden was tempted to take control back.

Nathan grabbed the overhead, bracing himself. Even though inertial dampening systems removed the forces of flight, the body often replaced them. Just seeing things outside shift suddenly could throw you off balance.

Thrusters fired, and the shuttle slipped through

an opening in the Atlantis's hull that barely seemed large enough for them to pass. A second later, the inside of the bay outside flashed blue-white as the Atlantis jumped away. The lights in the bay were red but changed to pale blue a moment later, indicating the space was repressurizing.

"Keep things warm," Nathan stated as he turned to exit. "I want to be ready to depart on a moment's notice."

"I'll keep her fires burning, Captain," Aiden assured him.

* * *

"Oops," Josh commented as they came out of the jump. "Looks like we're early."

"Better early than late," Nikolas commented. *"I just want to get out of this thing and stretch my legs. Maybe even close my eyes for an hour."*

"I'm going straight to mess," Josh declared. "I've been eating nothing but flight rations for two days now."

"I like flight rations," Nikolas said.

"That's cuz you never tasted Neli's 'clean out the galley' stew."

"That doesn't sound very appetizing."

"Don't knock it till you've tried it," Josh insisted. "Kusya said she just put a batch on the line today."

"I thought you didn't like Neli's cooking?"

"I just say that to piss her off," Josh admitted.

His cockpit filled with blue-white light, and the Aurora appeared before him, already rolling into her next turn.

"I can smell that stew now," Josh said as he turned to follow the Aurora, increasing his forward thrust to start closing on her stern.

"Dragons One and Two, combat landings," Sima

ordered over comms. "We've got gunships on our tail. Dudder and Mop almost didn't get aboard."

"Got it," Josh replied. "Sweetie, you've got the landing," Josh instructed his AI.

"*Understood. Executing combat landing.*"

"Let's get down quick, Remo."

"*Just make sure you stay on your half of the landing bay,*" Nikolas joked.

Josh glanced out his forward windows as his AI dropped his fighter down behind the Aurora, lining up for a rapid landing cycle on the landing deck located on her stern, between her main drive nacelles.

"*On final, ten seconds to touchdown.*"

Threat alert lights began flashing on Josh's tactical display, located in the pedestal between his legs. He glanced down at the view screen as it suddenly filled up with dozens of small icons, all of them barreling toward the Aurora from all directions. "Fuck. Abort! Abort!" Josh ordered, grabbing his flight controls. "I've got the controls," he added as he pulled back hard on his flight control stick and gunned his throttles.

The Aurora rolled to the left as Josh's nose came up.

"Dragons! Jump Three! Jump Three!" Sima warned.

The Aurora disappeared behind a flash of blue-white light, leaving Josh and Nikolas alone, with more than fifty incoming missiles headed their way.

A quick glance at his tactical display showed him that Nikolas had maneuvered in opposing fashion, pitching down and going to full power. This would split the target selection algorithms between the two fighters.

"Time to go, Remo," Josh insisted.

"Meet you at Omega Four," Nikolas replied, just before the icon representing his Dragon fighter disappeared from Josh's tactical display.

Josh came out of his pitch-up maneuver and immediately rolled left, touching his jump button a second later to escape. His jump flashed washed over him, and Josh started a turn toward the Omega Four rendezvous point that Nikolas had referenced. But before he could punch in the coordinates, twenty-plus missiles appeared on his display.

"Twenty inbound," his AI warned. *"Three seconds to impact."*

Josh had already reached for the jump button before his AI had completed her warning call. He jumped his fighter ahead five light seconds, then rolled into a starboard turn. The twenty icons that had been on his threat display had vanished when he had jumped but reappeared a few seconds later. "What the fuck?"

"They're still with us," his AI warned.

"Are these..."

"Jump tracking? It appears so," his AI confirmed.

Josh pressed his jump button again, barely escaping destruction. "If so, they can't have much range," he decided, verbalizing his thoughts aloud as usual. "We have to out-jump them", he added as he dialed up a one-light-year jump. He waited for the missiles to reappear, but didn't have to wait long. Again they jumped in only a few seconds from impact, forcing him to jump yet again.

When his jump flash faded, he didn't bother taking evasive maneuvers, instead dialing up a five-light-year jump, and jumping once more as the missiles returned.

Josh dialed up a ten-light-year jump just in case,

but after waiting a full ten seconds, no jump missiles appeared. "Looks like that did it," he decided. "Sweetie, plot a course to Omega Four and get us there. Aurora, Dragon One. Time to point Three?"

"*Dragon One, Aurora,*" Sima replied. "*Forty seconds.*"

"Be advised, the enemy has jump-following missiles. But it looks like their range is limited to maybe a few light years."

"*Thanks, we just discovered the same,*" Sima answered.

"*Jumping to Omega Four,*" his AI announced as the jump flash washed over them.

"Hey, Reems, did they chase you as well?"

"*A-firm,*" Nikolas replied. "It took three point five light years to lose them."

"We've got about twenty seconds to get to jump point Three."

"*We are way long, Josh,*" Nikolas pointed out. "*I'm getting low on propellant.*"

"Yeah, me too," Josh admitted. "Sweetie, calculate the lowest consumption turns and jumps to reach the target jump point in Aurora's current Delta Five Two that will get us there in fifteen seconds and still have enough propellant to land."

"*Done, but there are problems,*" his AI warned.

"Execute."

"*Executing,*" his AI confirmed as it began a turn. "*Would you like to hear the problems?*"

"Let me guess. We're not going to have enough propellant left to land?"

"*Your wingman will, but we'll run out of propellant during our turn to final,*" his AI explained. "*The Aurora will have to adjust her course and speed in order to safely recover this ship.*"

"That's impossible," Josh protested. "The stern is too far from the ship's center of gravity to have that precise of control, especially if she's still got gunships on her ass."

"*That is why we'll be landing on her main flight deck.*"

"Oh that's so much better," Josh moaned.

"*Don't worry, Josh,*" Nikolas said. "*They'll just match your course and speed, and then thrust up to get close enough for the flight deck's gravity fields to get hold of you and pull you in. Basic rendezvous and docking.*"

"With gunships attacking," Josh added.

"*Just to make it a little more exciting, right?*"

"Just another first in space jock history by Josh Hayes," Josh said, rolling his eyes as his AI finished their final turn and jumped both ships.

The jump flash cleared a second later, followed by another as the Aurora jumped in directly in front of them.

"*Both Dragons are on parallel courses. Dragon Two is low and starboard,*" his AI reported. "*Dragon Two will land first on the Dragon recovery deck. Then the Aurora will maneuver into position to pull you in.*"

"*Don't worry, Josh. You've got this.*"

"I'm not worried at all," Josh insisted.

"*See you on deck, boss,*" Nikolas said.

"Aurora, Dragon Two, on final, combat landing."

"*Dragon Two, Aurora, cleared for landing,*" Sima replied over comms.

Nikolas extended his landing gear but didn't fold in his wings like usual. Combat landings meant quick and dirty, and Dragons only had full maneuverability when their wings were fully extended. He glanced down at his auxiliary flight display, which currently showed his approach corridor to landing. He was slightly high, but chose not to adjust his flight path just yet. He was still low enough to slip into the landing bay, and he didn't want to use the last few seconds of propellant he had left unless he had no other choice.

"*Ten seconds to touchdown,*" his AI reported. "*You are slightly high but still within safety margins. Shall I correct?*"

"Negative."

The threat warning light on his tactical console began blinking furiously, drawing his attention to the tactical display screen. In rapid succession, more than a dozen inbound missiles appeared.

"Josh! Incoming!" Nikolas warned over comms as the Aurora's point-defense turrets opened fire, laying out explosive intercept flak in the paths of the incoming weapons.

"*One of the inbounds has locked onto us,*" Josh's AI reported. "*Impact in five seconds.*"

"Uh, Aurora? I could use a little help here."

"*We're fully engaged here,*" Sima replied. "*Recommend you jump clear.*"

Josh glanced out his front window. The Aurora had already started translating upward. "Negative. I don't have a clear jump line!"

"*Impact in five seconds,*" his AI warned.

Nikolas fired his translation thrusters, causing his fighter to pop up above the Aurora's dorsal surface. "Micro jump! Put us between Josh and the incoming!"

His AI responded immediately, the jump flash washing over them. Nikolas immediately pitched his nose up, using the last of his propellant to end his pitch maneuver, opening fire with his forward torpedo cannons. At the same time, his AI also engaged their forward-facing turrets, but it was like trying to hit the head of a pin coming straight at you, with another pin.

"Two seconds!" his AI reported. "Jump..."

The missile exploded only meters away, and the ship shook, shifting to port violently as something slammed into them. Warning lights began lighting up as critical systems began failing. In the blink of an eye, running out of propellant had become the least of his problems.

"*Mayday-mayday-mayday,*" Nikolas announced over comms.

Josh shifted his view overhead just as Dragon Two exploded. "Remo!" Josh yelled over comms. "Aurora! Dragon Two is down!"

"Two meters and falling," his AI warned.

Josh grabbed his grav-lift throttle, easing it up just enough to soften his touchdown on the Aurora's flight deck. A jump flash washed over him as the Aurora jumped away. "Wait!" he exclaimed. "What about Nikolas!"

"*Dragon One, confirm touchdown,*" Sima insisted.

"I'm fucking down, okay! Now what about my wingman?"

"*I'm fine, Josh!*" Nikolas announced over comms. "*My AI punched me out as my ship exploded. We jumped five light years out.*"

"*Dragon Two, be advised. We're redirecting the Tara to pick you up,*" Sima reported. "*ETA three minutes.*"

"*Did you make it down?*" Nikolas asked.

"I did thanks to you," Josh replied, starting to relax a bit.

"*Just doing my job, boss,*" Nikolas bragged.

"We really gotta get those refueling drones built," Josh added.

* * *

"Welcome aboard, Captain Scott." Ghatazhak officers rarely smiled, at least not without good reason.

"Sonoda, right?" Nathan replied.

"I'm surprised you remember."

"Well for us it's only been a couple months," Nathan replied. "And you're a *commander* now?"

"I'm the ship's second officer," the commander explained. "General Telles asked me to welcome all of you and to convey that he awaits you all on the bridge."

"Then I suppose I should give this to you," Nathan said, handing a bag to the commander.

"And this is?" Commander Sonoda asked, accepting the bag.

"An AICC node that provides encrypted comms with all Free Fleet ships, like the Aurora," Nathan explained. "I thought you might find it useful in the future."

"I'll give it to our chief engineer to clear."

"Clear?" Nathan wondered.

"We have very strict comms security within the Ghatazhak fleet."

"You have a *fleet?*"

"Well it's more like a single warship and several support vessels. I'm sure Lieutenant Cefalo can make it work."

"Cefalo?" Jessica said. "I don't remember a Cefalo."

"He is not *technically* a Ghatazhak," the commander explained. "In fact, he is Dusahn."

"Dusahn?" Nathan questioned, surprised.

"He has been instrumental in the resurrection and overhaul of the Atlantis."

"And you trust him?" Jessica asked.

"As much as any other Ghatazhak," the commander assured her. "Besides, he is probably the *only* Dusahn left in the universe, so who would he sell us out to?"

"Good point," Nathan agreed.

"What's all the commotion?" Jessica asked, noticing troops in specialized combat pressure suits that she didn't recognize heading for somewhere in a hurry.

"Jess," the commander greeted, reaching out to shake her hand. "It is good to see you again as well. We are about to start another op. The general will explain." The commander went over to Kit and his men, giving each of them a quick but hearty hug. "Never thought I'd be so happy to see your punk ass," he told Kit.

Kit smiled broadly. "You're looking pretty good for an old man," he joked. "I can't wait to hear what you guys have been up to."

"You as well." The commander turned back to

Nathan and the others. "There is a transport station just past the bulkhead. Just step in and say 'bridge'." Now if you'll excuse me, I have other duties to attend to."

"Of course," Nathan replied.

"This is so damned cool I can't believe it," Jessica exclaimed. "The Ghatazhak with their *own warship.*"

"Don't get too excited," Nathan told her as they made their way forward down the center corridor. "This ship is older than the *original* Aurora."

"I don't know, Captain," Kit said. "Everything looks pretty new to me."

They passed out of the hangar bay, stopping at the transport station the commander had mentioned.

Nathan stepped up to the doors, which opened automatically. "Looks like an elevator," he said, stepping inside.

Jessica, Breyanna, Kit, and the other three Ghatazhak in his squad followed Nathan into the elevator car, the doors closing once they were all inside.

"*State destination,*" a stern female voice stated.

"Uh, bridge?"

"*Of course,*" the voice replied. "*General Telles is expecting you, Captain Scott. We will arrive in fifteen seconds.*"

"Is it my imagination, or does she sound like an older version of Deliza Ta'Akar?" Jessica said.

"*You are correct,*" the voice replied. "*The voice of our benefactor was chosen for the Atlantis's AI.*"

"Benefactor?" Nathan wondered.

"Hey, are we going sideways?" Kit asked.

"He's right, we *are* going sideways," Mori agreed.

The doors slid open, revealing the ship's bridge.

"We need elevators that go sideways," Jessica

said as she passed Nathan, the first one to exit the elevator. "Telles, you son of a gun. Why am I not surprised that you're still alive five centuries later?"

General Telles turned to face Jessica, embracing her as she approached. "Jess."

Jessica pulled back looking him over. "My God, you don't look a day older. None of you do," she realized, quickly taking in the familiar faces on the Atlantis bridge.

General Telles shook the hands of his four long-lost men. "We have missed you all," he told them. He turned to Nathan. "Captain Scott," he said, exhibiting one of his rare smiles.

"Lucius," Nathan said, embracing his old friend. "Thanks for the save."

"Our pleasure," the general assured him. He turned to Breyanna. "I take it this young lady is the person who came out of the creation pod?"

"I'm pretty sure it was a medical SA pod," Nathan corrected.

"I can see how you would think so," the general said. He stepped over to Breyanna, examining her closely. "Incredible."

"You're not so bad yourself, pops," Breyanna snarked.

"General Telles, this is Breyanna," Nathan introduced.

"A pleasure to finally meet you," the general stated. "Several people have given their lives to get you here."

"I don't understand."

"Did you say *creation pod*?" Jessica remembered.

"I did. Where is it?"

"Still on the Traverna," Jessica replied. "In the

reactor room, tucked underneath the ship's main power reactor."

"That's what I feared," the general said. "That's why they're still attacking both us *and* the Aurora. They're trying to keep us distracted while they retrieve that pod."

"That's what your teams are preparing for isn't it," Jessica realized.

"I don't understand," Nathan said. "Why is that pod so important? Isn't it *Breyanna* they're after?"

"In part, yes," the general explained. "But the pod that *created* her is what really matters."

"Created her?" Nathan asked, surprised.

"That is correct," the general acknowledged. "You see, Miss Breyanna is neither a naturally born human nor a clone. In fact, she is the first successful bio-synth."

Nathan was speechless, as were the others.

Breyanna was not silent. "I'm a *what?*"

"I apologize for being indelicate, ma'am, but the body you currently occupy was *created* in that pod."

"It didn't look like any clone pod I've ever seen," Jessica stated.

"Her body was created using a process similar to one used to create replacement organs, only on a much more complex scale."

"You're saying I'm not human?" Breyanna demanded.

"Under the strictest definition, no you are not. But this is neither the time nor place for such a debate," the general insisted. "We are about to launch a B and C."

"General," the tactical officer called. "All teams are ready for deployment. Recon drones confirm the

Maturo is approaching the Traverna. However, they have yet to deploy any boarding teams."

General Telles did not look pleased.

Nathan leaned into Jessica. "B and C?" he asked under his breath.

"Board and capture," Jessica whispered back.

"Of course," Nathan replied, realizing it was obvious.

"Unless we engage the Maturo and draw her away, our odds of mission success are unacceptable," Captain Kellen added as he approached. "Good to see you, Jess, Captain Scott."

"Has *everyone* been promoted?" Kit asked.

"Only as needed to maintain command structures, Lieutenant," Captain Kellen explained. "It is good to see you as well, Lieutenant. Gentlemen." Captain Kellen turned to General Telles. "Your orders, General?"

"Engage the Maturo," General Telles instructed. "Hold the assault teams until I give the word."

"Yes, General."

"Can we get back to me *not* being human?" Breyanna demanded.

"Captain, if they can create human host bodies like we create parts for the Aurora, they could genetically tweak them and give them all kinds of attributes," Jessica warned. "Increased strength, better senses, the ability to function in atmospheres that we cannot."

"And in a fraction of the time required to achieve the same results through cloning," Nathan realized.

"Imagine an army that can't be killed...*ever.*"

"I'm afraid it's more insidious than that," General Telles stated.

"More insidious than an army of invincible super-soldiers?" Nathan asked. "What could possibly be worse than that?"

General Telles paused a moment. Not for dramatic effect, but because he knew that what he was about to tell them would seem unbelievable at best. "We have reason to believe that the Alliance plans to use bio-synth bodies to host AI consciousness."

"Yup, that would be worse," Jessica agreed. "Humans have a natural aversion to killing. Even Ghatazhak have to be trained to turn off that instinct to preserve life. With an AI, their forces would be completely compliant."

"One AI consciousness could control an entire platoon," Nathan realized.

"The delays inherent with command and control of large forces would be measured in nanoseconds," Jessica added.

"If they equipped the hosts with AICC nodes, such forces could be controlled over an entire galaxy," Nathan surmised, becoming even more concerned.

"You are both thinking on too small a scale," General Telles told them.

Nathan and Jessica both looked at him.

"What is the one thing that must be done to create a lasting, totalitarian, communist regime?" the general asked Nathan.

"Get control of the population's hearts and minds," Jessica replied. "Usually through an exhaustive propaganda campaign involving state-owned media and public education."

"Yes, but that's not the answer I was looking for," the general replied.

"You execute all resistance," Nathan stated, a cold chill washing over him. "But we're talking about trillions of people."

"Quadrillions actually," the general corrected.

"You can't execute that many people without creating incredible backlash," Jessica argued.

"She's right," Nathan confirmed. "History shows that the more brutal a regime, the more likely it is to be overthrown."

"But what if all resistance were to be removed *without* the population's awareness?" General Telles postulated.

"How is that even possible?" Jessica asked.

"You replace their human forms with bio-synth copies," Breyanna stated.

Nathan and Jessica both looked at her.

"To transfer a human consciousness into an android body, you had to convert their consciousness into code that could run on that hardware. At that point, their consciousness can be tampered with and made to think and feel whatever they wanted. That's why using android bodies to host human consciousness was made illegal."

"The same problem exists with the use of a bio-synthetic human host body," General Telles explained. "The human consciousness must be broken down to trillions of bits, each mapped to a physical location in the source brain, and its biochemical structure recorded, enabling it to be put into the same state in the bio-synth host body. During this process, consciousness can be altered. The individual's entire belief structure tailored to meet the Alliance's needs."

"They could even rearrange memory storage to increase recall efficiencies," Breyanna added.

"Recall efficiency?" Nathan asked.

"You know how you memorize a list of something. Like when you were a kid, and you had to memorize calculation tables and such. Doing so moves those memories into more rapidly accessible locations, so they can more easily be recalled. That's how savants work, only on a far deeper level."

"You would, in essence, not only be creating a super-race," the general explained. "But a super *obedient* super-race."

"But why not just make a race of androids?" Jessica asked.

"Because AI lacks human instinct," Nathan reminded her.

"And human instinct comes from life experience," the general added. "It is the uniqueness of each individual's own instinct that makes humanity the superior form of intelligence. Preserve that while creating absolute obedience, and you have a society that can never be equaled."

"But why would anyone agree to be transferred to a bio-synth body?" Nathan wondered.

"Eternal life, absolute health, superior abilities," Breyanna stated. "Just to name a few."

"Can they even procreate?" Jessica asked.

"Theoretically yes," General Telles replied. "A bio-synth body is identical to a natural human body. In fact, even a doctor with state-of-the-art medical sensors could not tell the difference. And because it is *manufactured*, it is far easier to adjust its design. Evolution would occur at any point it was desired. One could even *evolve* in their own lifetime. Especially considering that they would be immortal, as long as they maintain access to replacement host bodies."

Nathan was silent for a moment. What the general was telling them was beyond anything he could have imagined. "What's your plan?" he finally asked.

"Miss Breyanna is proof that the prototype works. We intend to capture that pod and use it to counter the Alliance."

"How?" Nathan asked.

"By sharing the knowledge of its existence with the entire galaxy," General Telles replied.

"That's not enough," Nathan argued. "How many people do you think would sell their soul for eternal life?"

"How many people do you think would not?" the general countered.

"If you want to prevent this from being implemented on the scale you describe, you're going to have to *defeat* the Alliance. Is that even possible?"

"Two days ago, my answer would have been 'no'," the general replied. "But now, here you stand."

"I don't see how our existence changes anything," Nathan admitted.

"Trust me, it does," the general replied. "But for now, we must capture that pod. We will never have this opportunity again."

CHAPTER TEN

"I should be on one of the assault teams," Jessica insisted. "I've already defended the Traverna against one boarding action. I know the layout."

"Those were corporate security types," General Telles pointed out. "Zhulati assault troops are an entirely different matter."

"There are only so many ways to fight in a long corridor divided by bulkheads," Jessica argued. "I beat them down before with only Vlad and Doctor Barra."

"I was there too, you know," Nathan reminded her.

"Oh yeah, and Pirate Captain Scott, scourge of the cosmos, was there sword and all."

"Our B and C teams have been training together for quite some time," the general said.

"It's not like I don't know how you guys work," Jessica argued.

General Telles looked to Captain Rezhik. "It's your call, Torren."

Captain Rezhik looked at Jessica. "Only if you agree to shadow your squad leader."

"Agreed," Jessica immediately replied.

"And you do not speak unless you are asked a question."

"You got it."

"And you do not fire your weapon, *any* weapon, without authorization."

"What if I'm being fired on?" Jessica challenged.

Torren looked her squarely in the eyes. "You take cover and wait for orders."

"So I'm basically a spectator," Jessica complained.

"A spectator with a gun," Torren corrected.

"A gun I can't use," Jessica grumbled.

"Those are the terms. We *can* do this without you, Lieutenant Commander."

"Understood, sir," Jessica acknowledged respectfully.

Torren turned to Kit. "Lieutenant, you and your team take Lieutenant Commander Nash to ready room six. Two decks down, four bulkheads aft, and to starboard, so she can get properly suited up."

"Why us?" Kit asked.

"So that you and your team can suit up as well. Lieutenant Commander Nash will be *your* shadow."

"Wait, why do they get to go full op?" Jessica demanded.

"Because we may have to B and C the Zhulati warship as well. So we can use an extra squad. And Lieutenant Vasya and his men are accustomed to your high jinks and are less likely to shoot you when you disobey an order, like I would."

Jessica couldn't help but smile. "I'm all yours, Vasya."

"Let's move out," Kit ordered, heading for the exit.

Jessica fell in behind Kit, winking at Torren on the way out. "You know you love me, Captain."

Torren did not reply.

"Are you sure about this?" General Telles asked.

"Our lost boys will do fine," Captain Rezhik assured him.

"Can you teach *me* how to control her like that?" Nathan asked the captain.

"I can try," Captain Rezhik remarked as he passed.

"How do you plan to get the pod out of the ship?" Nathan asked.

"We have developed many new methods over the last few centuries," General Telles assured him.

"I can't wait to hear about them."

"*Escape jump complete,*" the Aurora's AI reported.

"Did the Tara make it aboard?" Cameron asked her comms officer.

"Affirmative, sir. They are aboard with Ensign Sorenson."

"How the hell are they tracking us down so quickly?"

"They obviously have more advanced jump tracing methods than most," Laza opined.

"Based on past intercepts, we've got about ninety seconds until another batch of missiles appears," Cameron stated.

"*Recommend we use Captain Scott's trick and use a star's corona to mask our jump signature,*" their AI suggested.

"Will our shields protect us, considering their current condition?" Cameron asked.

"*If I channel more of our shield energy to our windward side, I believe so. However, I recommend evacuating all outer compartments.*"

"Radiation protocols," Cameron realized.

"*Correct.*"

"New contacts," Laza announced. "Impact in six seconds."

"Confirm all our people have returned?" Cameron asked her comms officer.

"Affirmative."

"*Executing escape jump,*" the Aurora's AI reported as the jump flash washed over the bridge.

"How far to the nearest appropriate star?" Cameron asked.

"*Thirty-seven point three light years.*"

"Very well. Change course and jump us there as soon as possible," Cameron instructed. "Let's end this cat and mouse game."

Jessica stood still as the auto-don system quickly encased her in her combat pressure suit one component at a time. The cycle finished, and she started to step off the platform.

"You're not done yet," Kit warned. He looked up as a large component was lowered down onto his shoulders, locking onto his body armor and then clamping around his waist.

"What the hell is this?" Jessica asked as the same backpack was lowered onto her.

"Space CMU," Kit replied.

"Sweet. How do I pilot it?"

"Just think where you want to go, and your AI will do the rest."

"Why do we need it?" Jessica wondered.

"How do you think we're getting over to the Traverna?" Mori said.

"Boarding shuttle?"

"Where's the fun in that?" Kit chuckled.

Jessica finally stepped off the donning pad. "This thing's pretty well balanced. But how are we going to get around inside with this on?"

"We don't," Kit stated. "We jettison these things once we reach the Traverna."

"What happens if we're unable to capture the ship?" Jessica wondered.

"We're not looking to capture the ship, Jess," Kit explained. "Just the pod."

"There are some pieces missing in this plan," Jessica commented.

"Let's move out!" Captain Rezhik barked as he passed, having already suited himself up. "One minute to deployment."

"B and C teams are ready for deployment," the Atlantis's comms officer reported.

Nathan stood at the back of the Atlantis's bridge. He was not accustomed to being a spectator during such a battle.

The Atlantis was unlike any ship Nathan had ever seen. On the outside she looked like an old Dusahn heavy cruiser, but inside she was a completely different ship. No ship had ever looked cleaner and more efficient *on the inside*. Of course considering it was for the Ghatazhak, that was not surprising.

Even the bridge was a shining example of minimalism. A center command chair flanked by two standing consoles, with two auxiliary sit-down stations on either side. There was only one door onto the bridge, and that was from the transport system.

The entire bridge was surrounded by a ring of large view screens that provided a three-hundred-and-sixty-degree view. Above them, a second ring of smaller view screens displayed critical information.

The command chair was a station unto itself, with wide sidearms and angled side panels, all of which were covered with touch screens.

The odd thing was that there was no helm station.

"How do you fly this thing?" Nathan asked.

"From the command chair," the general said, taking his seat. He touched a small button on the right side, and the touch screens to the left and right at the forward ends of the armrests disappeared, retracting into the arms. Fully articulated control sticks popped up in their place, an attitude controller on the right, and a throttle quadrant on the left. "Of course these are rarely used. Our AI usually pilots the ship."

"How'd you get your hands on an AI?" Nathan asked.

"The Dusahn were using AIs to run their ships decades before the rest of us. It took minimal effort to retool it to meet our needs. It operates the entire ship. I only need to tell it what I want, and it gets it done. Half the time it anticipates my orders before I give them. In fact, if every officer on the bridge were to become incapacitated, our AI would complete the mission."

"Ours is more inclined to save our hides than complete the mission," Nathan stated.

"Our AI's priority is the safety of the ship, not of its occupants," the general explained. "You see, each of us has at least two backup host bodies in SA. If one of us gets killed in battle, his last consciousness backup file can be downloaded into the new host, and he can be back to work in an hour."

"What if the Atlantis is lost?" Nathan wondered. "Does that mean all of you are lost as well?"

"We have three more host body repositories hidden on strategically located worlds," the general explained. "These ensure the Ghatazhak will live on, even if this ship and all her hands were lost."

"That's a lot of effort to go to," Nathan observed. "Why not just train more Ghatazhak?"

"Thousands of Ghatazhak are not the answer," the general stated. "Besides, the logistics of operating a small, well-trained force are far less demanding than that of an army. And at least with the Ghatazhak, a small force is just as lethal."

"I can't argue with that" Nathan admitted.

"Atlantis, shields up, weapons hot and free. Initiate insertion jump," General Telles ordered.

"You're not going to call for battle stations first?"

General Telles smiled. "The Ghatazhak are always ready for battle, Captain. You know that."

A blue-white band encircling the bridge just above the view screens glowed brightly for a few seconds, then faded.

"What's that?" Nathan wondered.

"This ship does not create a jump flash. Blue jump indicator lights located all over the ship glow to indicate a jump so that everyone knows a jump occurred. Everyone knows where we are at all times."

"I see."

"*The Traverna is dead ahead, six kilometers out,*" the Atlantis's AI reported. "*The Maturo is closing on her now, from her port side, slightly above, three kilometers out.*"

"Launch all combat drones," the general ordered. "Task them with keeping any enemy boarding forces from reaching the Traverna. And as soon as we're within gun range, open fire on the Maturo."

"New contacts," Laza reported from the Aurora's sensor station.

"More missiles?" Cameron asked.

"Negative. Gunships. Six of them. They're

maneuvering in behind us. They've probably detected that our aft shields are still not back to full strength."

"Aurora, how soon can we pull our little disappearing act?" Cameron asked.

"*Thirty-three seconds to get the angle for best effect.*"

"Disappearing act?" Josh asked as he entered the bridge, still in his flight suit.

The ship shook from incoming fire.

"*Aft shields down to sixty percent,*" Aurora reported.

"You're not tired of that outfit yet?" Cameron asked Josh.

"I assumed you'd be relaunching us sooner or later," Josh said. "Besides, it makes me look cool."

The ship shook again, forcing Cameron to grab the tactical console to prevent herself from losing her balance.

"*Aft shields at forty percent. Transition jump in fifteen seconds.*"

"What's the plan, boss?" Josh asked, feeling a bit useless.

"First we shake this tail, then we stage someplace where we can jump back and help if needed," Cameron explained.

"The Aurora's not taking the lead?"

"This one's the Ghatazhak's play." Cameron glanced at him as the ship continued to shake. "Get everyone ready to deploy, just in case."

"You got it, boss," Josh replied, turning to exit.

"*Aft shields down to twenty percent,*" Aurora warned. "*Transitioning to star's corona in three......two......one...*"

The jump flash washed over the Aurora's bridge, quickly replaced with the bright light of the star which now filled every window on the bridge. Cameron covered her eyes until the filtering systems dialed down the brightness.

"*We are in the star's corona*," Aurora reported. "*Main propulsion to full power. Escape jump in thirty seconds.*"

The ship was no longer shaking from incoming weapons fire.

"Gunships have jumped to follow," Laza reported. "But they're staying out of the corona and are beyond range of their weapons."

"They still have jump missiles," Cameron reminded her.

"It is unlikely that a targeting system can clearly discern a target against the radiation of the star."

"Good point." Cameron turned to her comms officer. "Did we get all outer compartments evacuated?"

"Yes, sir."

"What about the Dragon pilots? Their launch tubes are outboard."

"They're holding up in the cockpit ready room," Sima explained. "I advised them to wait until we're out of the corona before returning to the ships."

"Good thinking."

"*Hull temperatures rising,*" Aurora warned.

"What about our shields?"

"*They are holding better than anticipated.*"

"How long until we can jump?"

"*The gunships are faster than we thought. The more distance between us and them, the more the star's corona will scramble our jump signature.*"

"Then steer us closer to the star," Cameron ordered. "Jump just before hull temperatures reach critical."

"Understood."

Cameron stood silently staring at the star outside. Even with the filters at maximum, it was too bright to look at. She could see the swirling gases of the star, and the numerous eruptions on its surface. It was both captivating and terrifying. "Such power," she said under her breath.

———————

The Maturo closed to within half a kilometer of the Traverna before turning to port to parallel the disabled vessel. But the incoming fire from the larger, more powerful Ghatazhak ship was quickly draining its shields. Soon, it would be forced to jump away to avoid destruction.

Four small shuttles dropped out from the bottom of the Maturo, immediately turning toward the Traverna and accelerating. Seconds later, while still under fire, the Zhulati warship jumped away.

———————

Jessica shot out of the tube and into space, the launch applying just enough force to move her quickly clear of the Atlantis. In front of her were Kit, Mori, and the rest of their team. Behind her and to her left were the other eight Ghatazhak who would be boarding the Traverna.

Jessica's CMU activated automatically, adjusting her attitude and firing her thrusters to steer toward the Traverna and increase her rate of closure.

Before her, the crippled cargo ship grew larger in size as they approached. Zhulati boarding pods were being intercepted by combat drones deployed from the Atlantis a minute earlier. The drones zeroed in on the four Zhulati boarding pods attempting to reach the Traverna, with as many as eight of the much smaller drones targeting each pod. The pods fought back, their automated defensive turrets firing incessantly, but the tiny drones were too quick and too well armed. The drones' superior firepower quickly overwhelmed the boarding pods' shields, and when they failed, their hulls were immediately penetrated. The boarding pods either broke apart, flinging their occupants out into space, or just exploded, leaving nothing but debris and body parts.

———————

"Still no contacts," Laza reported from the Aurora's sensor station.

"Well it's only been a minute," Cameron said. "Sima, go ahead and order our Dragon pilots to their ships."

"Aye, sir."

"Aurora, plot a jump back to the Nishida system just in case."

"*Right away, Captain,*" the Aurora's AI acknowledged.

Cameron tapped her comm-panel. "Cheng, Bridge."

"*I'm a little busy right now,*" Vladimir snapped back.

"How long until we have full shields back?"

"*Five minutes if you can avoid jumping,*" Vladimir replied. "*Jumps interrupt the recharge cycle for about twenty seconds. I can get it down to two and a half minutes by using power from our jump banks.*"

"Aurora, distance back to the Nishida system?" Cameron inquired.

"One hundred twenty-seven point three four light years."

"Current single-jump range?"

"Seven hundred fifty-two light years, not including our emergency jump banks."

"Vlad, go ahead and use the energy in our jump banks," Cameron said over her comm-set. "Just make sure you leave us two hundred light years of jump juice."

"Harasho," Vladimir replied, ending the call.

"Captain," Sima called from the comm-station. "The Atlantis has installed the AICC node that Captain Scott gave them. I have Captain Scott on the line now."

"Finally," Cameron said, switching over to the AICC channel on her command chair comm-panel. "Nathan, Cam. What's your status?"

"The Atlantis just reached the Traverna, but so did the Zhulati. The Atlantis's drones can keep the Zhulati boarding pods away for now, and that cruiser's guns are no match for the Ghatazhak's shields."

"I don't understand," Cameron admitted. "What's so important about the Traverna?"

"It's that SA pod," Nathan explained. *"It's a long story, but Telles believes that pod to be a game changer. He's already deployed sixteen Ghatazhak to board the Traverna and retrieve that pod. Jess went with them."*

"I see," Cameron replied, a look of concentration on her face.

"How's the ship?" Nathan asked. *"Did you recover all our shuttles and Dragons?"*

"It took a while to shake the Zhulati from our tail, but it looks like we've finally lost them. All shuttles are on deck, except for the Mirai of course. And all Dragons have been re-upped and are sitting in the launch tubes with pilots, ready for immediate redeployment."

"*Very good.*"

"Oh, and we lost another Dragon ship."

"*Who?*"

"Nikolas," Cameron replied. "He's fine, back in the cockpit waiting for launch."

"So no spares left," Nathan surmised.

"Are you sure you don't want us back there to help?" Cameron offered. "Our shields will be back up in two or three minutes."

"*Negative, stay put,*" Nathan insisted. "*Telles seems confident that they can manage things. One thing's for sure, this ship has some killer shields.*"

"Well ask them for that tech when you get the opportunity. We could use the upgrade."

"*I will. Meanwhile, they're setting up to provide constant battle telemetry to you over the AICC node so you'll be aware every step of the way.*"

"Good to hear."

"*Gotta run, Cam. Our people are about to touch down.*"

Cameron slumped back in her command chair, feeling a moment of relief. "Contacts?" she asked, fearing that feeling would be taken away.

"Still nothing," Laza replied. "How does the saying go? 'I think we lost them?'"

"Something like that," Cameron replied.

———

"*Jumping in three seconds,*" Jessica's suit AI warned. "*Two......one...*"

The latest Ghatazhak jump gear also made no

flash. Jessica's only indication was a small, pale blue light that flashed on the inside of her visor when the transition occurred. Suddenly, the Traverna was no longer a tiny, oblong, off-white dot in the distance. Now she was close enough to make out her basic form and was visibly growing closer with each passing second.

"*Stand by for CMU separation,*" her AI announced.

"What? Why?"

"*Relax, Jess,*" Kit told her over comms. "*CMUs are going to act as decoys. Besides, we're on terminal intercept with a disabled ship.*"

"You could've warned me *before* we deployed."

"*Would you have changed your mind?*" Kit asked.

"No, but you know how I feel about surprises."

"*We go cold when our CMUs disconnect,*" Kit instructed. "*That way, the CMUs are targeted instead of us. And don't worry about our closure rate. The suits can handle it.*"

"Of course they can," Jessica mumbled.

"*CMU separation in three......two......one...*"

Jessica felt the click as her combat maneuvering unit disengaged from her combat suit. A second later, it fired its thrusters again, steering away and ahead of her and the other Ghatazhak, while maintaining course for the Traverna.

"*Activating stealth mode,*" her suit AI announced. Most of the status lights and displays on the inside of her helmet visor disappeared, leaving nothing but the range indicator, closure rate, and estimated time of impact displayed along the bottom edge.

"*Maturo has returned,*" the Atlantis's AI reported.

Nathan glanced at the displays above the forward view screens. Between the data displayed on the contact itself, as well as the enhancements around the target on the view screens simulating windows, he instantly had a full understanding of the enemy cruiser's position and movement relative to both the Traverna *and* the Atlantis. One of the screens even showed an animation of the Traverna, as if a camera was only a few hundred meters away. It was all the same information that he had access to from the Aurora's command chair, but somehow, it was far quicker and easier to understand. There were even multiple views of the enemy ship, as well as several possible attack paths it could take, all of them provided by the ship's AI and based on all available data for the engagements thus far, as well as historical battle intelligence on Zhulati warships. That's when Nathan realized it. Displayed before him was everything that he always saw in his head during such engagements. It was even things he *felt*. But it was all laid out in front of him so that if he lost his concentration, he could easily regain his situational awareness without effort. Somehow the Ghatazhak had created the perfect combat AI for General Telles and the Atlantis.

Nathan's train of thought was suddenly derailed.

"*Maturo is launching more boarding pods,*" the Atlantis's AI reported. "*They are launching combat drones as well.*"

Nathan noticed the concern on the general's face. "What is it?"

"Those drones will be targeting both our drones *and* our boarding teams."

"Then we should abort," Nathan urged.

"We cannot allow the prototype to return to Alliance control," the general insisted.

"Then put a nuke in that ship and we all go home."

"We still have one more trick up our sleeve," the general insisted.

Nathan watched the tactical display as the enemy drones began their attack. Just as the general had feared, the Zhulati drones fired on both the Ghatazhak drones and their boarding teams as they coasted toward the Traverna. One by one, icons representing both drones and soldiers began disappearing from the display as the enemy drones destroyed them. "They're dropping like flies!" Nathan exclaimed. "You have to abort!"

"Captain," General Telles warned calmly. "It will be okay."

"How can you say that?"

"Those icons are the CMUs, not the soldiers themselves."

"But they're connected *to* the soldiers!"

"They were," the general explained, another confident near-smile appearing on his face.

———————

Jessica watched in fear and amazement as drones and their CMUs were picked off in front of them, one by one. The Traverna was getting closer, and in seconds, they would be touching down on the exterior of her hull, assuming the enemy drones did not kill them first.

As they closed on the ship, the dance between combat drones was no longer in front of them, but all around them. Energy bolts streaked past from all sides and in all directions, any one of which could easily hit them. The Ghatazhak combat suits had incredibly good shields, but they couldn't stand up against multiple blasts from drones designed to attack ships.

Every instinct told her to activate her suit's automated defenses in order to fight back. But that would only attract the attention of those drones. They were tiny blips of human flesh encased in composite armor that was undetectable by typical sensors, especially against the infinite void of space. But the moment they reached the Traverna, their bio-signatures on the *outside* of its hull would make them easy to spot.

Jessica scanned the approach quickly, picking out all the other members of their assault team. None of them were so much as flinching as they drifted through space toward the disabled cargo ship. Every one of them probably felt the same way, wanting to go to guns.

The first of the Ghatazhak reached the Traverna, touching down confidently and immediately moving to cover positions on the outside of the hull. Still they did not open fire on the enemy drones. Doing so would cause the focus of the drones to turn to the ship itself and would lead to Ghatazhak deaths. Furthermore, as long as their people were not being targeted, there was no reason to fire. The mission was more important than any one of them.

So instead, as they touched down the Ghatazhak found cover and then found the existing breaches in the Traverna's hull, disappearing through them one by one.

As more Ghatazhak reached the Traverna, a few of the Zhulati drones seemed to take notice and began targeting the intruders. But the Ghatazhak moved quickly and surely, moving from one bulge in the hull to another, reducing their exposure to the incoming fire as much as possible.

But more and more drones were refocusing their weapons toward the hull of the Traverna. Unfortunately, Kit's team was not yet down, and Jessica was behind them, the last to touch down. She spotted Mori and Kit, trapped in a depression in the Traverna's hull, unable to move due to a Zhulati drone that had taken up a stationary position only a few meters away from the ship.

Jessica powered her suit back up, raising her arms and opening fire with her wrist-mounted plasma cannons. In seconds she destroyed the drone, followed by two more before she finally touched down herself.

Unlike the others, Jessica didn't bother to take cover, instead choosing to run like hell along the hull, reaching one of the existing breaches and dropping into it just as one of the Zhulati drones peppered the area where she had last stood.

"Goddamn that was fun!" she exclaimed, now safely inside the ship. "Shake your ass, boys! We've got work to do!"

"The Maturo has returned," Commander Sonoda reported from the standing operations station just aft and starboard of the command chair.

Nathan glanced at the overhead displays again, quickly scanning the windows next. The Traverna was dead ahead and slightly below the Atlantis, which was holding position about five hundred meters out. Despite its proximity, it still appeared quite small.

But it was encircled by a data ring projected on the view screen by the ship's AI, making it easier to spot.

This time, the Maturo was at a bearing of zero four zero mark one five and was just over a kilometer away from the Traverna, putting her about sixteen hundred meters from the Atlantis. Without that data ring, she would have been difficult to discern against the starry background.

"They're launching more boarding pods," the commander added.

"Status of our boarding teams?" the general inquired.

"All seventeen of them are down and entering the Traverna. No one left in transit."

"Atlantis, all weapons on the Maturo. All drones on the boarding pods," the general instructed calmly.

There was no acknowledgment from their AI. Everything that was happening was displayed on the view screens. The targeting data and power settings for every one of their guns was available, as were the results of every impact of every blast fired. He could even see the status of the Maturo's shield strength, broken down to every panel. Even the announcements from his subordinates were more of a formality than a necessity. The captain was already aware of the information before its report was completed. The Atlantis was a top-notch warship, designed for one purpose and one purpose only...to win battles.

"Maturo has jumped away," Commander Sonoda reported. "Six boarding pods were launched, four have been intercepted. Two more are still attempting to get around our drones."

"They will fail," the general stated confidently, looking at Nathan.

"Thank God you guys are on our side," Nathan stated.

Jessica stood guard just under the hull breach she had dropped through. Flashbacks of defending against men who had dropped through this very same breach two days ago kept popping into her mind. She had killed four men in this very spot. Had they not spaced the bodies, they would still be there. Instead, there were only the stains from their blood and tissue that had been blasted all over the walls.

Kit came dropping through the breach next, taking a position facing forward, opposite Jessica. He glanced back, spotting the gruesome markers of the previous battle. "Your work?"

"It wasn't pretty."

Mori was the next down through the breach, falling in next to Jessica. He also spotted the blood. "I see you've been here before."

Kit looked forward, spotting another area further down the corridor covered in even more blood. "You do that too?"

"That one was mostly Nathan," she replied. "With a sword no less."

"No shit," Kit chuckled as Jokay and Abdur dropped in.

"Last ones in hold here," Kit instructed. "Mori and I will go to the reactor room and figure out how to get the pod out." He moved over to Jessica and Mori. "Since you already bloodied the place, you may as well lead the way."

The threat alert indicator on the center overhead view screen flashed. As the newly arrived target was encircled on the main windows, details on the contact filled out on another overhead.

"Maturo has returned," the commander announced calmly. "Four more pods have been launched."

The Atlantis had already begun firing on the returned Zhulati warship, sending streams of energy bolts its way.

The general glanced at the status screens, noting that their combat drones were already on their way to intercept the incoming Zhulati boarding pods.

"They are determined," Nathan commented.

"Not because they need that pod," Breyanna, who had been mostly silent until now, declared. "They can always make another. They just don't want us to have it."

Nathan suddenly became more concerned. Up until now, this had seemed like a cakewalk for the Ghatazhak and the Atlantis. "If they can't get in and capture that ship..."

"They'll destroy it," the general finished for him. "Do not worry, Captain. We have anticipated this as well."

———

Jessica advanced aft down the main corridor, quickly but cautiously, her weapon held up and ready. When she reached the power generation room, she paused at the hatch, waiting for Kit and Mori to take their positions for entry. Once they were set, Jessica moved inside, sweeping the compartment, finding it empty as they had hoped.

Kit and Mori entered next.

"Is that it?" Kit asked, pointing to the pod tucked under the power reactor.

"That's it," Jessica replied.

"It's bigger than I imagined," Mori admitted. "How are we going to get it out?"

"Well they got it in here, so..." Jessica said.

Kit turned and looked back at the hatch. "It looks like the entire hatch bulkhead can be removed. It would fit through then."

"*Two, One,*" Captain Rezhik called over comms. "*Status?*"

"We found the pod, right where Jess said it would be," Kit reported. "But we're going to have to disassemble the hatch bulkhead to get the thing into the main corridor and back to the aft loading hatch."

"*How long?*"

"Five maybe ten minutes."

"*Strike, Telles,*" the general interrupted. "*Can you blow the bulkhead?*"

"Negative, sir," Kit replied. "Heavy duty, radiation shielded. We'll have to kill the gravity just to manage the damned thing. The amount of explosive force needed to blow this bulkhead would destroy everything in the compartment."

"*Get moving then,*" the general instructed. "*Rezhik, do you need additional manpower?*"

"*Negative,*" Captain Rezhik replied. "*I'll send a couple of men from my team to help them. Just keep those boarding pods away.*"

"*Will do.*"

Kit looked at Jessica and Mori. "Grab some power wrenches."

"*Vasya, Rezhik. I'll send two men to relieve Jokay and Abdur so they can help you.*"

"Sounds good," Kit agreed as he picked up a

power wrench and joined Jessica and Mori. "Jokay, as soon as you are relieved, find engineering and figure out how to shut off the gravity."

————————

A split second after the Atlantis's sensors detected the Maturo's return to the area, its main guns opened fire, sending a barrage of red-orange plasma and rail gun slugs pouring into the Zhulati cruiser's shields.

"You have to give them credit for their perseverance," Commander Sonoda declared. "They're launching *eight* boarding pods this time."

"They can't have many left, can they?" Nathan asked.

"The Maturo *is* their flagship, but I can't imagine they could hold that many more. They've already lost sixteen pods."

"That's *sixty-four* men," Nathan said, shocked.

"Assuming they loaded each pod to the maximum, yes."

Nathan just shook his head.

"Do not worry, Captain. Every one of those men have backup host bodies, just like us. It is one of the perks of being a Zhulati," the general explained.

"Cloning is illegal in Alliance space," Breyanna stated.

"Loopholes in Alliance law," General Telles explained. "In the interests of 'national security'."

"Maturo has jumped away again," the commander reported. "One boarding pod *has* reached the Traverna. Ventral side, just forward of midship. Captain Rezhik has been notified."

"Have they breached?" the general asked.

"Unknown," the commander replied.

"Warn Kit."

"Already done, sir."

"Is this a problem?" Nathan asked.

"Shouldn't be as long as no *more* boarding pods make it down," the general replied.

"How do you plan on getting that pod out of there?"

"Same way they got it in," the general told him. "Assuming there is time."

Captain Rezhik and his team made their way around the outside of the Traverna's hull, making their way to the Zhulati boarding pod that had attached itself to the underside of the ship, just forward of her midship line.

As the captain crested the ventral edge, he could clearly see the boarding pod. With two of his men on each side, all of them opened fire, blowing the pod open with unexpected ease.

"Strike Leader to all Strikers," the captain called over comms. "Bandits are inside, repeat, bandits are inside." He turned to the rest of his men. "Second squad enters here and chases. First squad with me. No more pods can get through."

The Atlantis's bridge suddenly rocked violently, rocking again two seconds later.

"Zhulati battleship," Commander Sonoda announced.

"They opened fire the moment they came out of the jump," Captain Kellen said.

"The Maturo must have fed them precise tracking

and targeting for them to jump in so close," the general added as he tapped his comm-panel. "Rezhik, Telles."

"*Go, General.*"

"Party crasher, heavy. Anticipate heavy push to take target. Possible Jaxak."

"*Understood,*" Captain Rezhik replied.

"What's a Jaxak?" Nathan asked, gripping the side rail tightly to avoid being knocked off his feet by the incoming fire.

"It's our code for a full mission abort and escape to recovery positions."

"But if they get that pod back..."

"They will be producing bio-synth Zhulati by the thousands in a few months' time and replacing citizens within a year."

"*Shield strength falling,*" their AI reported.

"Capturing that pod keeps us on an even footing," the general continued. "We can never match their hardware production, but that pod at least ensures our survival by vastly reducing the cost and complexity of creating and maintaining cloned reserve host bodies."

"Not to mention the ability to adjust genetics as needed," Breyanna realized.

Nathan looked at her, unsure of her meaning.

"I'd never held a gun before now," she explained. "Nor had I ever physically attacked and incapacitated someone. Yet I was able to do so as if I had been training for years."

"And she is just an existing consciousness transferred into a new host," the general said. "Imagine if they figure out how to *create* a consciousness to put into it."

"You're talking about *creating* life," Nathan realized. "Intelligent, *sentient* life."

"Preprogrammed to be loyal, obedient, and lethal," the general added. "Atlantis, time to shield failure?"

"Five minutes, thirteen seconds at current rate of fire."

"They could fire *more*?" Breyanna wondered, also holding on to the railing to stay on her feet.

"They're holding back because we're so close to the Traverna," Nathan explained. "They're afraid debris will take *it* out as well."

"Atlantis, turn into the target," the general ordered.

"To reduce target size, right?" Breyanna realized.

"Correct," Nathan confirmed.

"I shouldn't know that," she admitted. "I shouldn't *understand* any of this!"

———

Smoke began pouring out of Mori's power wrench, causing him to abort his efforts. "Damn! This isn't working, Kit. The bulkhead must be tweaked for the bolts to be this locked up."

Jokay tossed his power wrench aside. "This one's burnt out as well."

"Jesus!" Kit exclaimed. "There are only six bolts left!"

"The only way to get these bolts free is to torch the heads off," Mori explained. "Even then, we're going to have to pry the bulkhead off."

"Shit," Kit cursed, tapping his helmet comms. "Rezhik, Vasya. This is a bust. We can't get this thing out of here in less than half an hour at best."

———

General Telles was not a man to show his emotions, but he was obviously displeased. "Jaxak. Blow the package on departure."

"*Copy Jaxak,*" Rezhik acknowledged. "*Blow on departure.*"

"Captain, wait," Breyanna urged. "You said the pod was tucked under the ship's primary reactor, right?"

"Yes, but..."

"The Traverna is a Boron-class cargo jumper. That reactor is a top-mounted ZPED that uses low density containment fields that are cheaper to produce."

"What does this have to do with..."

"In order for a low-density containment ZPED powered ship to operate in Alliance space, it has to have an auto-eject system that *jumps* the entire power compartment, reactor and all, at least one light year from the ship, in case of catastrophic failure of the fields that keep the zero-point energy singularity from expanding out of control."

"How do you know all of this?" Nathan wondered.

"I just *do*," Breyanna insisted.

The Maturo jumped in on the far side of the Traverna from the Atlantis as the Ghatazhak warship continued its uneven exchange of weapons fire. With the enemy busy defending itself, the Zhulati flagship was able to maneuver for a close pass over the opposite side of the cargo ship, deploying four more boarding pods before jumping clear again.

"Captain, I am receiving some curious data streams from the Atlantis's AI," the Aurora's AI reported.

"What kind of streams?"

"It has detected a pattern to the Maturo's hit and run tactics. It believes it can predict their next arrival point."

"Is it correct?" Cameron asked.

"I estimate a ninety-three percent probability of success."

Cameron grinned, which was something she rarely did, especially during battle. "Looks like we may be able to help out after all."

———————

"Are you sure about this?" General Telles asked Breyanna, a deadly serious look in his eyes.

"I am," she replied.

"They'll have to withstand considerable G-forces during ejection," Nathan warned.

"About fifteen Gs," Breyanna stated. "Don't ask me how I know. I couldn't tell you."

Telles looked to his second in command.

"Our suits are rated for twelve," Captain Kellen stated. "Worst case, they pass out."

"Worst case is the entire compartment falls apart in the process," Telles corrected. "Shield strength?" he asked as the ship continued to rock from incoming fire.

"Sixty percent and falling," their AI reported. *"Three minutes, twenty-two seconds to failure."*

General Telles looked to Nathan, hoping for some sign of endorsement from his old friend.

Nathan only shrugged indifferently. "It's your call, Lucius."

General Telles did something he never did. He sighed. He then touched his comm-panel. "Rezhik, Telles. Fall back inside and hold. Signal Delta."

"*Understand Delta,*" Captain Rezhik replied calmly.

"What's 'signal Delta'?" Nathan asked, fearing the answer.

"Hold position to their deaths," Telles replied, just as calmly as Captain Rezhik.

"You're asking them to sacrifice themselves?" Breyanna exclaimed in disbelief.

"Death is only a temporary state for the Ghatazhak," General Telles replied solemnly. "Painful but temporary."

"Jess doesn't have a backup body," Nathan pointed out.

"I am aware," the general replied.

Captain Rezhik hunkered down next to the Traverna's aft hull breach, opening fire on one of the breach pods that had just attached itself to the ship. In order to quickly breach the hull, the pods had to divert all power to their plasma cutters, leaving their shields inoperative for ten seconds. This was the only time the pods could be destroyed by handheld weapons.

A five second stream of steady fire at full power and focused on the same spot did the trick, and the captain's attack was successful. The hull of the boarding pod ripped open, and two Zhulati soldiers were ejected by the sudden decompression of the pod. The soldiers, themselves also clad in pressurized combat armor, opened fire as they tumbled uncontrollably away from the damaged breach pod, barely able to hold decent aim for more than a moment with each revolution.

Rezhik shifted his aim, firing on the two soldiers, along with two of his men from inside the Traverna's hull breach. His first shot glanced off the left soldier's personal shielding, but his second and third shots found the second soldier as he passed behind the first. The second soldier had failed to activate his personal shield prior to being ejected and paid the ultimate price for his negligence.

A jump flash lit up the hull, drawing Rezhik's attention upward. The Maturo passed overhead, stern to bow, no more than two hundred meters away. Four more boarding pods dropped from her port hangar bay, descending quickly toward the Traverna.

Eight more, much smaller, flashes of light revealed the arrival of incoming ordnance. Jump missiles. But they weren't headed his way. They were barreling toward the Maturo. Four of them reached their target, detonating as they impacted the Maturo's shields. The Zhulati cruiser's shields flashed, collapsing a second later, leaving that section of the ship fully vulnerable to the remaining missiles less than two seconds behind.

Unfortunately, the Maturo had the presence of mind to jump clear before the second wave arrived.

Another group of flashes revealed the four Dragons that had launched the missiles. They quickly jumped again, in pursuit of the Zhulati flagship.

Two more Dragons appeared to stern, and the Dragons streaked over him, no more than twenty meters distant. They opened fire, destroying three of the four pods descending toward the Traverna.

"*Four inside!*" one of his men warned over comms. Rezhik had his orders and stepped into the breach, pulled down by the ship's artificial gravity.

Inside, he was met with arms fire zipping past either side as Zhulati troops already inside attempted to advance on their position. "Fall back!" he ordered, pulling a plasma grenade from its position on his left thigh. His men did as ordered, walking quickly backward, passing him on either side as bolts of energy ricocheted off the walks. Two of his men fell, their personal shields failing from the overwhelming amount of energy being sent their way. But Captain Rezhik felt no remorse, no sorrow. He activated the grenade's fuse, then tossed it toward the enemy, turning and running afterward.

———————

Josh looked upward through his canopy as his Dragon fighter passed over the aft breach on the Traverna's dorsal aspect. A flash of red-orange light was visible through the breach as he streaked past, with debris being ejected through the breach itself.

"*Shit!*" Nikolas exclaimed. "*Did you see that?*"

"Plasma grenade," Josh replied.

"*Ours or theirs?*"

"I don't care," Josh replied, pulling his nose up and pressing the jump button to escape the incoming fire from the Zhulati battleship.

"*How can you not care?*"

"It's not my job to care," Josh explained. "My job is to kill whatever they *tell* me to kill. Caring gets in the way of that."

———————

"*Shields down to forty percent,*" the Atlantis's AI warned. "*Incoming fire has increased.*"

"Move closer and put us directly between that battleship and the Traverna," General Telles instructed.

"*Revised time to shield failure, one minute,*" their AI warned, as if inferring that moving closer to the enemy had been an unwise decision.

"If we jump away before they manage to eject the reactor compartment, they'll see the ejection. They'll know."

"It is a gamble," the general replied calmly.

"But your AI..."

"Executes our commands," the general stated firmly. "It does not make decisions for us."

"I completely agree," Nathan defended. "It's just that the Ghatazhak are always so analytical, and if I didn't know better, I'd swear you're following your gut right now."

"A lot has changed over the last five centuries," the general assured him. "Including my gut."

Josh came out of the jump still hot on the tail of the Maturo, which was already executing a turn to jump back to the Traverna, just as the Atlantis's AI had predicted and then relayed through the Aurora's AI.

Josh immediately toggled the launch button on his flight control stick, holding course as two more ship busters dropped from his weapons bay and streaked forward on fiery tails.

Josh quickly rolled left just as the two missiles launched by his wingman streaked past. He immediately turned back, holding course alongside the Maturo as she banked hard right and jumped away, barely avoiding the approaching ordnance.

"Speak to me, sweetie," Josh begged his AI.

"*Bearing zero zero three by zero one zero. Range two light minutes.*"

"*Stay on her, Josh,*" Nikolas urged.

"Like stink on shit," Josh replied as he pressed his jump button.

"*Like what?*"

Josh just grinned as his threat alarm flashed once again. The Maturo was again directly ahead of him, turning hard and diving, anticipating another attack. "We've got her on the run, Reems!" Josh declared as he fired his last two missiles and peeled off. "Dragon Three, Dragon One. We're empty. You're up."

"*Dragon Three copies,*" Talisha replied over comms. "*We'll intercept on her return jump.*"

"Execute," Cameron ordered, sitting in her command chair with her eyes fixed on the forward view screen.

The jump flash washed over the bridge, and the Traverna, the Atlantis, and the Zhulati battleship were now directly in front of them, closing rapidly.

"Put us between the Atlantis and that battleship," Cameron instructed her AI.

The bridge shook as the battleship redirected some of its firepower toward the Aurora.

"*All power diverted toward gunward shields,*" the Aurora's AI reported.

"Three more boarding pods just attached to the

Traverna's hull," Laza reported from the sensor station. "The Ghatazhak will be overrun."

"Jess, Cam," Cameron called over her comm-set as Vladimir charged onto the bridge.

"*I'm a little busy trying to figure out how to eject this fucking thing, Cam,*" Jessica snapped. "*Not to mention the place is crawling with Zhulati, and our boys are dropping like flies just outside the hatch!*"

"Shut up and listen!" Vladimir demanded. "Back side of the reactor, between the lateral vertical coolant lines, there's a small, unmarked cover. Open it and pull the red handle out and then up. That will initiate a manual compartment jettison and jump, or at least it should."

"*Whattaya mean should?*"

"Just do it!"

"Good luck, Jess," Cameron added.

———————

"Fucking great," Jessica muttered as she made her way around to the back side of the reactor. She found the panel right where Vladimir had said it would be. A push on the lower edge of the cover caused it to pop open and swing upward. She pulled the red handle out but held it in place, not jamming it upward. "Rezhik!" she called over her comm-set. "We'll open the hatch and you guys jump inside! We'll all eject together!"

"*Negative!*" Rezhik ordered, intense weapons fire nearly overpowering his words. "Jettison now! That's an order!" he added.

"Yes, sir!" Jessica replied. "Hang on!" she warned Kit and the other three members of their team. "We're about to get squashed!"

"See you on the other side," Captain Rezhik called over comms.

Without hesitation or remorse, Jessica pulled the handle upward.

"What are you doing, Captain Taylor?" General Telles inquired over comms as the Aurora slid into position between the Atlantis and the Zhulati battleship.

"Taking the initiative, General," Cameron replied. *"Now do what you're going to do quickly. We can't take this much pounding for long."*

"The Traverna's reactor compartment is ejecting," Commander Sonoda reported.

"Atlantis, four nukes into the Traverna on my mark," General Telles instructed. "Aurora, jump on my go."

"Reactor compartment is charging its jump systems," the commander added. "Estimate jump in three..."

"Launch missiles," the general instructed.

"Two..."

One of the view screens above the main windows showed four torpedoes armed with nuclear warheads leaving the Atlantis's launch tubes, heading for the Traverna with an estimated impact time of three seconds.

"One..."

"See you on the other side, gentlemen," the general said to himself.

"Reactor is jumping," the commander announced.

"Aurora, jump now," the general instructed over comms. "Atlantis, jump as well," he added, noticing that the countdown to impact was at one second and then zero.

The blue light that encircled the bridge flashed once, indicating the jump.

"Atlantis. Lock all jump missile batteries on that battleship's last known position. When ready, launch in waves. One missile per battery, cycle every fifteen seconds. Maximum yields, one-hundred-meter arrival ranges."

"*Executing,*" their AI acknowledged.

"Aurora, Atlantis. Would you mind retrieving that reactor compartment for us? We're a little busy raining terror on that battleship from afar."

"*We're on it, General,*" Cameron replied. "*How much time do we have?*"

"Two minutes."

"*Oh no problem. I was afraid you were going to say one,*" Cameron joked.

"*First wave of missiles away,*" the Atlantis's AI reported.

"You may recall your Dragons as well," the General told her.

"*I already have, sir,*" Cameron assured him. "*We'll update you when we have the package.*"

General Telles stood from his command chair, turning to face Nathan and Breyanna.

"So that's it?" Breyanna wondered. "It's over?"

"For now," the general replied. "But we have much to discuss, the three of us."

"Why me?" Breyanna wondered.

"Because you are the key to understanding the capabilities of this technology," the general explained. "In fact, you just might be the key to preventing the Alliance from taking over the galaxy and destroying the entire human race."

"That's insane," Nathan argued. "Why would they want to destroy *themselves?*"

"Because the Alliance is no longer controlled by humanity," the General stated. "It has been hijacked by a consortium of the most powerful corporations in the galaxy. And those corporations are controlled, in whole or in part, by AIs. You see, Captain, humanity has inadvertently lost control of its own destiny. We intend to correct that error."

Thank you for reading this story.
(*A review would be greatly appreciated!*)
Visit us online at
frontierssaga.com
or on Facebook
Want to be notified when
new episodes are published?
Join our mailing list!
frontierssaga.com/mailinglist/

Printed in Great Britain
by Amazon

62770755R00160